THE CYPRESS CLUB

THE CYPRESS CLUB

Jeff Wiemiller

gatekeeper press
Columbus, Ohio

The Cypress Club

Published by Gatekeeper Press
2167 Stringtown Rd, Suite 109
Columbus, OH 43123-2989
www.GatekeeperPress.com

The interior formatting, typesetting, and editorial work for this book are entirely the product of the author. Gatekeeper Press did not participate in and is not responsible for any aspect of these elements.

Library of Congress Control Number: 2021938467

ISBN (hardcover): 9781662914058
ISBN (paperback): 9781662914065
eISBN: 9781662914072

one

The last thing Ben's grandmother said to him was how much he'd regret it if he didn't attempt to improve things with his mom. "Don't give up on her," Helen had insisted about her only daughter. "Even if I may have."

It had felt like a double punch to the gut, knowing both that time was running out for Grandma and that all he'd have left of her was this request hanging over his head. A request he regarded as more than a mere suggestion. If it came from Grandma, it was to be an assignment, a duty even, incapable of being ignored.

To Ben, regret felt like something akin to landing on the receiving end of a lazy friendship: it was frustrating, often long-lasting, sometimes even safe. But its continuation required a certain level of passivity, and at a point, the mounting work it took to change course—or his disappointment in himself for not yet having done so—tended to only fuel the problem. In effect, he was unlikely to glean much in terms of real value as a participant. He'd just end up resenting that friend. Or, absurdly, he'd regret all the regretting he was doing. Best to cut the cord.

It wasn't that he and his mother didn't get along, exactly. In fact, they had been rather close for a time. For the better part of his childhood, not unlike most other little boys his age, Ben was his mother's best friend. And as such, he knew her best. Like a baby barometer, early on he learned to quickly and accurately register shifts in her often volatile mood. He was the first to notice when she was upset or unhappy, and accordingly the first to then offer a hug or gentle compliment in hope of easing her troubles. "Your hair looks real pretty, Mom," he'd say, nestling his little head under her arm. The tactic never failed to cheer her up.

Eventually, however, Ben noticed his male peers begin insisting on some distance with their moms—refusing good-bye kisses, limiting conversation, and generally crouching in embarrassment if they were ever forced to be seen with her in public. But that somewhat sad yet possibly inevitable quest for detachment in adolescence never really developed in Ben. If anything, it was his mother who gradually withdrew from *him*.

First, she began excluding him from her semiweekly trips to the mall (homework came first), then announced she no longer enjoyed their favorite television program (the townsfolk on *Dr. Quinn, Medicine Woman* were unrealistically PC for nineteenth-century frontiersmen). And in what may have been her most perplexing move, she dropped him as her doubles partner at their local country club after he made the high school tennis team. He was "too good" now.

I'm not crazy, he'd resign himself to saying when failing to understand what he'd done wrong. What a thought at seventeen! There'd been nothing traumatic about their breach. No blowout argument or painful reprimand for delinquency. And without the adequate tools of communication to effectively navigate a relationship whose slope had grown slippery so gradually, he just kept it in. Maybe it was part of growing up—his mother's not so subtle way of coaxing him out from behind her skirt and into a world filled with what he found to be far too many possibilities. A dose of "tough love," as it were. Ben couldn't say he never gave it a thought these days, twenty years later. But it had been a while since he'd bothered to examine how her behavior never really seemed to add up when it came to him. He'd grown accustomed to some space from all that melancholic, destinationless thinking.

And now Grandma had gone ahead and unsealed the proverbial can of worms. She knew full well Ben couldn't disregard a deathbed request. He wasn't angry with her for that; it was probably for the best, actually. He likely wouldn't have launched an effort to reconnect with his mother at all had Grandma not made the suggestion. This weekend's trip to Palm Beach for Mom and Dad's fortieth anniversary might just be the opportunity he needed to begin honoring her wishes. Or at least he kept trying to convince himself of that.

Most cooped-up Minnesotans would jump at an excuse to visit Florida this time of year. Back in Minneapolis, Ben was used to March temperatures that ranged anywhere from being able to enjoy one or two "T-shirt weather" days, to practically needing a ski mask if you hoped to avoid frostbite merely crossing the street. With the past few weeks having edged much closer to the latter, he couldn't help but feel a little guilty now, not being more excited to escape the cold—even if he never was one to truly relish the sunshine.

The truth was, he'd been dreading the impending trip. Yes, he probably could have come up with some justifiable reason for staying home after the fact, had the prospect of visiting really been too much to bear. But he'd sealed his fate at Christmas. A tearful toast from Mom invoking Grandma's recent passing had sparked in him a somewhat tipsy moment of sentimentality. And after raising his glass of mulled wine, he'd promised her he'd be there. To say he didn't feel like it now, while honest, was likely to cause more headache than it was worth.

His twin sister, Abby, had been decidedly unsympathetic to his concerns. Ben had arrived at her annual New Year's Eve party a little early, hoping she'd offer some angle for wiggling out of his commitment. It took one brief mention of their mother for Abby to immediately know where he was headed.

"You're going," she told him. "It's time."

"What the hell is that supposed to mean?"

Abby paused her arranging of a catered vegetable tray and tipped her head at Ben. "Come on, B." Ben only stared at her in annoyed confusion. "Now that Grandma's gone? You're not going to want to keep things like this with Mom." Abby returned her eyes to the tray and quipped, "It'll drive you nuts not having that maternal validation."

Ben stiffened, his natural response when his psychologist sister occasionally veered off into doctor-patient territory with him. She'd said this so nonchalantly, like it should be obvious. As if everyone knew his relationship with Grandma had somehow grown into some protective blanket, shielding him from any chance of closeness with their mother. It was unnerving to know his apprehensions about it were not exclusive to his own thinking.

Ben grimaced and took a sip of his sauvignon blanc. "Ugh, you are out of control."

Abby brandished that know-it-all smirk she knew got under her brother's skin.

"Things aren't that bad," he protested.

Abby had to laugh. "Girl, get serious!" she teased. "You could barely look at her at Christmas. They're not going to be around forever, you know."

Ben noticed her eyeing his glass. At Thanksgiving, Abby had announced that she and her husband, Terry, were expecting their third child. It was hard for Ben to imagine going without for a week, much less nine months, as was Abby's current hardship.

He had already abandoned his argument. "How have you managed to sidestep this all these years?" he asked.

Abby shrugged. "I was never that close with her. There's nothing to patch up between us."

Ben didn't know whether to feel bolstered or saddened by this sober observation.

"So, stop whining and just *go*," she added.

He smiled, as though conceding defeat. "Is this how you talk to all your patients?"

"No. I'm much more blunt with them." With that, Abby snatched Ben's glass and took a tiny sip of his wine. She closed her eyes and let the taste linger for a few seconds. Ben clutched his chest and manufactured a scandalized gasp.

Abby's words from that night revisited him now. More, any diagnostic implication they held bubbled to the surface of his apparently unexamined psyche. It was true Grandma had held an important place in his life. Abby viewed this as simply filling the maternal void that plagued him. Standard "mommy issues" from her clinical perspective, no doubt. But he knew it went deeper than that. His sister's estimations notwithstanding, Grandma had been more than a replacement for any wanting affections. She had been a tether. A tether to sanity and at least some shred of self-worth. Which, if he were honest, meant life. In her way, she'd provided the ability for him to believe that any gulf between mother and son wasn't because of *him*.

Only a few months into Grandma's absence, however, doubts had begun creeping in. So, unsure of his route and finding himself repeatedly tipping his nose to give his underarm a paranoid sniff, here he was.

Just as his rental car was finally managing to gain some ground in the humidity battle, Ben felt a few beads of sweat returning to his forehead when he saw a sign ahead that read *The Cypress Club, Second Left.* The retirement community his parents had chosen was a recent upgrade from their previous home. He'd visited Citrus Hill just once since they had moved to Florida four years prior, and had already considered it a fairly upscale place. While perhaps a bit stuffy, the people were nice enough, and he was satisfied that Mom and Dad had plenty of activities and friends to keep them occupied.

His mother had reportedly desired a change last year, however, and with housing prices still favoring buyers in the area, she and his father took advantage and purchased what she described as a more "comfortable" home, not far from Citrus Hill. From the few bizarre anecdotes she'd offered Ben over the phone about their new residence, he'd been left with the unsettling impression that his parents had made the leap from a quietly affluent retirement village to a pretentious, one-percenter-packed compound.

Easing the vehicle onto the stone-paved driveway, Ben's first look at the club's entrance did little to disabuse him from his worries. An imposing cast iron gate loomed beyond the attendant's booth, almost inspiring him to turn back now. He rolled down his window and cautiously approached the house-like structure, where an unsmiling man with an indecipherable badge sized him up and down.

"May I help you?" the man grumbled.

"I'm here to visit—"

"Name?"

Ben blinked repeatedly, surprised by the man's abruptness. "Ben. Ben Apt."

The attendant scanned his clipboard. Ben could see his brow furrowing above his sunglasses, as if irritated by the very presence of a guest.

"Apt. Apt. Apt," the attendant repeated to himself. There was a long pause before he asked, "Ben Apt?"

"Correct."

"Who did you say you were visiting?"

"I didn't say," Ben shot back. Then he finally answered, "My parents. Jim and Betty Apt."

After a brief review of his list, the man looked up and studied Ben closely. "I only see a Jim and *Betsy* Apt."

"Yep. That's them," Ben confirmed, peeking at his watch.

Within a few weeks of moving to The Cypress Club, Ben's mother, Betty, had begun introducing herself as Betsy. She justified this to her two children by telling them it was due to there being so many other women she'd met at the club with the same name. The slight variation would help minimize mix-ups, she'd assured them.

"I.D., please," demanded the attendant.

Ben fished out his wallet from his back pocket and handed the man his license. The attendant examined it for what seemed like an unnecessarily long time.

"Is this your vehicle?" the man asked, gruffly.

"Yeah, I guess. It's a—"

"How long are you staying?"

Ben had to think. He purposely took his time. "Three nights."

The attendant ripped a yellow receipt from the top of a pad and extended it to Ben, along with his I.D.

"What, no strip search?" Ben asked.

"I beg your pardon?"

"Never mind."

The man hesitated before allowing Ben to accept the items. "Put this tag on your dash and follow the signs up the hill for visitor parking," he said, pointing toward the gate. "A valet will guide you from there."

"Great. Thanks," said Ben, finding a smile. "This has been lovely."

His comment elicited no reaction from the attendant, only a thumbing gesture directing Ben to keep moving forward. The massive gate opened away from him, and Ben cautiously rolled in with his basic compact. At the airport, the chattering agent who'd secured him his rental car had pursued him to the lot to recommend one of their full-sized SUVs. "It can fit an entire Jet Ski!" the overzealous employee had chirped. With the flick of a finger, Ben had managed to shoo her away and promptly selected something he'd deemed more practical. Coasting through the cavernous entrance now, he realized that gas-guzzling monstrosity he'd been so loath to choose could have easily fit through the gate six times over.

As promised, a very eager fellow approached Ben's vehicle and greeted him with wide eyes and a toothy grin. "Welcome to

The Cypress Club!" he beamed. "My name's Ramón. If you'd be so kind as to step out of your vehicle, I'd be happy to safely park it for you, sir."

Ben recoiled as Ramón brusquely occupied his personal space. "Thank you." He set the parking brake and quickly exited the car.

Ramón squinted and pointed to a sidewalk off to the left. Ben opened his wallet, regrettably finding no cash for a tip. Ramón only shook his head, assuring him it was no problem. After an apologetic smile, Ben stepped away and watched as his rental car gradually disappeared around a corner in the opposite direction.

The air was heavy. Walking fast only made him warmer, but he wanted to get out of the sun as quickly as possible. He lifted the bottom of his T-shirt to cool the sweaty small of his back, then followed the signs for the main clubhouse. Under his feet, the path was oddly paved with an Oz-like yellowish brick. Ben thought of his boyfriend, Jake, who'd scolded him shortly after they'd begun dating for having never seen *The Wizard of Oz*, Jake's favorite film. Ben smirked, half wondering now if the narrow road he was on was somehow going to lead to an intoxicating field of scarlet poppies.

It hadn't been Ben's preference to make the trip alone. When he'd second-guessed his decision in the weeks leading up to it, Jake—whom Ben suspected was in cahoots with Abby—had strongly encouraged him to stick to his plan. In Jake's experience, Ben had always acted a bit funny whenever he was about to spend time with his mom. But since Grandma's passing, he'd apparently been more irritable in general, to the point of being difficult to be around. In a "funk," as Jake had put it.

The trip, and hopefully some catharsis with his mother, could be a good way of jumpstarting his mood, Ben was urged. Still, Jake's words left him with a sense that he thought it was more than just a good idea—that if Ben didn't come back from the weekend with at least some sign of resolution, there would be cause for worry. As an accountant in the middle of tax season, however, Jake was swamped with returns, and couldn't justify getting away for a long weekend. His absence thus deprived Ben of half of his otherwise reliable pair of parental buffers.

The other was literally Ben's other half—Abby, of course. She would be staying home that weekend as well, enjoying the convenient excuse of now being six months pregnant. For most women, Ben had reminded her, reaching your second trimester wasn't an absolute dealbreaker for flying domestically. But Abby had experienced slightly elevated blood pressure during her second pregnancy three years ago. Although her obstetrician had assured her that her levels were well within the normal range this time around, she cited this precaution as reason enough to forego traveling.

On either side of the path, a tall wall of junipers screened Ben's view until the walkway finally opened, revealing his destination. He stood facing a palatial structure, fronted with four white pillars which elicited a lurid comparison to a plantation home in the antebellum South. Pausing a moment, he caught his breath and took in the building's enormity before cautiously entering through its glass doors.

Beyond the foyer, Ben was met with a grand room that rose three stories to a domed glass ceiling. He tipped his head back for a moment to inspect the detail. At the far end of the room, a succession of at least a dozen live palm trees lined the wall, below which laid an array of orange and pink tropical blooms planted in a marble podium. An enormous fiber optic chandelier dangled from the glass ceiling, its strands hovering vertically like horse tails over a complicated fountain, which Ben could only assume complemented a display of liquid neon fireworks set to music each evening. Everything smelled of chlorine and mango.

A smartly dressed gentleman flashing an unnervingly broad smile welcomed Ben at the check-in counter. "Good afternoon, sir," he said. "Welcome to The Cypress Club of Palm Beach. My name's Clark. How may I assist you today?"

"I'm checking in," Ben replied, resting his hands on the counter. "I'm staying with my parents, Jim and Betty—er, Betsy Apt."

"I'll be happy to assist you with that, Mr. Apt. If you don't mind waiting a moment while I find your name in our guest registration list." Clark busily tapped away at his keyboard until one final smack of the Enter key. "Here we are, Mr. Apt! Am I correct in assuming you've entrusted your vehicle with our valet, Ramón?"

"Yep."

"Wonderful. And was your luggage in the vehicle as well?"

Ben hesitated, transfixed by Clark's ability to not blink. "Yes. He said I could just let you know."

"That is absolutely correct. Your belongings will be at your parents' villa when you arrive. I can have someone escort you."

Villa? "That'd be great," said Ben.

Clark never broke his smile. His face had to be exhausted by now, Ben decided. Whenever forced to pose with Jake or some other friend who insisted on capturing the perfect selfie, his own cheeks could last only about ten seconds before feeling sore.

Clark handed Ben a plastic card with a magnetic strip on the back. "This will provide you access to the majority of our club's complimentary amenities," he explained. "The golf courses do require an additional fee, but if you're accompanied by either of your parents, we'll be more than happy to waive that."

Ben wasn't unfamiliar with the workings of guest services at places like this. His family had been members of a small country club for years back in Minnesota. Still, he couldn't help but feel a bit dazed by the inflated hospitality he was being shown, first by Ramón and now Clark. After his prickly encounter with the uptight attendant at the entrance gate, he had already braced for a less than generous welcome with each new person he met. It was as if the club were barricaded to prevent anyone on the outside from getting in. But once you actually breached its uninviting facade, the members would do everything in their power to make sure you never wanted to leave.

He turned to observe residents, mostly women, briskly entering and exiting through one of two arched doorways on either end of the room. Arm in arm, they went about their afternoon business, each clutching a large purse or beach bag in her free hand. Several others pushed medium-sized dogs in curious little strollers, pausing their gossip only long enough to smile coquettishly at Ben when they passed him at the fountain. He raised an eyebrow at the comical similarity in their platinum hairdos, and he counted only about one brunette per twenty among the bustling heads that bounced by.

Suddenly, Ben heard his name being shouted by a familiar voice behind him. "Benny? Benny?! Is that you?!" Sporting an off-the-shoulder floral blouse and a mid-length pencil skirt and heels, Betsy darted up to the concierge's desk and wrapped her arms around Ben in a semi-reciprocated embrace. "You got in earlier than expected!" she squealed.

"No delays for a change," Ben said, unable to match is mother's enthusiasm. "You were right about how close it is to the airport."

"Isn't that great? Your father and I love how convenient it is," Betsy said. "It's one of the main reasons we chose The Cypress Club."

Ben hopped to avoid a doggie stroller from catching his toe. "Jeez," he griped. "Whatever happened to leashes?"

"Pet paws aren't allowed on this flooring," Betsy replied. "They leave prints."

"Oh," Ben said, raising his chin a little in confusion. Then he took a deep breath and added, "Jake's sorry he couldn't make it. March is crunch time for tax season."

"Sure, sure," Betsy said quickly, as if to avoid further discussion of Jake. "It's important he get his work done." Ben watched as she teased her hair a little and adjusted the sleeves on her blouse.

He'd always considered his mom a pretty lady. She had the same bright blue eyes as her mother, along with Helen's youthful cheekbones which somehow never seemed to have succumbed to the pull of gravity. She looked tan and trim—she'd always liked her walks—and despite being a lifelong brunette, for some reason she'd begun bleaching her hair last fall. He was aware of the facelift she'd gifted herself for her sixtieth birthday and, while not a big fan of the idea, he'd conceded that she looked better afterward.

Today, however, he detected something different about her appearance compared to when he'd last seen her around the holidays. Although her skin still showed far fewer lines than one might expect for a person nearing seventy, certain areas no longer seemed to move naturally. Her eyes appeared slightly asymmetric in size now; the right one narrowed to a pronounced squint when she smiled, and her eyebrows didn't move at all. But it took Ben a moment to identify what exactly seemed off about her mouth. While her lips did look fuller, somehow that little divot above her upper lip had completely disappeared, pulled tight into flatness, making her nose look thinner and longer. Her makeup had been meticulously applied, but Ben thought she wore far too much of it, especially for midafternoon. In an obvious attempt to make herself look younger, he realized, his mom, with her apparent second facelift of the decade, had only managed to render her appearance a bit odd.

A prim man in a bow tie who had been accompanying Betsy finally caught up with her. Ben quickly discerned by the man's pinched cheeks that he'd had his own share of work done as well, though a little more difficult to pinpoint than Betsy's. He gave Ben a thorough visual dress-down.

"Oh," Betsy said, noticing her companion next to her. "Dwayne, this is my son, Ben." She ushered Dwayne closer. "Dwayne's been helping me organize details for tomorrow."

"Nice to meet you," said Ben, reaching out his hand. He detected a hint of gray sprinkled in the tightly trimmed sides of Dwayne's head. He had probably been cute at one point, Ben decided—before all the work had moved him one step closer to looking like an alien, that is.

Dwayne gave a peculiar grin. "The pleasure's mine, of course." He accepted Ben's hand and held it just long enough to make Ben uncomfortable. "So, made the trip for the big fiesta, huh?"

"Mmm-hmm," Ben answered, annoyed he was already being flirted with.

"Have you been to Palm Beach before?"

"Nope. First time. Boca's the closest I've been." Ben tried to keep his responses as short as possible.

Dwayne waved his arm toward the fountain like a game show model and said, "This room we're in will be completely transformed tomorrow night."

Ben peered at Betsy. "I'm sure it'll be *fabulous*," he said.

"I know you'll find plenty to keep you busy at the club, but there are also some great places to visit if you want to explore the city more," Dwayne offered. "Let me know if you need any recommendations. This can be an exciting city with a proper guide."

Ben shifted his stance restlessly and looked away from Dwayne, as if to admire the room for the first time.

"Dwayne knows everything there is to know about this town," Betsy gushed. She proceeded to recite a litany of restaurants, boutiques and theaters she presumed anyone who visited Palm Beach would be dying to experience.

"Mom," Ben interrupted, "I'm only here a couple days. I figured I'd probably just hang around here for most of the weekend." He nodded slowly. "Enjoy the pool."

Betsy paused, then smiled at Ben encouragingly. "Of course, sweetie," she said. "But are you sure you don't want at least a few ideas of things to do?"

Ben watched Betsy and Dwayne for a moment, unsure why his mom was pushing this. The knowing glances she and Dwayne exchanged made it obvious they'd already been talking about him before he arrived. "I really think I'm good, Ma," he said finally.

Betsy exhaled. "Suit yourself," she said. "But you really should chat with Dwayne about this at some point. At least for the next time you visit."

"Okay," Ben said, hoping this concession would end their conversation.

With Ben's lack of interest apparent, Dwayne gave Betsy an air kiss and promised he'd check back one last time in the morning. "Don't worry, darling," he reassured her, "it's going to be wonderful."

Uncertain but hopeful, Betsy bit her lower lip. Dwayne turned back to Ben, then with an annoyed smirk said, "It was so nice to meet you, Ben. I hope you enjoy your stay." There was an uncomfortable silence.

An old woman suddenly screamed as her miniature dachshund escaped from its stroller and dashed past Ben. A cacophony of high-pitched barks echoed through the room and the atmosphere quickly turned to one of a prison break—the fluffy inmates hooting and hollering in excitement at the idea of anyone daring to breach the confines of their cell.

Unphased, Dwayne bent down to pick up the pink bow that had flown off the dog's head. "And my offer stands," he added. "Just let your mother know if you'd like some suggestions about the area." He handed the bow to Ben.

A bit disoriented, Ben accepted it quickly, careful to avoid even the slightest contact during the exchange. Dwayne gave a little shrug, then winked at Betsy before departing.

Ben held his mother's unsmiling gaze briefly. Together, they watched Dwayne take his time sashaying toward the front doors, as if witnessing his departure were some event worthy enough to bypass even a few moments of interaction with each other.

A young staff member had gone after the dachshund. Ben extended his arm as she passed to relieve himself of the tiny twist of pink ribbon Dwayne had so awkwardly bestowed on him. He monitored the silly chase for a few moments, then turned back to find Betsy had stepped away and was now occupied at the concierge's desk. He stuffed his hands in his pockets and squinted back at the front doors, unable to shake the unsettling feeling that this wasn't the last of what he'd be forced to foil.

two

Betsy had Clark secure them a golf cart, the essential mode of transportation for traversing the club's grounds. Along the pristinely kept paths, Ben spotted sapphire ponds and pools left and right, each paired with a small gazebo affording shade over a welcoming wooden bench. A myriad of carts and caddies scattered the lush fairways of two eighteen-hole golf courses. Betsy lifted a hand from the wheel to wave and shout greetings at folks as they passed, and most waved back.

In spite of what Ben had thought was already an obvious display of disinterest, Betsy continued to chatter away about Dwayne and how indispensable he'd become in preparing for the big anniversary party. She took care in providing a detailed résumé, which included where Dwayne grew up and the name of an evidently prestigious design school he'd attended somewhere in New England. Ben was about to cut her off in protest when his pocket buzzed with a message alert. He raised his phone to find a text from an unknown number.

Great to meet you Ben. Let me know if you change your mind. Dwayne.

Ben groaned. "You gave him my number?"

"Well, yeah," Betsy replied, innocently. "I thought that in case you two didn't meet today it'd be easier." She glanced at

Ben. His head was down, still eyeing his phone. "I just wanted to make sure you and Dwayne could connect."

"I don't want to connect, Ma."

"That's fine," Betsy said, shaking her head. "You don't have to respond to it, then."

Ben had had several boyfriends over the years. He came out to his parents when he was seventeen, and while Betsy had avoided him for two weeks immediately afterward, she hadn't been staunchly unsupportive about it. In fact, when she liked the guy Ben happened to be dating—or more accurately, when she liked the *job* of the guy Ben happened to be dating—she was very supportive. She was jubilant when he brought home Mitch, an intellectual property attorney, one Easter. It didn't matter that Mitch wasn't particularly friendly or that he got hammered before dessert was served. Betsy fawned over him. She couldn't be bothered to make an effort with Justin. A sweet, unassuming guy, Justin worked at a non-profit for homeless youth, a nonstarter for Betsy. Jake, as an accountant in a small tax firm, was middle ground. Tolerable, but forgettable.

Regardless of the reason for Betsy's approval or non-approval of Ben's boyfriends, her fluctuating levels of acceptance had been a perplexing experience for him. It had been understandable that his mom would act a bit unsure of how to behave around him for a while, right after he came out. When he began dating, Ben watched her progress through the typical tricky phases a parent goes through for how to introduce a gay child's companion. First "friend," of course. Then the big leap to "boyfriend." This was a particularly tough one for Betsy. The term made it impossible for her to deny that a sexual reason existed for her son to have chosen to live with a man.

"Partner" was actually a welcome relief for her. For insurance purposes three years prior, Ben and Jake had uneventfully signed documents to become domestic partners. And despite their tendency to still call each other "boyfriend," Betsy could again feel relatively comfortable with this more neutral term at her disposal. When Ben noticed her occasionally reverting back to calling Jake his friend or roommate, he'd gently remind her and she'd eventually acquiesce, assuring him that she was sorry and had just forgotten. While Ben couldn't be certain of his mom's apparent matchmaking intentions with Dwayne, today's bizarre encounter had only added to his confusion.

Continuing to wind their way through the grounds, Betsy surprised Ben by switching gears to let him in on some of the latest gossip floating around the club. He drew a hand to his face as he listened to how Esther Caldwell had recently gotten a DUI following a mimosa-soaked brunch with some girlfriends. Or how last month at Ed and Connie Lambert's granddaughter's wedding reception, a groomsman had stolen four pin flags from course two and fiendishly staked them in someone's previously perfect yard. And then there was Betsy's cards partner, Sue Wilkins. Betsy had suspected Sue was one of the three or four women rumored to have recently contracted an STD from a yet to be identified resident Casanova. She was tipped off after a game of bridge, when Sue confided in her about a possible yeast infection—an overly vivid piece of information which Ben, cringing, assured his mother would have been absolutely fine to leave out.

They passed a series of grand homes. Most appeared similar in make, but a handful stood out as a tad more unique, ever so slightly managing to sidestep the perception of redundancy. For most of his childhood, Ben had grown up in a fairly affluent suburb southwest of Minneapolis and was used to a large house. He and his sister each had large bedrooms with walk-in closets. There was an office—Betsy called it a den—and an impressive yard which his parents paid to keep meticulously landscaped. A middle-aged Ukrainian woman named Irina came weekly to dust, vacuum and clean the bathrooms.

Both his parents had expressed confusion when Ben continued to rent a small apartment for many years after college. He and his sister had each been gifted a hefty sum upon graduating, which would have served very nicely as a down payment on a sizable house. Ben chose to save his, however, allowing it to appreciate until he and Jake were prepared to purchase their modest condo downtown, in full.

As they approached the villa, Ben realized his parents' new house was something very different. He had thought that when people retire they tended to downsize, the way Jim and Betsy had done at Citrus Hill. Instead, what stood before him now was a huge, Mediterranean-style McMansion. Door-sized windows covered a majority of the home's facade. A balcony extended from what looked like a large bedroom on the second floor. The garage consisted of three stalls—more than ample space for the Apts' single vehicle and golf cart. Curled around the west side of the home, a gleaming pool was complimented by a covered patio with enough padded lounge chairs to seat fifteen. The tidy hedges looked like something out of an arboretum. Ben's suitcase sat under the arched front doorway.

Betsy stepped off the cart and stood with her hands on her hips. "What do you think?" she asked proudly.

Ben hesitated before replying. "It's...really big," he said.

"It's not *that* big," Betsy insisted. "The garage size just gives it the illusion of being big. You saw some of the houses we passed. We're sort of middle of the road for size here."

Ben continued to ogle the home's massive exterior. "How many bedrooms does it have?"

"Five," Betsy shrugged.

"*Five?* Jeez, Mom. For what?"

"What do you mean, 'for what?'"

"It's just you and Dad. Why on earth do you need five bedrooms?"

Betsy frowned. "We have guests who stay with us occasionally, and we figured that if you or Abby and the girls were ever here at the same time, it'd be nice for everyone to have their own space. And one of the rooms we've converted to a den for your father. Besides, not many other houses that were available here had a pool this nice."

This was the first time Ben had been to Florida in two years. Abby hadn't visited in three, and never with her husband, Terry. Since their father's retirement, they would see their parents around the holidays, when Jim and Betsy typically came back to Minnesota and stayed for about a week. Betsy would craft grandiose plans to have the whole family come down in the spring, but balked if Abby ever actually attempted to solidify plans, providing excuses like "the pools weren't really designed for young children," or "I'm sure fall isn't a good time to disrupt the girls' routine." After a while, Ben and Abby just started coming up with their own excuses for not going. It felt better to say "no" than to feel unwanted.

Ben had to question whether his mother's insistence on his presence that weekend was fully genuine. He wasn't sure how to react when hearing her mention the possibility of them all being together again. If she were serious, he might feel a little funny about this being only his second trip to Florida. And although he already regretted the hint of disapproval in his voice over the size of the house, its effect had obviously landed, as Betsy's cheerful demeanor distinctly mellowed when they stepped inside.

"Your father's napping," she said. "I'd prefer not to wake him."

"No problem," Ben said, trying to find things to agree on.

He was grateful for the climate-controlled chill that welcomed him upon entering the house. He gazed up into the entryway to examine the interior. It smelled like paint. The walls were all a light tan color with an ivory crown molding. Each of the lamps and wall hangings were either brown or gray, matching the similarly toned sofa filling the living room. He liked the vaulted ceilings, but other than that, the place appeared rather cookie-cutter and gave the feeling more of a new hotel than someone's home. After seeing his mother's reaction to his astonishment at the house's size, however, Ben figured it was best to pull his punches in the critique department, and remained silent.

"We've got you set up in here, sweetheart," said Betsy, stopping in front of one of the bedrooms.

"Whoa. King-sized bed," Ben said, smiling in the doorway. His intention wasn't to criticize. He was genuinely excited about having such a large bed all to himself for the weekend. But he instantly realized his mistake when he heard Betsy's frustrated exhale. "This is great, Mom. Really. Thank you." He suddenly realized how overly agreeable he was behaving at this point—an impulse to diffuse conflict he hadn't felt the need to employ much in recent years. He squeezed the handle on his suitcase until his knuckles whitened.

Betsy had wrapped her arms around herself. "Go ahead and get yourself settled," she replied. Her blank expression was one usually reserved for when Ben had said something particularly smart-alecky. "I'm actually feeling a bit tired myself. I might lie down for a while before dinner." Then she added with a slight smile, "We have reservations at the club's best restaurant at six."

"Perfect!" Ben said, aware of how earnest this too sounded.

Betsy briskly stepped across the entryway toward her own bedroom. "You should nap too," she directed, and closed the door behind her.

Ben stood in place for a few moments, watching the door to his parents' room, beat. What a brilliant start he'd managed to work out for himself. He raised his shoulders to take in a deep breath, then loosened his grip on his suitcase and slowly wheeled it behind him into his room.

～

Ben suspected his exhaustion was more than just the heat and two glasses of wine he'd enjoyed on the plane. Regardless, at least he'd have little trouble following his mother's instructions to rest. He swept aside half of the nearly dozen accent pillows on his bed, then plopped down and sent off a text to Jake to let him know he'd made it safely. Just as he was about to close his eyes, his phone, resting on his stomach beneath his folded hands, began to buzz.

"Hey, handsome," Ben said, almost in a whisper. He put his phone on speaker then set it back on his belly.

"Hi, babe! I'm in the car on my way home from work so didn't want to text," Jake explained. "How's it going so far?"

It was a loaded question. Jake was already looking for good news on his progress. "Not bad. I was just trying to rest my eyes for a bit before dinner."

"Do you want me to let you go?"

"No, no. It's fine." Ben sat up a little in bed. "How was your day?" he added, shifting focus from himself.

"Crazy, of course." Jake sighed. "I'll have to go in for a while this weekend."

Ben had seen relatively little of his partner since the start of the year. Seventy-hour weeks had become the norm between February and April for Jake.

"Aw, yuck. I'm sorry."

"Eh, it's the season," Jake said. "But I don't feel like talking about work. Tell me about the club. Is it just obscene?"

Ben ran his fingers through his hair. "Nah," he said. "It's okay so far."

"Seen any black people yet?"

"Jeez, Jake," Ben laughed. "No. As a matter of fact I haven't."

"Shocker," Jake scoffed.

"I've only been here an hour."

"Well, from your parents' description, it didn't strike me as a particularly diverse place."

"So nothing like Minnesota then, huh?" Ben playfully challenged.

Jake ignored this. "I defy you to spot a single person of color there this weekend."

"Done."

"Who *doesn't* work there."

"Ugh," Ben groaned. "Fine. Will you take my word for it, or will you need photographic proof, you weirdo?"

"I'll take your word for it," Jake said, satisfied. They both giggled then like little boys.

But Jake had ample cause to inquire about the demographics. Born in Haiti to a white father and black mother, he knew all too well the uneasy feeling of stepping into an environment like The Cypress Club, the almost dull lack of representation among its residents. And while Ben was disappointed his boyfriend's demanding work schedule prevented him from joining that weekend, he understood how Jake might have ultimately preferred staying home regardless.

"I have to admit," Ben continued, "the club really is incredible. It sort of feels like I stepped into Disneyland."

"Ew."

"Only it's old people walking around with creepy smiles on their faces instead of costumed characters."

"Oh my God," Jake howled. "Well, they probably can't help it if their faces are all frozen from the Botox."

"Right?" Ben agreed, chuckling a little too.

Ben's laughter slowed then, reminded of his mother's new appearance. Not long before this trip, he and Jake had been poking fun at Jim and Betsy's circle of friends in Florida after they'd seen a series of photos Betsy had posted online. All the women had that "surgered" look to them, as Ben called it. Anyone who saw the photos would easily be able to tell that Betsy had had work done, too. But when compared to the others in the photo, her appearance had retained a reasonable level of normalcy. Whatever procedures she had elected to undergo between then and now, however, Ben determined, had decidedly shifted her into the same category as her friends. He cringed slightly when considering how Jake would react if he saw her now.

"The club's ridiculously fancy," Ben continued, opting not to mention Betsy's latest "work." "Picture the nicest day spa you've ever been to and then just living there."

"Wow," Jake said.

"Yeah. And everything's big. Like, really big."

"I can only imagine," said Jake. He paused a moment, then asked, making sure to emphasize Betsy's recent rebranding. "So, how *are* Jim and Betsy?"

"Haven't talked to Dad yet. He's napping. Mom is...good?"

"Well, that sounds convincing," Jake teased. "Was she crabby or something?" There was a hint of concern in his voice.

"No, she was actually in a super good mood when I met up with her at the main building. Of course she gossiped the entire way to the house. Oh, excuse me. Villa."

"Oh, Lord," Jake laughed. "So, what was it?"

"I don't know. She just seems sort of—"

"What?" Jake interrupted, anxious for a bit of gossip of his own.

Ben lowered his voice slightly, as if hesitant to divulge anything negative about his mother this early into the trip. "...different, I guess. She's always been a bit of a busybody, but she was on total hyperdrive this afternoon. She talked for like fifteen straight minutes on the ride here." He slumped against the firm pillows then. "I don't know. Maybe it's just standard operating procedure for the people in this place."

"I hate to break it to you, babe, but that's not new," said Jake, as if disappointed to learn that Betsy, to him at least, sounded the same.

"What do you mean?"

"Your mom being annoying."

"She's not that bad," Ben laughed.

"Come on," Jake egged. "Fifteen minutes is nothing for her."

"To finish a story?"

"To finish a sentence."

"Stop."

"Without taking a breath."

"All right, all right," Ben said, trying to muffle his voice. "She'll hear me."

He was strangely relieved that Jake seemed to think his mother hadn't changed much.

"I imagine it's kind of like returning to high school with a bunch of cliques forming and everyone knowing everything about each other," Jake suggested. "That place sounds just right for her."

"Yeah, I suppose," Ben said. For some reason he was reluctant to agree with this just yet. Then he added, "When I arrived, she introduced me to her party planner and wouldn't shut up about him."

"How do you mean?"

"She kept insisting that he and I chat about things to do in the city."

"That's kind of weird," Jake said.

"I know," Ben quickly agreed. His tone was playful. "I was like 'Mom, are you trying to get us to hook up?'"

"What do you mean 'hook up'?"

"I don't mean she actually wanted us to hook up," Ben said, backtracking a little. "She just wanted us to talk. I guess he knows the city well."

"Was he gay?" Jake asked, serious now.

Ben squirmed on the bed. "Probably," he said. "I mean, the guy was wearing a pink bow tie and foundation. I think it's safe to assume he's family." He was trying not to sound exasperated.

"And your mom was hoping to set you two up?"

Ben wished he hadn't brought up Dwayne at all now. It had seemed like a fun example of the nonsense he might expect to run into that weekend. But Jake was taking it entirely differently. "It wasn't as calculated as that, Jake," Ben said. "She probably just thought that since we were both gay, it was like a rule that we hang out or something. She meant no harm." Ben recalled an occasion when his mother insisted on introducing one of his college friends to a fellow member of her book club, after discovering the two were both one-sixteenth Ojibwe.

"Was he cute?" Jake asked. It felt like an accusation.

"Christ, Jake. No." Ben sighed. "He was like over fifty and plastic. Not exactly my type." He instantly regretted saying this.

"So you have a type now?"

"Are you seriously worried that I'm going to hook up with my mom's fucking party planner? Good God. I'm sorry I even mentioned it."

"Please don't try to turn this into me being the paranoid jealous boyfriend," Jake contended. "I'm just saying it's bizarre that the first thing you and your mom talk about when you get there is getting set up with one of her friends."

"I'm sorry, but that's just ridiculous. It was a purely one-sided conversation. I did absolutely nothing to give this guy or my mom any impression that I was even remotely interested."

"You know I'm not just being ridiculous," Jake replied, more softly.

There was a brief silence. Ben lowered his voice to match Jake's, but couldn't hide his frustration. "Do we really have to do this again? Now?" he asked, almost pleading. "What do you want me to say, Jake? That I called my mom ahead of time to make sure she had someone lined up for me to fuck as soon as I landed?"

There was another, uncomfortably long silence. "No," Jake replied. "Let's just forget about it."

Ben grit his teeth and closed his eyes tightly. He already wished he could redo half the conversation with his mom earlier, and the last thing he wanted or needed now was for his boyfriend to be mad at him. But he couldn't take back his reaction to Jake's apparent worries about Dwayne.

"Jake, I'm sorry," Ben offered as calmly as he could. "I didn't mean to put it on you."

"It's fine. Really," Jake insisted. "I'm sure I'm overreacting." He sighed then. "Maybe you should consider taking this guy up on his offer. I mean if it'll help with your mom..."

"Absolutely not."

Jake's silence signaled Ben had answered correctly. Finally he said, "I should probably get going anyway. I need to stop at the grocery store."

"Okay," said Ben, drained by where the conversation had led.

"Tell your dad hi."

Ben raised a hand to his forehead. "Will do," he said. He tried to lighten his voice a little. "Give the cats a spanking for me."

"We'll miss you this weekend," Jake replied, and hung up.

Ben threw his phone onto the bed. Dinner was in under two hours and he was dreading the effort it would take to get himself in the mood to be passably social. He realized Betsy was probably right about trying to nap beforehand, but a stubborn restlessness lingered after his conversation with Jake, and he worried he'd be incapable of settling down enough to doze off. He recovered his phone and guessed right on his parents' Wi-Fi password: uncreatively a variation of his and Abby's birth date. Surfing one of his preferred porn sites, he unzipped his snug jeans and duly finished himself off to a clip showcasing the aloof intertwinings of three impossibly perfect Brazilians. Sleep easily followed.

three

Ben awoke from his nap at five-thirty, the sun still beaming warmly through the bedroom window. There was little time before dinner, and he knew he better get moving if he wanted to shower and change without making his parents wait. He had hoped his irritation at what he considered Jake's needless worrying would be solved by the nap. Instead, he felt more tired than when he'd fallen asleep, and with a headache now to boot. He eventually dragged himself to the bathroom, where after figuring out the right combination of temperature and pressure from the four dials on the wall, he enjoyed a small boost of energy under the cool spray of the rainfall shower head.

Even from a distance, Ben was counting on Jake's support to get him through the weekend. But as he changed into a crisp polo and finally a pair of shorts, he couldn't shake their thorny exchange from his mind. He was seething from how defensive he'd let himself get. Moreover, it bothered him how irrational Jake had been on the phone—the immediacy of the accusations when he'd done nothing wrong. His interaction with Dwayne had been completely one-sided, and Jake's lack of trust over something so trivial seemed wildly unfair under these circumstances.

The truth was, Ben knew Jake's misgivings about him travelling alone to Florida were not without merit. They'd endured a tumultuous period last summer at the close of Jake's softball season. Jake and his teammate Oliver had sort of hit it off as friends, and the two began including each other in their free time outside softball. They'd plan game nights and movie nights, or grab drinks on Fridays after work. By the nervous way Jake behaved around Oliver, the way he spoke about his wit or how sweet it was when he'd helped an opposing team's player off the field after an injury, it was obvious to Ben that Jake had developed a little crush. He couldn't really blame him. Oliver was kind and self-deprecatingly funny. It would be difficult not to feel something for him.

More remarkable to Ben, however, were Oliver's astonishingly good looks. With his athletic build, irresistible dimples, and head of wavy hair that always made him look like he'd just stepped off a yacht, everyone wanted him. It wasn't uncommon among their group of friends and acquaintances to develop little side crushes on other guys, even when they were in relationships. As far as Ben knew, few ever acted on it. Yet he began to make a point of clearing his schedule to ensure he was in attendance for as many of Jake's games as possible.

At the end of each season, all the teams in the softball league met for a banquet dinner and closing party. Awards were presented for best team in each division, most valuable player, most improved, most "fabulous" uniforms, and best team cheer. To no one's surprise last summer, Oliver was named MVP of the A division. Small groups from a few teams would also compete in brief drag skits they put together, with winners decided by the loudness of applause received from the audience. Jake's troupe's performance came in a close second.

Ben had intended to join Jake for the banquet, but his grandmother had unexpectedly been hospitalized with a bout of pneumonia, and he chose to skip the event to be with her. After he was assured that she was in no danger and would be released in the morning, Ben met up with Jake and their friends at a nearby bar, where the party had inevitably spilled over.

By that point in the night, Jake's usually contained interest in Oliver had become much less reserved. Ben noticed how Jake drunkenly laughed at everything Oliver said, regardless of its level of humor. When Oliver playfully teased Jake about how tipsy he was getting or that he could still see traces of his eyeliner left over from the drag skit, Jake coyly smacked him on the chest with the back of his hand and only giggled more. Oliver hadn't been nearly as intoxicated, and could see that Ben was nearby, watching intently. The two exchanged looks occasionally, monitoring each other's reactions.

Ben's concern over his boyfriend's flirtation somewhat cooled when it became clear that Oliver's interests that night rested unmistakably on him, not Jake. It started with long-held glances, then with Oliver gradually moving closer and taking every opportunity to make physical contact, either with a brush to Ben's back or cozying up shoulder to shoulder as they both stood at the bar waiting for a drink. Ben was handsome too, and with his tall, trim frame and dirty blond hair, he'd had his own cast of admirers around the scene.

At bar close, Jake boldly invited Oliver back to their place, ostensibly for a nightcap. Ben hadn't thought it was a good idea, but Jake's drunken insistence coupled with Oliver's quick agreement left him with little capacity to protest. Back at their condo, it didn't take long for Jake to pass out on the sofa. Ben was tired and distracted. But Oliver's earnest interest to hear about his grandma was disarming, and the two ended up chatting for a while. When Oliver inched closer to rest a consoling hand on Ben's thigh, Ben didn't fight the move for a kiss. And as those lips, as if on a mission, worked their way to Ben's waist, Ben only closed his eyes, tipped back his head, and enjoyed the delirium of full, if brief, escape.

He had considered keeping the encounter a secret. Although multiple people had seen the three of them leave the bar together, he and Jake weren't known to have an open relationship; and if rumors swirled, he could have easily passed it off as typical speculation from nosy queers. Jake wouldn't have remembered the events of the night regardless. But Ben had always been honest with him, and although he felt like his vulnerability may have been taken advantage of that night, it felt only right to explain what happened with Oliver.

Unsurprisingly, Jake was hurt, even stunned, by the news. The two had never discussed the possibility of branching out sexually with other people. Worse yet, the fact that Jake was himself very fond of Oliver made Ben's perceived betrayal doubly difficult. Not only had he been cheated on by his partner, but it also became clear that Oliver didn't think of Jake the same way Jake did about him. Even if nothing were ever to come of Jake's interest in Oliver, Ben understood that it wouldn't feel good to know that a guy you not so secretly liked was far more interested in your boyfriend than in you.

The fact that Ben had actually been sober was the one untruth he felt necessary to leave intact. He figured that with enough apologizing and a promise to never do it again, Jake would forgive him, and they'd move on. Absolution seemed to have come with time. But Ben worried the recovery of

Jake's trust may never, the possibility of which today's phone conversation had somewhat painfully reminded him.

~~~

Ben hurried out of his room a little sheepishly, knowing he was cutting it close for their reservation. His parents were waiting in the living room. Betsy flipped through the pages of a magazine to distract herself from the television, which Jim had tuned to a golf tournament.

"Lazarus!" Jim hollered. He stood up to shake Ben's hand then wrapped his other arm around him in a bro hug.

Ben was a little surprised by just how happy he was to see his dad. It bordered on relief, as if he'd forgotten there would be someone else he knew this weekend besides Mom. "Hey, Pops. It's great to see you," he said.

Betsy lifted her eyes from her magazine, unsmiling. "We should probably get going."

"I haven't made us late for dinner, have I?" asked Ben.

"Oh, we're fine," Jim assured him, slapping Ben on the shoulder. "Our table's not going anywhere. You hungry?"

"Famished."

"We'll leave soon," Jim said, then motioned toward the living room. "Sit down and visit with us a bit. We've got a few minutes." Betsy pursed her lips and reopened her magazine.

Ben noticed his dad had put on a few pounds since the holidays. He'd grown a bit of a paunch in recent years, nothing drastic. Still, his belly and face were a little rounder today, even for him. But Ben found the extra weight only made his father look more himself—as if he were always on the verge of a smile. And thanks to a minor skin condition, Jim's naturally plump cheeks were rosy year-round. Ben and his sister had taken to teasing their father in recent years with the suggestion that if he'd just grow out his beard, he could make a few extra bucks each December playing Santa Claus at a local mall. Jim would only wave it off, laughing with a self-mocking "ho-ho-ho."

Ben sat across from his parents on one end of the large, U-shaped sofa. He eyed the room, able to study it more closely than when he'd arrived.

"So, how've you been?" Jim asked.

"Good. Busy," Ben said. "Not as busy as Jake is this time of year, of course. But it's been steady at the clinic." Ben glanced at Betsy, then back at Jim. "He says hi, by the way."

"Oh, good," Jim replied, cheerfully. "Tell him hello from us as well. We'll miss him this weekend."

Jim had always been more conversational about Jake than had Betsy. There were times early on where he'd tend to speak of him more as one of Ben's colleagues or old college buddies, rather than his partner. It was only around Betsy and their friends when that would happen, Ben had noticed. But Jim had since come around. A couple of years ago, even when Jake had insisted he wasn't taking on new clients, Jim persuaded him to add the Apts to his accounts. As a favor, Jake agreed. With a few previously unknown deductions, Jake had also found a way to save Jim's business a boatload of cash. And ever since, Jim had placed Jake near the top of his favorites list, which thrilled and relieved Ben.

"So, things are good at that clinic of yours?" Jim asked.

Ben paused and smiled. "Yes, I like it there."

Jim nodded, his attention going back and forth from the TV. An orthopedic surgeon before retiring, Jim had taken great pride in the fact that both Ben and Abby had followed in his footsteps into the health field. Each had attended the University of Minnesota—Abby becoming a clinical psychologist, while Ben went on to the physician assistant program at Augsburg after undergrad.

Having been on the front end in developing a minimally invasive procedure for hip replacements, Jim had built an incredibly lucrative practice in the Twin Cities. His technique ensured a much more rapid recovery with less pain, an appealing outcome that had patients lining up at the door on a six-month waiting list to see him.

Ben's decision not to attend medical school at all had always been a sore spot for Betsy. She'd helped out in the clinic as a receptionist from time to time, and assumed their son would want nothing more than to take over the family business after Jim retired. When Ben agreed to join Jim's practice after finishing PA school, his parents were excited about that possibility. His tenure lasted only six months, however. Ben just couldn't picture himself enduring the monotony of suturing up hip after hip four mornings a week while his father scrubbed out and moved on to their next anesthetized customer. And to his mother's disappointment, he resigned and opted for a position at a family practice clinic on Minneapolis's unglamorous north side.

Sensing the conversation might revisit that history, Ben looked around the room, trying to think of something else they could talk about. It occurred to him that with how matchy-matchy everything was, the home's decor and furnishings seemed to be predetermined upon purchase. "Where's all your stuff?"

"What stuff?" asked Betsy.

"All the old stuff you had back home."

"You didn't expect us to move all that old furniture down to Florida with us, did you?" Betsy replied, crossing her legs. "Anyway, it wouldn't fit the layout of this place, Benny."

"No, I don't mean the furniture. You still had a few of your travel mementos at your place in Citrus Hill. I figured maybe there wasn't enough room for everything then, but there seems to be plenty of space now. Don't you miss having some of those things around?"

"It was just simpler to keep everything in its place back home," Betsy said.

Despite spending less than a week there over the holidays, the Apts had maintained ownership of their home not far from Minneapolis. They hired a service to look after it all year long, as Betsy preferred that no one actually live there while they were in Florida. For decades, she had relished collecting expensive souvenirs from her travels with Jim, many of which she had proudly kept on display in their home. A three-foot red vase she'd shipped over from Shanghai had welcomed guests in the entryway. In the living room, a rough slab of petrified wood from Rio served as the centerpiece for the coffee table, while several small, ivory busts she'd acquired in Athens of some Greek philosophers had been perched on the mantle of their piano for as long as Ben could remember. At times, it had felt a bit like growing up in a museum, always being told not to touch anything. It wasn't until adulthood that he gained some appreciation for how unique those objects made their home feel.

He saw the joy they brought his mom when she'd inevitably provide their lengthy backstories to whomever she could corner into accepting a tour.

Ben glanced at his father, who had begun to doze off. Betsy nudged him, then tossed her magazine onto the coffee table, a closer look at which made Ben now realize was, somewhat ironically, a copy of *Good Housekeeping*. He had never expected his parents to stay in his childhood home forever, but presumed that wherever they ended up, it would still show hints of their own tastes. None of the expensive prints on the walls or various knickknacks on the end tables in this new place even remotely resembled anything personal, however. There were no books. No plants—no real ones, anyway. Not a single family photo was visible. With its design that looked like it had been conveniently clipped from a coastal living catalog, Ben was puzzled and a bit disappointed at the hollowed-out hutch in which his parents had chosen to live out their golden years.

His appetite all but disappeared.

～～

They made it to The Blue Fin fifteen minutes past their reservation time.

"Sorry we're a bit late, Saul," Jim said, shaking the host's hand as they entered.

"Not at all, Mr. Apt," replied Saul, waving off the slight tardiness. "I'll be happy to show you to your table. The rest of your party has already been seated."

Ben whipped his head away from the enormous aquarium he'd been admiring in the entryway and grabbed Betsy's elbow.

"The rest of our party?" he asked, a slight look of panic on his face.

"Yes. Our friends the Gundersons. Remember?" Betsy replied, shaking her head. "We sort of have a standing reservation with them on Friday nights. I mentioned that, didn't I?" Ben only glared at her as she peered ahead into the crowded dining room. "Well, Benny, I can't very well ask them to leave now."

"Are you sure I won't be intruding?" Ben quipped.

"Nonsense," Betsy smiled, as if Ben were serious. Then she whispered as she linked her arm with his, "Sweetie, you'll like Dan and Ruth. They have a son who's a doctor too."

"Wonderful," Ben sighed. "I'm sure I'll hear all about him."

Winding their way past the other tables, Ben could feel the room's eyes studying him. His youthful presence in a room full of Boomers seemed to cause a bit of a buzz amongst its diners. When they reached their table, he sat down as quickly and inconspicuously as he could. His parents took their time reconnecting with the Gundersons, as if the foursome hadn't seen each other in ages. Jim shook hands with Dan and slapped the side of his shoulder, while Betsy and Ruth embraced and complimented each other on their outfits. When Dan kissed Betsy on both cheeks and hugged her for what seemed like an unnecessarily long time, Ben couldn't help but check his father's reaction. He didn't seem to notice. Ben dragged his hand across the back of his neck, then managed to grab the attention of a passing waiter and promptly ordered a gin and tonic.

"Well, this must be Benjamin!" Ruth squealed, taking her seat. "It's so nice to finally meet you. Your mom has told us so many wonderful things about you and your sister."

Slouching, Ben offered a bashful wave from across the table. "Hi," he said.

The Gundersons both appeared friendly. In addition to being a little more plump than most of the women he'd seen since arriving, Ruth stood out in dark-rimmed glasses. Ben quickly identified her auburn bob, with its bangs stopping just above her eyebrows, as an expensive wig. She was more conservatively dressed than his mom, opting for capris and a pink summer sweater. Dan, a retired orthodontist, smiled with a brightness one would expect from someone in his profession. His shiny teeth sharply contrasted with the leathery texture of his tanned face. Ben guessed his age to be similar to Ruth's, but his obvious penchant for sunshine left him looking about fifteen years older.

"I understand you work in a primary care office in Minneapolis?" said Dan, jumping right in.

"That's right," Ben replied.

"What kind of patients do you mostly see?"

"Your typical family medicine patients, I guess. A lot of chronic things like high blood pressure and diabetes. I work in an underserved area of Minneapolis, so there tend to be a lot of issues managing treatable illnesses."

"Oh, heavens," Ruth gasped.

"What do you mean by *underserved*?" Dan asked, squinting.

Ben hesitated, a little perplexed. "Poor."

By the repulsed look on Dan's face, it was as if Ben had just detailed what it would be like working in a leper colony. Ruth uncomfortably fiddled with her place settings, unsure how to respond.

Betsy hurried to offer a more palatable topic. "Ben was rated one of the area's top doctors by *Twin Cities Magazine* last year," she bragged.

"Oh my goodness!" Ruth said, perking up.

"Well, I'm not a doctor, actually," Ben quickly corrected. "I'm a PA." Then to Betsy, "And I wasn't personally named as one of the top providers by the magazine. I was just mentioned as part of the team of physicians I work with."

Betsy, a little embarrassed, glanced at Ruth and quickly added with a nervous smile, "Oh, Benny, you're just being modest."

"Yes, your mother's right, I'm sure," Ruth insisted.

Ben's clarification, while accurate, was in fact a bit modest. He had worked closely with several physicians at his clinic to improve how patients are educated about their blood sugar levels. The research he'd conducted had been published in the *Journal of Endocrinology* and changed certain standards for diabetes care nationwide.

"Did you ever consider going on to medical school?" asked Dan.

"Going on?" Ben repeated.

Ruth smiled and said, "Yes, now that you've gained experience in the medical field? I expect you'd want to be able to do the same things as the doctors in your office."

"I already do," Ben said, growing irritated.

While used to regularly fielding similar questions from people unfamiliar with his job, something about the Gundersons' naiveté made Ben particularly annoyed about having to explain that being a PA wasn't merely a stepping stone to becoming a physician. He leaned back in his chair and looked over each shoulder, hoping to spot the waiter on his way to the table with his drink.

Betsy shook her head. "It's no use, you two," she said, laughing like it was no big deal. "I've tried."

Ben shrunk a little in his seat.

Noticing the effect of Betsy's comment, Jim cleared his throat and attempted to change the subject. "Tell us about Eli's new job."

"Oh, yes!" Ruth exclaimed, locking eyes with Ben then. "Our son Eli is currently a radiologist in Indianapolis, but he just accepted a faculty position at the Mayo Clinic!"

With letters of recommendation from his instructors, Ben had been offered a job at the Mayo Clinic just after finishing PA school, but declined it without telling his parents. After driving to Rochester a couple of times for interviews, he concluded it was possibly the most boring city he'd ever visited.

"Good for him," Ben said. "Rochester's beautiful."

"You should give Ben his email," Betsy suggested.

"Good idea!" Ruth shrieked.

"That's not necessary," Ben interjected. But seeing their disappointed looks, he quickly added, "I can find him on the Mayo directory."

Both ladies flashed an appeased smile.

"Your mom mentioned there's a third grandchild on the way," Dan said, placing his napkin on his lap. "What about you, Ben? Married?"

"Nope."

"Girlfriend?" Ruth prodded, leaning in.

"Uh, no," Ben said. "Boyfriend."

Dan and Ruth's eyes widened and they both nodded slowly. Betsy obliviously poked her nose in her menu. After a few moments, Dan followed suit.

Ben glared at his mother. This felt like the second blow, and they hadn't even ordered their meals yet.

"And what does...he do?" Ruth asked softly, as if trying not to be overheard.

"Jake's an accountant," Ben said, deliberately louder.

"Well, that's nice," Ruth smiled. "It's a shame he wasn't able to make the trip with you."

"Yeah, it's sort of impossible for him to be away from work during tax season," Ben replied.

For the first time in his life, Ben wished he were an accountant too. The waiter came around with his drink and Ben swiftly scooped it off the tray with both hands. The rest of the table ordered a round as well, and just before the busy waiter escaped, Ben quietly requested a second gin and tonic.

As dinner progressed, Ben barely spoke. After the introductory peppering of questions, no one at the table seemed all that interested in hearing what he had to say, Jim and Betsy included. So for the most part, he was able to relax. He held his phone discreetly below the table to text his sister about their mother's little omission of the fact that he'd be dining with strangers.

You sound surprised, came Abby's response. She quickly added, *Has anyone asked you how much less you make than an MD yet?*

Ben had to stifle a laugh. The twins' little back-and-forth temporarily spared him from having to participate in the table's vapid topics. Dan generally led the charge, covering the growing preponderance of Latino wait staff, laxed club admission standards, and what a major inconvenience it was that the clay tennis courts would be unavailable this week due to resurfacing.

Only during their entrées, when the conversation veered into healthcare, did Ben think to lift his head and consider chiming in. Dan brought up how a few months ago he had tweaked his knee playing golf and the pain had been affecting his game. After getting an MRI and undergoing an arthroscopic procedure to remove some cartilage, he was proud to report that he had made it back on the greens within a month of the injury.

"It's a testament to a free-market healthcare system," Dan bellowed. "Can you imagine how long it would've taken me to even get the imaging done in Canada? Unless something had been obviously torn, there's no way they would've ordered an MRI that soon. I'd probably still be waiting, much less done with surgery."

Betsy and Ruth nodded in agreement, both sipping chardonnay. Ruth liked ice cubes in hers.

"That's right," Ruth joined. "Dan's really been working hard on his swing this year. Imagine all that time he'd have missed being unable to play."

Betsy was nodding more enthusiastically now. "It's silly to think how in the twenty-first century they could make anyone wait months for something that required a surgery," she said. Then poking Jim's elbow, she added, "Remember that time I twisted my ankle in Melbourne? They just sent me home with an ice pack!"

Ben had been providing Abby with the play-by-play. She knew affordable access to healthcare was a particularly touchy subject for her brother.

How many drinks have you had? she asked.

On my third.

Oh shit. Will you put your phone on speaker?!?!

Ben rested his elbows on the table. "The pain prevented you from playing?" he asked Dan.

The two couples looked up from their plates, surprised to hear Ben's voice.

"Well, not exactly," Dan replied, glancing at the others. "It was mostly on my drives. I wasn't able to get a full swing with the amount of twisting it required on my knee."

"You had to shorten your swing just on driving?"

"Sometimes, yes."

"So...not all the time?"

Dan paused. "On occasion I didn't feel it much," he admitted.

"How bad was the pain when you felt it?"

"It could be sharp."

"But it wasn't always sharp?" Ben asked. Then, before Dan could answer, "How long did it last?"

"I don't know. Just a few seconds, I guess."

Jim chuckled nervously. "Jeez, son," he said, checking the ladies. "What's with the third degree?"

Ben scratched his neck. "I'm just curious about the extent of Dan's activity limitations from the knee pain, that's all. Sounds like the pain was only intermittent and brief when taking a full swing off the tee."

"It was a meniscus tear, Ben," Dan said, more serious now. "It had to be fixed."

"Bucket-handle tear?" Ben asked.

Dan sighed. "It was diagnosed as a degenerative tear, I believe."

"Interesting," Ben smiled. "One of the ortho docs I often refer patients to sent me an article a few months ago that showed the long-term benefits of physical therapy over surgery for degenerative meniscus tears. Was that an option they offered you?"

"They may have mentioned something about PT," Dan said, going back to his meal. "I figured it was never going to go away on its own, so I might as well have it taken care of now."

"I think that's pretty standard, Ben," Jim said, smiling as if he hoped this would put an end to it. "Take it from a surgeon. Knee arthroscopies typically have really good outcomes."

"Yes, when they're performed for the right reason," Ben argued. "And when's the last time you performed a knee surgery, Dad? 1982?"

Jim sat up a little, taken off guard by his son's pointed retort.

"Some current studies suggest that simply introducing a surgical scope into the knee joint space can speed up the degenerative process and exacerbate arthritis," Ben described. "Of course, there's no other option if a meniscus tear is traumatic and large." He turned to Dan. "But that's not the kind you had."

The ladies were trying to look anywhere other than at Ben or Dan.

Ben was feeling the alcohol by now and didn't resist the boldness it afforded him. "Now you're probably going to require a knee replacement sooner than you would have otherwise, had you instead just opted for a few weeks of rehab. Plus," he shrugged, "when all is said and done, it likely would've cost less than a tenth of what was spent on the surgery. Think your golf game suffered before? I'd be surprised if you're golfing at all in two years."

Ruth gasped, pressing her hand over her chest. The other three remained silent but looked equally stunned.

Ben shook the ice in his glass and gulped back the last of his gin and tonic before abruptly tossing his napkin on the table. "*That's* the true testament of a free-market healthcare system," he said. And with that, he excused himself to the restroom.

~

When Ben returned, his parents and the Gundersons were standing, ready to leave. The check had already been paid and the two couples had said their goodbyes. Dan cordially shook Ben's hand and told him to take care. Ruth offered a small smile, but said nothing.

Waiting outside the restaurant, Jim stood a few steps ahead of both Ben and Betsy, ready to accept the keys from the speedy valet when he pulled up. Betsy was quiet, her head down and her arms crossed. Ben grabbed his phone from his pocket.

"Would you put that thing away," Betsy ordered.

Ben looked up with a scrunched face. "What's the matter?" he asked, incredulously.

"You've been on it all night. It's rude."

Ben returned to his phone. "You didn't seem to mind during dinner."

"Well, I did," Betsy insisted. "You barely so much as lifted your head to acknowledge the rest of the table."

"I'm afraid I didn't have much to add to your topics of conversation."

"Until your mean comments to Dan, anyway."

"Mean?" Ben slowly asked. "You think I was *mean?*"

"You just met Dan, and you had the nerve to question his personal health decisions? Why would you do that? Dan and Ruth are our friends, Benny. I don't appreciate them being insulted."

"Knock it off, you two," Jim snapped from the curb.

It was unlike his father to raise his voice, and Ben quickly took notice of the irritation. He closed his eyes and inhaled deeply. "Mom, I'm sorry if you felt I was rude," he said. "I didn't mean to insult anyone."

"I don't just *feel* you were rude," Betsy scolded. "You *were* rude."

"Okay, I'm sorry if I *was* rude. It was just difficult to hold back after the things Dan was saying."

"What things?" Betsy demanded.

"I don't know. Just a lot of stuff. You guys were talking about the ethnicity of the employees and how rough you have it if something at the club is closed for a day. When Dan started shitting on single-payer healthcare…I guess I just sort of reached my limit of nonsense."

Betsy's jaw dropped, silently dumbfounded. When the car pulled up, she hopped into the front seat and slammed the door.

Jim slipped the valet a twenty, then turned to Ben with a grave look as if to ask, *What have you done?*

four

Jim offered Ben a finger of bourbon, and the two chatted over their nightcaps in the living room. Betsy continued her pout in the kitchen, noisily opening and closing cabinet doors as she emptied the dishwasher. Jim hollered to her from the living room, asking if she wanted him to open a bottle of wine, but she declined. "Damn," he whispered. "Why is she this upset?"

"I don't know," Ben said. "I already apologized for ruffling Dan's feathers at dinner."

"Eh, Dan will be fine," Jim said, swatting at the air. "I'll see him at golf in the morning. Ruth will probably try to make her feel bad about it for a while, but she'll get over it too. Your mother just gets anxious about people not liking her."

This relaxed Ben a little, despite the continued clamoring of dishes. He looked over his shoulder in the direction of the kitchen, hoping he could grab Betsy's attention. Jim made a jerking motion with his head, prompting Ben to get in there and attempt to make peace. Begrudgingly, Ben shuffled past the sofa into the kitchen and sat himself on one of the tall stools, quietly resting his drink on the granite island. On a small step with her back to him, Betsy pretended to reorganize a shelf.

"Need any help, Ma?" Ben asked.

"No. I'm fine, honey." Betsy continued fussing with the contents of the cabinet, moving mugs back and forth onto either side of the shelf. Ben gave her a few moments, thinking she'd finish up and turn around.

"I feel like you're still upset about dinner."

"Not at all, Benny," Betsy said. Then, redoubling her efforts in the cabinet, "I just need to get this done."

Ben extended his neck to the side, trying to see around her. "What are you doing?"

"This cabinet needs a new liner."

"Tonight?"

"What's wrong with tonight?" Betsy asked, a hint of disdain in her voice.

"Nothing. Just that Dad and I are hanging out in the living room and you're in here doing something that seems like it could be done any other night I'm not in Florida."

Betsy stopped and carefully lowered herself from the stepstool. She paused with her head down before turning to face Ben. "I don't understand why you feel such a need to criticize," she said softly. "We spend a lot of time with Dan and Ruth. How do you think it makes me and your dad look when you're so impolite like that?"

Ben's face sagged. What he wanted to tell her was how humiliating it had been at dinner when she'd felt the need to dress up the nature of his job, or that among the "so many things" she'd already told the Gundersons about him, it couldn't possibly have included the small detail that he was, in fact, gay.

"Mom, I already apologized," he said. "I know I got a little prickly with Dan, but I really don't think I was all that rude."

"Yes, you were. And now I'll be left to smooth things over with them tomorrow." Betsy let out an agitated exhale. "I just hope they still come to the party."

"Wait...you're worried they'll skip your party because of me?"

"I don't know," Betsy muttered, tears beginning to well in her eyes. "Maybe."

"Mom, you guys are good friends, right? I can't imagine they'd hold that kind of grudge over something so minor."

Betsy only sniffled, then dabbed at the corners of her eyes.

"Do you want me to call them? Or have Dad say something?"

"No, I'll take care of it," Betsy said, firmly.

As soon as Ben offered to take this minor step to rectify the situation, Betsy's dour mood decidedly lightened. His capitulation was apparently evidence enough for her that she had landed her point and won the argument. Ben walked around the island to give his mother an apologetic hug. "You sure everything's okay?" he asked.

"Of course, sweetie," Betsy said, grinning.

Ben produced a relieved smile and the two separated.

"But I do have a little favor to ask," Betsy added.

"Okay..." Ben cautiously replied, returning to his seat.

"We're one short for our mixed doubles match tomorrow morning."

Oh shit. Ben waited for Betsy to continue, hoping she somehow wouldn't ask what he knew was coming.

She bit her lower lip, then folded her hands at her chest as if in prayer. "Would you be able to fill in and be my partner?"

Ben instantly regretted how casually he had opened himself to her request. "*Tomorrow* morning?" he asked, playing dumb in an effort to stall.

"I'd ask your father, of course, but he has a tee time with some buddies. Plus, his doctor told him not to overdo it with his arrhythmia."

"What happened to your usual partner?"

"George had to leave town this week for his mother's funeral in Tucson," Betsy explained.

Ben searched for polite excuses, knowing he wasn't really in a position to refuse. "Won't it be a little unfair for me to be your partner?" he proposed.

"Oh, it's just for fun, Benny," Betsy scoffed. "Nobody will mind if you fill in. It'll be a good challenge."

"I didn't really bring the right shoes."

"You were wearing sneakers when you arrived this afternoon, weren't you?" she wondered, wide-eyed. "If not, you and your dad wear the same size. I'm sure we could find something that would work for you."

Out of excuses, Ben fought back a frown. He shouldn't be fighting this so much. It was an opportunity to spend some quality time with Mom. It's what he was here for, right? But he remained silent a little while, providing one last chance for Betsy to withdraw the request. Realizing she would not, he slumped on one of the stools. "We're not playing the Gundersons, are we?"

"No!" Betsy laughed.

"Okay then," Ben sighed, defeated. "What time do I have to be ready?"

Betsy gave a little clap and hopped in place a few times. "Oh, yay!" she exclaimed. "Al and Liza will be excited you're joining. We have the court from seven to eight-thirty. This'll be fun, Benny!"

"Sheesh," Ben said, raising his brow. "So much for sleeping in."

"Oh, come on," Betsy prodded. "It's not that early. We'll have a nice breakfast afterward and you can spend the rest of the day lounging around the pool if you want."

With her mission accomplished, Betsy walked around the island and stood behind Ben. She placed her hands gently on his shoulders and stood on her tiptoes to kiss the back of his head. Then she mumbled something about there being little time to complete her nightly facial compress before bed, so she would say goodnight. Tomorrow was a big day.

Ben and Jim stayed up a while longer, enjoying a second bourbon. Hearing Ben had smoothed things over with Betsy, Jim smiled in relief that a major conflict had been averted. He mentioned how Betsy had apparently been rather anxious in the weeks leading up to their party. Even a minor squabble, he feared, could turn the weekend into a nightmare for everyone involved. They just had to keep her happy for one more day. Like partnered cops, they would need to lean heavily on each other to navigate the dangerous trenches that were Betsy's increasingly (as Ben was learning) pendulous moods. It actually bothered Ben a bit, the extent to which his father was now participating in any need to manage her behavior. But ultimately, Ben couldn't really blame him. It was the path of least resistance. And when it came to Mom, sometimes it was the best anyone could hope to do—from an energy standpoint at least—not to mention someone as historically non-confrontational as Dad.

Jim went on to describe how he had already offered to step in the following morning as Betsy's doubles partner. "For crying out loud, I golf eight times a week," he said. "It wouldn't have been a big deal to duck out of my round for one morning to help her out. Besides, my heart is fine. The doctor only cautioned against overly strenuous lifting for a while. Taking a few steps here and there in a doubles match is hardly that."

But Betsy had insisted he keep his tee time. In Ben's experience, his mother's interest in tennis always seemed like nothing more than an opportunity to get in some exercise while she gossiped. It puzzled him a bit that she'd be so adamant in suggesting he be the one who filled in, and not Jim. Why was he so reluctant to consider that perhaps Mom really did just want to spend some time with her son? If that were the case, Ben wished she could just come right out and say it, instead of employing some sort of setup or angle.

He and his dad both shrugged it off in the end, happy that relative peace had been restored for the time being. After finishing their third round of bourbon and chatting briefly about Ben's work, Jim finally decided it was time for him to call it a night as well. He stumbled a little when getting up, then paused a moment. "I really appreciate you making the trip down here, Benny," he said. "You know it means a lot to your mother."

Ben nodded once to acknowledge Jim's gentle thank-you.

"I know you had some reservations about how things were handled with Grandma," Jim added. "It'll be good for you and your mom to spend some time together this weekend."

"So everyone keeps telling me."

After a brief silence, Jim rested a comforting hand on Ben's shoulder.

Ben looked up at his father from the sofa, then smiled softly and said, "Sleep well, Dad."

~~~

To Ben, Grandma Helen had always felt like his biggest fan. For as long as he could remember, she seemed to find subtle ways to pay extra special attention to him. Whenever he and Abby visited her little hobby farm just a few miles from their childhood home, he'd notice the welcome hug he received was always held ever so slightly longer than the one given his sister. "How's my little sassafras today?" Grandma would beam, getting down on one knee to match Ben's eye level.

First stop was always the kitchen, where waiting inside a hen-shaped jar would be a pile of enormous peanut butter cookies. She'd lift the ceramic head off the chicken and lower the bottom portion to reveal the tasty treats. As the "big" sister—by two minutes—Abby invariably positioned herself first in line. Before Ben even reached into the jar, Betsy would be ushering Abby over to a table to avoid too many falling crumbs. Grandma would then give Ben a wink and insist, "Grab two. Full bellies make for a thankful heart." She had a way of putting things that sounded warm and almost musical to him, and this always made Ben smile.

When Abby insisted on horse camp the summer the twins turned ten, Ben spent three to four mornings a week at Grandma's. Betsy would drop him off before meeting up with her tennis pals, and the day would start in the garden. Helen maintained an enormous vegetable plot that required daily attention. For as long as Ben could remember, her backyard was overrun with row after row of green beans, lettuce, squash, peppers, potatoes, radishes, broccoli, carrots, cucumbers and cabbage, each with their own magnificent way of developing over the summer. It always amazed him to think how those pointy yellow flowers he'd see bloom each June could somehow transform into carvable pumpkins come October.

But of all Grandma's plants, it was her tomatoes that were her specialty. Fourteen varieties flourished under her care.

Romas for sauces or salads. Yellow pear, only because Ben thought they were pretty. And nothing but Cherokee purple for the best-tasting salsa.

"You know they're fruit," Grandma once said, plucking a cherry tomato from the vine and eyeing it between two fingers like a shiny penny.

"No they're not."

"Oh yes they are. A berry, in fact."

"But they're salty," Ben asserted. "And this is a vegetable garden."

"Well, tomatoes are imposters. They may not be sweet, but they hold their seeds inside. That makes them a fruit."

Ben paused his weeding for a moment and sat upright on his knees. A quizzical look lingered across his young face as he scanned the rows of plants. "Then what about the cucumbers? And green beans? Or the peppers?"

"All fruit."

Ben furrowed his brow at this notion. *That can't possibly be right, could it?* But Grandma had never misled him, so he accepted it and went back to the soil. "Maybe we should call this the fruit garden then," he added after some further thinking.

"Yes," Grandma agreed, smiling. "Let's."

Given his druthers, young Ben preferred spending his free time inside, reading, or sitting in front of the TV for countless hours, attempting to master the latest iteration of Super Mario Brothers to have hit the market. But with Grandma, being outside was fun. All the digging and picking offered an acceptable excuse to get a little dirty, even if his mother still groaned about having to remove the grass stains from his pants. And he learned something new every day.

Grandma would assign Ben to organizing their harvests into designated bags, which could then be hauled into the kitchen for washing, and finally the all-important canning process. Upon seeing a scattering of wet Ziploc bags turned inside-out to dry on the counter one afternoon, Betsy, exasperated at what she considered her mother's hopeless frugality, had once remarked, "Oh, Mom. Why don't you just buy some new ones? They're cheap!"

"You know how many I go through, Elizabeth," Helen had reminded her. "I'm not about to just throw away perfectly good bags when they can be washed and reused."

"Your grandmother should've been a nun," Betsy had once scoffed to her son. It wasn't until much later that Ben understood this comment hadn't been made to acknowledge some inclination toward piety or kindness. Rather, it had been said to denounce even the hint of any devotion to poverty.

By the time fall would come around, Grandma's cellar was a wall-to-wall smattering of shiny jars. A year's supply of vegetables, sauces, and purées were at the ready. She gave a lot of it away; Ben's grandfather had passed away shortly before he was born, and the amount of produce Grandma's garden yielded every year was far too much for her to consume alone. Still, many marveled at the sheer quantity she managed to turn out annually.

"I couldn't have done it without my partner," she'd announce.

This made Ben feel proud. She never said "helper" or "assistant." Certainly, Grandma did far more work than he in tending the garden each summer. But *partner* suggested a more equal share in the credit, and Ben was excited that she acknowledged his small role so generously.

Early one September in junior high, Ben had confided in Grandma that a few kids at school had teased him about how much time he'd spent that summer in his "fruit" garden. "Aptly named for fruity Apt," a wiseass classmate had snickered behind his back.

"You pay them *no* mind, you hear?" Grandma had insisted. "Those brats wouldn't know a fruit from a vegetable if it hit 'em upside the head."

Ben ignored Betsy's advice to simply consider decreasing his time on the farm. He looked forward to that shared experience with Grandma. Summer jobs and extracurriculars eventually made it challenging at times, but he continued to help out as often as he could through high school. It was Helen who had encouraged him to try out for the tennis team. And when he made varsity as the only sophomore, Helen was at every match. Even if she never quite got the hang of how to keep score, she could tell by Ben's demeanor whether or not he was doing well.

In the spring of his senior year, she caught him off guard by suggesting he ask the neighbor boy on his street to go to prom with him. He'd never explicitly divulged his crush, but Grandma had somehow inferred his interest, regardless. He'd often wondered if maybe Mom had figured it out and said something. The prospect of asking a guy had felt far too scandalous for Ben to ever seriously consider, however, and he eventually agreed to attend instead with his lab partner, Katie.

During college, Ben made a point of driving out on occasional weekends to help in the garden. While Grandma always encouraged him to check in at home, she never insisted on it. If Ben intended to spend the night, however, she would insist that he join her for church in the morning. He still remembered the psalm she made him memorize:

For you created my inmost being;
you knit me together in my mother's womb.
I praise you, for I am fearfully and wonderfully made.

Grandma maintained the farm with little to no help well into her eighties. She chopped her own wood for the large basement fireplace. She loved mowing her own lawn, and never gave up working in the garden. In the past few years, she'd even asked that Ben bring Jake along to help prepare the soil for winter, infusing mixtures of compost and bone meal after the final fall harvest. She'd sit on a little stool and point instructions with the end of a hoe. And despite once conceding that it was a decidedly "Lutheran" hymn, she would score the day's work by humming the chorus to "Bringing in the Sheaves." At the end of the day's work, she never failed to hand Jake a grocery bag filled with all the vegetables he needed to concoct a delicious batch of his mother's family recipe for soup joumou.

One week before her 94th birthday, a niggling cough progressed to her second bout of pneumonia in as many months, and Helen had to be hospitalized. At first responsive to treatment, her illness ultimately proved resistant to medications, and the infection quickly spread through the rest of her body. With a "do not resuscitate" clause established in her living will, a decision had been necessary on whether or not extraordinary means were to be taken to prolong her life, should she be left unable to breathe on her own.

As the eldest of Helen's three children, Betsy had been named the executor of her living will. After his parents moved to Florida, Ben had urged his mother to consider designating one of her brothers to oversee any of Grandma's medical decisions. His uncles were both local, and more than capable of handling the responsibility. But Betsy had insisted on continuing to oversee her mother's care.

When it became evident that Helen was not going to pull through, Betsy had authorized, by phone, medical staff inserting a breathing tube to prolong her life. The "do not resuscitate" order did not stipulate "do not intubate," Betsy had argued. This would ensure enough time for Betsy and Jim to return to Minnesota, regardless of the physical discomfort it may have caused Helen. As Grandma seesawed in and out of consciousness, nurses and respiratory therapists worked to maintain her airway until Betsy could sign the necessary paperwork. When she arrived, finally convinced of the hopelessness of the staff's efforts, Betsy had permitted the breathing tube to be removed. And Helen, with her tortured little lungs unable to inflate and deflate under their own power, passed within minutes.

~~~

Ben stirred, woken by a quiet voice repeating his name. His empty bourbon glass rolled from his chest onto the sofa when he tried to sit up a little.

Betsy stood behind him. She stepped to one of the end tables and switched off the small lamp. Ben made a slight groaning sound, then shifted to the edge of the sofa. His cheeks were damp. "Time for bed, Benny," she whispered.

Ben stood and brushed under his eyes with the back of his hand. He kept his head down. Betsy ushered him from the living room and guided him the few paces it took to reach the hallway. At the door to his bedroom, she drew a tissue from the pocket of her satin robe and placed it in his hand.

He had closed his eyes again, ready to sleep standing. "Thanks," he managed to mutter.

Betsy gently patted the small of his back and reached in front of him to turn the doorknob. There was just enough glow from the floodlights outside his window for him to find the bed. He plopped onto his stomach, asleep the moment his head disappeared into the giant pillow.

Betsy watched him for a few moments. She left his door ajar just a crack, the way he always used to like it, then silently tiptoed back to bed.

five

It had been fifteen years since Ben had picked up a racket. He had rarely played after high school, an occasional intramural league in college the only exception. When he'd originally agreed last night to play doubles with his mom, he assumed that he would be the youngest player on the court by at least two decades—in his mind, an unfair advantage. This morning, however, as he lethargically willed himself from the comfort of the supersized structure that would serve as his bed for the weekend, he registered each ever-increasing ache in his nearly forty-year-old joints, and seriously questioned his ability to take on an opponent of any age.

He couldn't shake the feeling that he'd been manipulated. At first, he thought maybe it was his own fault. He'd let himself engage with his own defensive reactions at dinner. The quick turnaround in his mother's disposition after he'd apologized for his behavior toward the Gundersons, however, made him wonder if she was really all that upset over the encounter. Or was it that she had merely seen an opening for something she wanted, and used it to her advantage? If she thought he would say "no" when asked about joining her for doubles, positioning herself as a victim could potentially be useful leverage in minimizing the chances of being denied.

Ben detested the silent treatment. More, he was annoyed at how much he allowed it to influence his actions, particularly when it came to his mom. He'd had plenty of practice dealing with others who chose a passive-aggressive approach to conflict, both in the workplace and in his romantic relationships. It was against his nature, as he saw it, to succumb to an immature practice of getting one's way without thoughtful, rational discussion. The effort it took, and the rift it so often created with the opposing party, however—his mother being no exception—made it more trouble than it seemed worth to insist on having a grown-up conversation about the problem. With certain folks, he'd concluded, if feelings were hurt you may as well be talking to a child.

So, as much as it pained him, he had learned to say he was wrong over time, even when he was certain he wasn't, for the sake of moving beyond disagreement, a compromise he let himself believe was born out of a need for self-preservation in a world full of emotional babies. What little good it did him now—woefully under-practiced and expected to wade seamlessly back into an arena that he feared would only give rise to wistful memories of Grandma, he was left facing a commitment this morning in which he had zero interest taking part.

He texted a heart emoji to Jake before leaving his room. Betsy was in the kitchen, wiping up a spill around the coffee maker. "Good morning, sunshine," she said, brightly yet quietly. Whether it was the ponytail under her visor or more subdued makeup, there was a greater resemblance to the mom he remembered, and this made Ben smile.

"Morning," he grumbled. He perched himself on a stool and sat up to peer over the island. "Is there a little of that left, by chance?" he asked.

"Of course, sweetie. It's for you." She was being extra nice, as if acknowledging she hadn't played fairly last night. She reached into the cabinet to grab a travel mug, then off they went in the golf cart.

The sun was just creeping above the palms. Its rise seemed to imbue the morning with a hint of optimism—a small if unexpected favor for which Ben was thankful nonetheless. With the afternoon swelter still hours away, he steadied his thermos with both hands and sipped carefully, basking in the glow as if he were back under the warmth of an inviting blanket.

He was surprised by how busy the club's grounds were at this hour. A steady stream of golf carts passed them on the path, their occupants automatically raising a hand in cheerful salutation. Four exquisitely groomed bocce ball courts bustled with vocal players bent over in billowing sun hats. Everywhere he looked, couples were leisurely getting in their morning walks or bike rides.

"It's busy here on the weekends," he said.

"Not especially," Betsy replied. "Every day is sort of like a weekend here, sweetie. Our schedules don't change much, aside from what activities the club offers on certain days. It's nice not having to think about planning things all the time."

"I guess this is a bit of a strange weekend for you guys, then."

"Definitely," replied Betsy. "I have to admit, it was a little difficult getting back into the mindset of watching the calendar in preparation for the party. But it's all worth it." She softened her voice a little then. "Especially having you here." Ben squirmed in his seat at Betsy's gushy remark.

"Your grandmother loved a good party," she added. There was a brief silence. This was the first time she'd mentioned Grandma.

"That she did," he agreed, nodding slowly.

"Do you remember her eightieth birthday?"

"You mean when she drank three Stingers and started a food fight from a crate full of beefsteak tomatoes? How could I forget?"

"I bet there are still a few stains on the walls in that garage!" They both laughed then. It felt nice to share something.

Ben stared ahead, still grinning. "She sure knew how to have a good time." Another silence. Ben pictured his grandmother's face. He thought there should be more to say, and wanted to hear his mother say it, but his stomach had tightened talking about her.

They remained quiet for a few moments, giving Ben a chance to enjoy another surge from the bitter brim of his thermos. He continued to marvel at the almost nondescript packs of residents milling about the grounds, their self-possessed nonchalance somehow making it seem like they'd always been there, and always would be. He fixed his coffee in a holder on the cart's dash. He glanced back at Betsy, trying to imagine her fully integrated into what he surmised might eventually feel like a certain banality to day-to-day life here. He cleared his throat, feeling the need to ask, "So…what *is* a typical week like for you guys here?"

"You might ask that with a little less contempt in your voice."

Ben shook his head. "No, no," he insisted. "I'm genuinely interested." He was trying.

Betsy eyed him for a moment, as if gauging his level of sincerity. She tilted her head back in thought. "Well, let's see," she said. "I play tennis three times a week. Your father usually has eighteen holes in by ten o'clock. We like to relax around the pool for a bit in the late morning before it gets too hot, then I make us lunch. I'll usually do a Pilates class or get a massage at the fitness center in the afternoon while your father naps. Oh, and they're starting a Zumba class soon, too, which I think sounds fun."

Ben flashed a smile and gave her a quick wink, feeling the need to endorse her enthusiasm.

"We like eating out for dinner," Betsy added. "Did you know the club has six restaurants?"

"Actually, I did. They were all listed on the back of the menu at dinner last night."

"It really makes it convenient with so many on site. We also have a handful of bars in the city center where we do our shopping," Betsy added, brightly. "I try to drag your father there sometimes. He usually just watches and sips his whiskey if his back's bothering him. But once in a while I can get him to join me for a dance or two at Cowboy Cal's."

"There's a country-western themed bar here?" Ben asked with a perplexed look.

"Yep!" Betsy beamed. "It's all decked out to look like a dude ranch in the Old West. Your dad really gets a kick out of it. It can get pretty rowdy some nights." Almost whispering, she added, "People here are a little less reserved than at Citrus Hill."

Betsy went on to explain how Cowboy Cal's had installed a mechanical bull two years ago. It had become very popular until too many drunken residents were getting seriously injured after being bucked off onto the mat. Worrying about lawsuits, the club evidently replaced it with a karaoke machine. "I don't have to drag your father to sing, that's for sure!" she laughed. "He's sort of become famous around here for his version of 'Ring of Fire.'"

"Sounds like there's not much reason for you guys to ever have to leave the club then," Ben suggested.

Betsy hesitated slightly before answering. "Well, that's kind of the idea, Benny."

Now she wanted to stay home all the time? When she lived fifteen hundred miles away? Ben was careful here. While it may have taken his parents out of the home far more than he would have preferred as a child, his mother's propensity for travel was something he liked about her as an adult. Despite what he suspected were often contrived reasons for it, he had to admit it was interesting, all the places she'd been and could talk about. To confine herself now to one square mile oddly felt like hurtful timing.

"You don't miss traveling?" *Or your children and grandchildren*, he wondered, but didn't ask.

"You know, I thought I would more," Betsy replied, almost indifferently. "You have to understand that after I agreed to postpone our wedding until your dad finished his surgical fellowship, he indulged all my travel interests. So, I took advantage of it as long as he was willing. The compromise was that we'd eventually move someplace where things could settle down. I knew it was coming." She shrugged then, as if in acceptance. "But I have to admit, I've sort of taken to it! There are so many folks here who have the same interests as your father and me. And the shops in the city center have everything we need. There's a Whole Foods, a Target. Even a CVS with a new Minute Clinic."

Her excitement was palpable. Enough that, at least temporarily, he was able to set aside any feelings of he and his sister having been further downgraded on their mother's priority list. In this moment, she was happy. She was light. And when she was like this, he was shown—or perhaps taunted—with the sliver of possibility that if he just spoke up, he could tell her anything. Confide. Impart something upon her he'd wanted to say or ask since, what, junior high? But ironically, the only way he'd found himself able to avoid getting in the way of that possibility so far this weekend, much less participate in it, was if he remained silent.

In the distance, Ben spotted a series of tennis courts surrounded by mesh-covered fencing, behind which already teemed a slew of eager players. As they approached, he glanced at Betsy. She too was silent, her posture now noticeably rigid. Suddenly jolted into attention, Ben had to brace himself as she brought the cart to a firm stop at the entrance. Betsy swallowed hard and turned, startling him slightly with a look of unexpected intensity. "We're here."

Off to the left was an area of tables, where under an umbrella Ben could see what he assumed were their two opponents. A woman stood intently swooping her racket around in big, circular motions, while the beer-bellied man next to her sat slumped, possibly asleep.

"Good morning, you two!" Betsy waved. "I found us a sub."

The woman stirred her dozing companion, leveling a quick smack to his chest with the back of her hand. Betsy introduced

Ben to Liza and Al, and the pair produced welcoming expressions for him.

Liza inspected Ben. "What happened to George?" she asked.

"He's in Tucson," Betsy replied.

Al remained seated but reached out to offer Ben a firm handshake. "I could've sworn I just saw him last night at bingo," he said, looking at Betsy.

Betsy grabbed the rackets from the back of the cart, as if too busy to answer at first. "Well, I wasn't exactly sure which day he was getting back," she explained. "But I wanted to give him some time after his mother's passing. No need to rush him back so soon."

Ben squinted at Betsy, then monitored the confused reactions of Al and Liza. He too had been under the impression that his mother's usual partner was still out of town, necessitating the replacement.

Liza didn't seem to care. With a piercing smile, she seized both Ben's hands and peered eerily into his eyes. "Welcome to paradise," she said in a raspy voice.

"Uh...thanks," Ben replied, trying not to let his discomfort show.

"The club is incredible, isn't it?" Liza continued, still clasping his hands. In what now seemed to be almost expected, her face was pulled tight. Enough gold necklaces hung around her tan neck to rival Mr. T, partially covering what to Ben resembled a fleshy sheet of crumpled tin foil. "I get so excited when someone new experiences the club for the first time," she added, gnashing a helpless piece of gum. "I've been here almost ten years, and I love it more every day."

Ben just nodded and smiled politely, waiting for Liza to let go. For such a scrawny lady, she had one hell of a sturdy grip. He managed to pull free and wrung his hands for a moment to restore the flow of blood, offering, "Well, it's been lovely so far."

"We're excited for you to join us this morning," Liza said. She motioned toward her partner and teased, "You'll have to try to go easy on old Al here, though."

"Aw hell," Al grumbled.

"Oh, I'm just kidding," Liza said, smacking him more gently this time.

"We're all just here for fun," Al barked, making the effort to stand now. "I'm sure Ben has no intention of blasting anybody off the court. Isn't that right, Ben?"

Ben could see Al was wearing a large brace on his left knee and a smaller one laced up on his right ankle. "Of course not," Ben laughed sympathetically, half wondering if he should have tried to help Al stand.

"Do you play a lot?" asked Liza.

"No," Ben replied quickly. He felt a little torn between giving the impression that he was a beginner and admitting that in reality he'd had a significant amount of experience on the court. The fact that he hasn't played in so long seemed like an appropriate warning in case he performed terribly and reduced the quality of their match. "But I was on the tennis team in high school," he granted, hoping this tidbit would adequately satisfy Liza's expectations.

Trying to downplay Ben's abilities, Betsy quickly added, "But that was many years ago."

Liza hoisted her racket bag across her back. "I'm sure you'll have no problem," she assured Ben.

The two teams warmed up side by side on their halves of the court, Betsy hitting with Liza, Ben with Al. Nervous at first, Ben was relieved that after a few strokes his swing seemed to be coming back fairly easily. More relieved, perhaps, that he didn't start to feel weepy when he stepped onto the court. The instant he caught a whiff from a fresh can of tennis balls—a scent that as a kid was so appealing it seemed wrong in some way, like gasoline or a box of markers in art class—he had thought of Grandma again, her waving arm omnipresent in the stands during warm-up at his high school matches. "Your baseball swing looked better today," she'd often comment, referring to what was a commonly used two-handed grip on his backhand side. Somehow even that motion felt secure today. Probably just motor memory, Ben told himself.

Although Al refused to take more than one step if Ben's returns were even slightly out of his reach, when he did manage to make contact, he was surprisingly proficient. Ben tried to slow the pace a bit in order to focus his shots directly at Al so he wouldn't have to move. From what he could tell, Liza and Betsy made no mistakes in their warm-up together. Betsy's swing, while consistent, looked very mechanical and almost designed, as if she were thinking about where to place her arm with every stroke. It was obvious she'd been taking additional lessons and was making an effort to adhere to every one of her instructor's suggestions. Bouncing in place in anticipation of each return, the clunky chains around Liza's neck jingled like a bag of loose silverware. She too had no trouble keeping the rally going; but in contrast to Betsy's deliberate movements, her strokes were dynamic and natural. She hit harder than Betsy and with greater accuracy.

After about ten minutes of hitting, Al announced it was time to start. He explained to Ben that they would play a ten-game "pro set," win by two, with a deciding tiebreak if the score reached ten-all. Each team took a minute at their respective bench to rehydrate before starting. Ben had relaxed a bit, more confident in his swing than he'd expected, and actually finding himself enjoying the opportunity to play again.

Betsy was quiet and very serious. Her eyes were focused on her racket strings as she meticulously adjusted any wayward strands that had moved out of place during warm-up.

"Everything okay, Ma?" Ben asked, seeing the severity of her gaze.

Betsy took a deep breath. "This is the one team I've never beaten at the club," she revealed, her eyes still on her strings. "I'd really like to do well."

"Oh," said Ben. "You hadn't mentioned that."

Betsy leaned in closer then, as if to reveal a secret. "We've come close so many times. But George always ends up being the weak link. He makes errors at the most critical times." Glaring over at her rivals, she added, "Today I might finally have a chance."

Unnerved a bit by her stare, the feeling of relief Ben had enjoyed after his hit with Al diminished a bit now. With his mother apparently expecting him to deliver a big win, the match was beginning to feel more like a high-stakes race, as if a loss could somehow ruin her. He'd never known her to be this cutthroat. Certainly not when they'd played together in the past. She'd been almost annoyed by the high quality of play Ben brought to the court—as if his natural improvements had made the game less fun for *her*.

Before he could say anything further, however, Betsy had made her way over to the service line, anxious to put the first ball in play. "Love-love!" she hollered in announcing the score, startling Ben slightly.

Their rallies were competitive. Liza and Al were very complimentary of any nice shots from their opponents. Betsy had to quietly scold Ben from time to time when he felt the need to apologize for any shots that were perhaps a little too good. She, too, praised her opponents' shots, though seemingly more as an afterthought than in a genuine spirit of good sportsmanship. She was out there to win.

The two teams traded games until Betsy sliced a drop shot out of Liza's reach, finally earning set point, up nine games to eight. She and Ben cheered. He hugged her and they both laughed in excitement. They made a good team! Pouncing on a short serve, Betsy smacked the next return straight at Al's feet. He barely got his racket on it but somehow managed a high lob that forced Ben to backpedal from the net behind the baseline. Off the bounce, Ben carefully swung, only to watch the ball clip the top of the net and fall back on his own side. Liza and Al both let out a groan, relieved they were still in it. Ben bent over and lowered his head in mock embarrassment, but smiled, knowing he'd missed an easy shot which would have given him and his mother the win. Hanging her head in disbelief, Betsy stood with her hands at her waist.

"You guys are lucky!" Ben joked, pointing across the net to where Al and Liza were chuckling. Liza gave an exaggerated fist pump, which made Ben laugh, too. He turned to Betsy then, who was clearly less than amused. "Sorry, Mom," he said. "Guess I took my eye off the ball." He put his hand in the air to offer a high five. "Let's get this one."

With a sour look on her face, Betsy said nothing and simply lowered her stance in preparation for the next point. Another quick error from Ben followed by an ace from Liza tied up the set again at 10-10.

The two teams took a brief water break before the tiebreaker. It was getting hot. Tall palms had provided a welcome shade for the first half hour of play, but the sun had risen now well above their fan-like canopy.

"I have to admit," Ben huffed, "I'm having fun."

Betsy slowly sipped her water, then lowered the bottle from her lips and gave Ben an unconvincing smile in agreement. "How about we try to clean things up a little?" she suggested.

Ben furrowed his brow. "Seriously?" he said. "You know I haven't played in like forever, right? I think I'm doing just fine." He snatched the bottle from Betsy.

"There were a few balls three games ago that I know you could've easily put away," she said, disgusted. Then, making a slow-motion gesture with her racket, "But you just tapped them back to Al like lollipops."

"Come on, Ma, gimme a break. What do you want me to do, smash Al in the gut? We're trying to get some good rallies going. It's more fun that way."

"I don't want to keep the rally going," Betsy sneered. "That's what practice is for. Now that I'm this close I don't want to let the win slip away. Now *let's go*." She adjusted her visor contentiously and hustled back to the court.

"Easy, Rambo," Ben cautioned to her back. He was discouraged. Things had been good there for a few minutes, affable even. He thought he was doing his part. Yet each furious stride Mom now took back to the court felt like another stone removed from the bridge he thought he was supposed to be rebuilding between them. He shook his head and wiped his face with a towel before joining her, the fun all but gone.

"All right," Liza called. "First to seven points, win by two!"

Heeding his mother's "advice," Ben decided to add a little extra zip to his shots. This caused Al to take more steps during the tiebreaker than he had in the entire match. Liza changed nothing, playing steadily and confidently, her strokes not letting her down. The points were close and again competitive. But shots that had drawn encouraging compliments earlier in the match were now recognized less enthusiastically, as everyone's focus seemed to heighten. The stakes grew higher as each team's score crept toward seven, until a sharp forehand from Betsy whizzed cross-court untouched, earning her and Ben another match point at six points to five.

In undramatic fashion, however, Ben proceeded to hit two consecutive shots out of bounds, followed by a double fault into the net, effectively handing the tiebreaker to Liza and Al, 8-6. Perhaps realizing it was a tough way to finish, Liza and Al subdued their cheers. Ben joined Betsy but said nothing as the two quietly moved toward the net to shake hands. He initiated high fives in lieu of handshakes, and Liza and Al both obliged.

"What a great match!" Liza exclaimed, coughing a little to catch her breath. "Well done, you two."

"Congrats, you guys," said Ben. "Well deserved." He bent over, feigning fatigue.

Al stooped to adjust one of his braces. "The knees will be feeling this one tomorrow," he said, cheerfully.

"Nice game," Betsy sulked. She kept a grip on her racket but offered a shake with her left hand. "My goodness, you two must be getting tired of winning by now."

"Not really," laughed Liza. Ben tried and failed to stifle a chuckle, which only increased Liza's laughter. "But I'm sure you'll get us someday," she assured Betsy. "Until then, another week atop the Glory Board!"

Betsy grit her teeth. "Oh, it doesn't really matter," she replied, unconvincingly. "It's just for fun, right?"

"That's right," Ben agreed, hoping she was serious.

At their bench, Ben toweled off his face again and guzzled an entire bottle of water. Betsy stood motionless, still holding her racket. "Benny," she said softly. "I need your help."

Ben stepped closer. "What's the matter?" he asked.

Betsy lifted her racket to reveal her dilemma. Her intense concentration had left her unable to pry her cramped hand from the racket grip. Ben sat her down on the bench to assist in delicately releasing her fingers one at a time. Betsy squinted in pain. "I'm fine," she said. "Just do it."

After her hand was free, Ben insisted she drink some water and gently massaged her palm for a bit while she sat. "It's okay, sweetie, really," she said, but didn't attempt to withdraw her hand.

"I don't mind."

They remained quiet for a few moments, both intent on the work Ben was doing on Betsy's sore, small muscles.

"Thanks for playing this morning, Benny," she said, her focus still on her hand.

"Of course, Mom." He studied her expression for a moment, the frenzy gone from her eyes as if a switch had been flipped. Then he asked, "What's this 'Glory Board?'"

Betsy hesitated. "It's...just this sort of leaderboard that keeps track of each week's winners and losers. The top names are listed in big, gold letters."

"Liza's at the top this week?"

"Every week." She paused. "There's one for golf too, but it's smaller. They're kept outside the fitness center."

"So every player sees it?"

"Every club member."

There was a brief silence. It suddenly felt like he was talking to a child who'd been picked last for a game of Capture the Flag. "And you were really hoping to see your name up there this week."

She only shrugged.

Ben closed his eyes. His mother hadn't wanted the chance to spend the morning with him. She hadn't really even needed a sub. What she'd needed was a puppet, someone to serve as an accessory in this ruse for self-aggrandizement. And yet somehow, as maddening as it was, all he could think to do was apologize for the mistakes he'd made during play.

"Sorry about those last few points. I'm not used to going for so much on my shots." He thought he saw her shake her head.

"I guess you can't win 'em all," she replied. She glanced over at the other bench then and said, "Say, I was meaning to mention something on the ride down here. If it happens to come up, don't mention to Liza who we had dinner with last night."

"The Gundersons? How come?"

Betsy took back her hand and held it close to her chest. She lowered her voice almost to a whisper. "It's nothing."

six

At Sunny Side, a bistro breakfast spot in the club, Betsy insisted their tennis troupe be seated outdoors. Shade and a gentle breeze kept the air comfortable, if still warm. The patio was filled with chatty club members, most of whom already seemed to be finishing their meals. Ben smiled at the other ladies, their standard morning uniform evidently a form-fitting, pricey tennis dress—skirts and polos if they'd been golfing. Many, like Betsy, had adorned their meticulously coiffed heads with bejeweled visors, fixed like tiaras among their mountains of hair with the precision of a fussy painter.

After a round of mimosas arrived, Betsy wasted no time in filling Liza in on the details of tonight's party, while Al picked Ben's brain about his multiple, niggling joint aches. Ben did his best to give Al his full attention, but found himself getting distracted by the lively back-and-forth between the two ladies.

Liza turned to Ben suddenly and yipped, "Sure nice of you to make the trip for your parents' party." She grabbed another piece of gum from her purse and tossed it in her mouth. Ben recognized the Nicorette package from the samples they offered to patients in his clinic who were trying to quit smoking.

"Of course," Ben replied, smiling. "It's hard to say no to a trip to Florida in March." Betsy wrinkled her nose at this.

"Well, Al and I are looking forward to it," said Liza.

Then she lifted an e-cigarette from the breast pocket of her tennis dress and took a large puff, a cloud of odorless vapor disappearing over the table as she exhaled. Between the gum and vaporizer, Ben was somewhat aghast at the amount of nicotine he knew Liza was ingesting.

Trying to justify his staring, he asked, "Do either of you have kids?"

"Oh, yeah," Liza said, as if it had been silly to ask. "I've got two boys in upstate New York and a daughter in Philly."

"Two myself," Al said. "Both still in Cleveland."

"Do you have them down here to visit often?"

Al replied, "Not too often, I guess."

"I don't invite them," Liza announced plainly, grabbing her drink from the table and reclining a bit in her chair.

"Oh," Ben chuckled. While Liza may have come on a bit strong at first, he had to admit he got a kick out of her candor. "Why is that?" he asked.

She shrugged. "I just don't want them here. Simple as that. I get up north to see them at least every year. But my late husband and I moved down here to be by ourselves. We raised our kids, and they've got their own families now."

Ben glanced at his mother. She was nodding. Liza had evidently taken the words right out of her mouth. *Hello?* he thought. *I'm sitting right here!*

Liza continued. "If we had stayed in New York, it would've been way too easy for us to just turn into free babysitters. I could already see it happening all around us, and that wasn't how we wanted to spend our retirement." She enjoyed another large puff on her vaporizer. "The grandkids are usually too busy on their iPhones or iTablet pads or whatever they're called to even notice I'm around anyway."

Ben cringed slightly. This was not unlike his experience with his own nieces. He and Jake had agreed early on in their relationship that while they both enjoyed children, they had no intention of ever having any of their own. It was only recently, after they'd seen a particularly gushy holiday movie about a large family that reconnects after years of estrangement, that Jake had begun throwing out little hints about possibly changing his mind on the subject.

"And you don't miss them?" Ben asked, one eye on Betsy.

"Well sure, sometimes," Liza said, exhaling another big cloud. "That's why I visit."

"But you're always ready to come back, aren't ya?" joked Al.

"Damn straight," said Liza. She raised a hand to offer Al a high five, which made him flinch. The two of them shared a little laugh.

Betsy smiled knowingly and stirred the ice in her water glass.

"You don't realize how peaceful it is not having small kids around until you're with them again," Al added. "It's an important part of what people are attracted to down here."

"Just not having children around?" Ben asked, the skepticism apparent in his voice. "Isn't that what it's like at all retirement communities?"

"Sort of," Al replied. "But at The Cypress Club, there are even restrictions for how long you can visit if you're under eighteen: two weeks. And you have to be over 55 to live in this zoning district."

Ben crossed his arms. "So, if I wanted to live in this area," he asked, "I couldn't buy a house because I'm not old enough?" He scanned the table briefly. "Is that even legal?"

"Well, technically you *could* purchase a home here," Al explained. "You just couldn't live in it until you're 55. And yes, it's legal. The age restrictions were approved by Congress in '95 when they amended the Fair Housing title of the Civil Rights Act." Ben's eyes widened at this unexpected bit of legislative history.

Liza sat up. "Al was an attorney, so he knows all this legal mumbo jumbo," she squawked, still puffing away.

"It's pretty great, actually," Al said, smiling. "Our property taxes are kept really low."

"How's that?" Ben asked, disturbed and fascinated at the same time.

"Well, the Cypress Club property isn't part of a school district. It's zoned that way on purpose. Why fork over thousands of dollars each year to pay for the schooling of kids who don't live in our neighborhood?"

"And this exclusionary zoning by age is legal too?" Ben assumed.

"Of course," replied Al.

Ben sat back and took this in for a moment before continuing his inquest. "What about all the employees of The Cypress Club, though?"

"The employees?" Al asked, lifting his cap to scratch his bald head.

"Yes," Ben said. He looked around the patio briefly. "It obviously takes a huge number of people to keep this place running every day. The wait staff, groundskeepers, the people who work at the stores in your city center. I imagine many of them have families and children?"

"Probably," said Al, not really understanding where Ben was going.

"So, it seems strange to me," Ben slowly suggested, "that in return for the work they do at The Cypress Club, the employees here don't get any support from the community they serve. Shouldn't that be a reasonable expectation? Like as part of the social contract?"

Betsy and Liza were ignoring the men now, preoccupied with their own conversation.

"Social contract?" Al scoffed. "It's business. Plain and simple. Folks here are paying to live how they want, and spending their hard-earned money on things that they'll actually benefit from."

Just as Ben was about to counter Al's reply, their server Maria politely interrupted to take everyone's order. After their food arrived, the topic returned to the upcoming party that night, and Liza pressed Betsy on the guest list. Betsy did her best to skirt around naming the Gundersons, but when Liza sensed she was deliberately leaving someone out, she pushed just enough for Betsy to relinquish. Ben had already forgotten his mother's vague request that he not mention their dinner with Ruth and Dan last night, and Liza didn't hesitate to expound on what could have made Betsy so cagey.

There had been a rumor swirling that Ruth Gunderson, along with several other Catholic women at the club, was quietly assembling a Good Friday prayer circle next month for the conversion of Jews. Liza, like a good portion of other residents, was Jewish, and understandably outraged at the very idea of such a stunt. Even with Betsy's repeated assurance that there was no truth in it, Liza was convinced otherwise.

"I can't believe it doesn't bother you more," Liza snarled, stabbing at the last bits of her omelet.

"Well, we don't even know if it's true," Betsy insisted. "Ruth's a friend. I just can't picture her doing something like that."

Liza gave Betsy a hard stare. "Have you asked her?"

"No," Betsy replied, lowering her head slightly.

"Well, you should. Because it's probably true," Liza said. "That bitch is convinced we need to be converted but has no problem keeping her fat trap shut about a bunch of pedophile priests."

Ben's mouth dropped in a surprised smile.

"What's next?" Liza moaned, "changing textbooks to remove all history of the Holocaust?"

"All right," Al scolded. "Keep your voice down."

"Well, I'm pissed," howled Liza. Then, turning to Betsy more calmly, she said, "We've got to stick together on these things."

Ben gave his mother a careful once-over. There was something different about the way Liza had said this.

"I'll talk to her," Betsy quietly promised, patting Liza's hand.

This seemed to pacify Liza, and she took her napkin to dab the wrinkly area above her top lip. The table was silent for a few moments. Ben continued to watch his mother before Liza suddenly blurted, "Oh my God!" Everyone at the table jumped slightly at this unexpected exclamation.

"What?!" Betsy asked, placing her hand over her heart. There were a few turned heads from the tables around them.

"I cannot believe I forgot to tell you this!" Liza said. She pulled her chair closer to the table and lowered her husky voice to a secretive purr. "Speaking of friends of yours, I ran into Sue Wilkins at Cal's last night."

Ben made eye contact with Betsy. "Your bridge partner?" he asked.

"That's right," Liza eagerly confirmed. "She was already tipsy when I got there at like seven. I guess she already knew that you and I were friends, because she came up to me and my two girlfriends and chatted us up for a while." Liza leaned toward Ben and with a hand hiding her mouth, whispered, "She ended up getting pretty hammered, actually." Ben nodded in pretend shock.

"Anyway," Liza continued, "when my girlfriends stepped away for a few minutes to use the restroom, Sue burst into tears and told me all about how she'd slept with Bud Gillespie and that he was the one spreading an STD!"

Betsy sat like a statue.

"Doesn't surprise me at all," Al boasted, holding a toothpick in his lips. Betsy broke her frozen posture enough to scowl at Al. "About Bud, I mean," he clarified. "That guy's always on the prowl."

Al reported how Bud, due to the number of sexual conquests he'd allegedly scored with the resident women, was quietly known among the men at The Cypress Club as "Bedroom Bud." The tee boxes and member locker rooms were always abuzz with tales of his escapades in debauchery. As one of the few single men at the club, Bud enjoyed almost legendary status among most of the male residents, as if a vicarious reminder of their depraved glory days. News of his identification as the serial disease-spreader, as it were, would be a huge revelation among the ladies, the story of which Liza had now annoyingly scooped from Betsy.

"Well, looks like you were right, Ma," said Ben.

"You suspected Sue?" Liza asked, befuddled. "How?"

Betsy was shuffling through her purse, as if uninterested. "It was just something she said last week that tipped me off," she replied casually. "I have to say, though, if I'm being honest, I really don't think it's appropriate we're discussing this."

"What's the big deal?" asked Liza.

Betsy pulled out her wallet and set it on the table. She gave a testy smile. "I just don't think it's any of our business." Liza blinked at Betsy several times, nonplussed. "Besides," she added, "whatever Sue had, I'm sure it's cleared up by now."

Maria dropped off the tab. Both Al and Betsy reached for the check, with Betsy managing to grab it first. "Breakfast is on us," she insisted.

"Oh, you don't have to do that," Liza said.

"Nope. Losers buy," Betsy griped. "That's the deal."

"I'm having trouble remembering the last time I bought a breakfast," Al chuckled, elbowing Liza.

Fixing her eyes on the table, Betsy signed the bill with her club number. "How nice for you," she said.

~~~

On their cloudless ride back to the house, Ben noticed Betsy was unusually quiet behind the wheel. "Thanks again for brunch, Ma," he said.

Betsy maintained her focus on the path. "You're welcome, sweetie," she replied.

There was a pause. "Liza and Al were fun."

"I'm glad you thought so, Benny."

Another pause. This one was longer. He was stuck on something Liza had said. "Are most of your friends here Jewish?" he asked.

"Al's not Jewish."

"Okay. Other than Al, then?"

Betsy hesitated. "I suppose."

"I imagine a good portion of the members here are Jewish, huh?"

"Well, it's Florida," Betsy said with a partial smile.

A third, even longer and more uncomfortable pause. "Do you and Ruth ever go to church together?" Ben asked.

Betsy glanced at him out the corner of her eye. "Sometimes," she said carefully.

"Does Liza know that?"

"If you're suggesting that I would join that awful prayer circle thing..." Betsy snapped.

"No, no, of course not," Ben assured her. "That's not what I meant." He waited a bit before continuing. He'd been walking a fine line in every conversation he'd had with her since arriving, and wanted desperately to avoid another squabble. But his curiosity was getting the better of him. "It's just the way Liza looked at you when she said you guys need to 'stick together on these things.' Like you should both be offended."

"Well, it *is* offensive!" Betsy griped. "And Liza and I are friends too. I'm sure she's just looking for some support."

"Yes, maybe," Ben said, unconvinced. He studied his mother for a few moments, giving her an opportunity to respond. When it was clear she would not, he simply said, "Mom." Nothing. "Mom?" he repeated, impatiently. Still quiet, Betsy only stared ahead and accelerated the golf cart slightly. Her silence and the blank expression on her face did little to assuage Ben's suspicions. He averted his eyes then, baffled. "You are unbelievable."

"What? What do you mean?"

"Oh, come off it, Ma. You're really not going to say it?"

"Say *what?*"

Ben waited, equally amazed by both her ignorance and audacity. Then he blurted finally, "Liza thinks we're Jewish!"

Betsy tightened her grip on the steering wheel and lowered her head, as if trying to sink out of sight. Ben paused, his eyes like saucers, as she started and stopped her speech three or four times, fumbling for the right way to begin explaining herself. "What's the difference?" was all she could manage.

"The difference?" Ben asked, amazed. "For one, we're Catholic, Mom." Despite his own severing from the Catholic Church in college, Ben sat now in utter disbelief, eager to hear what reason there could possibly be for his mother to perpetuate the preposterous lie he'd just unearthed.

"I don't see why it should matter," Betsy insisted.

"You don't find it even the least bit dishonest?"

"I've never told Liza that we're Jewish."

"But you've never told her that we're *not* Jewish."

Betsy increased their speed again, fast enough now that Ben was forced to grab ahold of the overhang to steady himself as they rounded curves. "Why does she think we're Jewish, Mom?" he pushed.

The response came slowly. "I don't know. She just assumed."

Ben could feel his face flushing. "Why, though? There had to be some reason."

Betsy rolled the cart to a slow stop and turned to Ben. Her expression was testy now. "Fine," she conceded, removing her hands from the wheel. "A few months ago, when Liza and I were scheduled to play tennis with each other for the first time, she had seen my name on the schedule and muttered something or other before our match about how Apt was a nice Yiddish name."

"Ugh," Ben groaned, putting a hand to his forehead. "It's German."

"I know, sweetie," Betsy said. "I didn't think much of it at the time, so it never occurred to me to correct her until she invited me to a luncheon later that week with some of her friends. It was after the dessert that I realized everyone there was Jewish."

"Okay. So..." Ben said, nodding heavily and repeatedly making a large circular motion with his hand. "Then what?"

Betsy tipped her head back and smiled with her eyes gently closed. "It was such a beautiful lunch, and her friends were just lovely. They were all so well-traveled and well-connected. Many were from the Midwest, actually," she said, glancing at Ben with her voice slightly brighter now. "Our interests seemed to overlap so much. I just felt really comfortable and enjoyed getting to know them."

Ben only glared at her.

"I guess I was just craving a good group of girlfriends down here," Betsy confessed. "They made me feel like I could talk with them about anything."

"Except the whole Jewish thing," Ben remarked.

"There really wasn't much discussion around that at first. Most of the talk surrounded activities and people at the club: our families, a few current events. When someone eventually brought up Israeli sovereignty in Jerusalem—"

"Oh, Christ."

"That's when I knew," Betsy said, slumping. "It was easy enough to just nod politely and agree with everyone. I guess I just didn't want to do anything that would prevent Liza from inviting me again."

"Mom, Judaism isn't a club," Ben scolded. "And don't you think you might be underestimating your friends a bit? Why are you assuming they'd automatically exclude you from their get-togethers because of your religion?"

Betsy crossed her arms, pouting. "I don't know, Benny. Besides, I'm not converting to Judaism," she sneered. She took her foot off the brake and they began moving again. "To be honest, I don't understand why you of all people are getting so worked up about this."

"I beg your pardon?" asked Ben.

"Well, I thought you were all into atheism now."

"Nobody's *into* atheism, Ma. It's not like yoga or K-pop." Betsy shot him a confused look. "And I can be an atheist and still care that my family isn't misrepresented."

Sensing this as a dig in reference to her mother, Betsy scowled at him. She waited, then said in an accusatory tone, "You're not the only one who lost Grandma, you know."

Ben had to pause, taken off-guard by this remark. Finally, he let out a tired breath. "What is *with* you down here?"

"Excuse me?" Betsy said, insulted.

"You make me participate in this tennis charade. You're pretending you're Jewish." He didn't dare mention the physical changes he'd noticed upon arriving.

"What on earth are you talking about? 'Charade.' I needed a sub! Heaven forbid I want to spend some time with you. You said you had fun."

Ben shook his head. "That's not the point..." he said, trailing off. She could flip things on a dime.

Betsy sped up as they neared the house. At the end of the driveway, a pair of gardeners laughingly chatted in Spanish while they placed pruning shears and a large bucket onto the tailgate of their shiny green truck. They shouted "good morning" when Betsy briefly waved. She pulled into the driveway and stopped the golf cart outside the garage. Keeping her hands on the steering wheel and eyes forward, she sternly said to Ben, "Leave this alone, Benny. I don't want to discuss it any further."

Exasperated, Ben only threw up his hands. His will to keep up the fight had expired. He watched Betsy struggle to retrieve their rackets from the back of the cart. When she finally managed to pull the bulky bag to the front seat, Ben reached out and gently rested a hand on her knee. "Just tell me one more thing, Ma," he said.

Betsy turned off the cart and tipped her head toward Ben with a frustrated sigh.

"Does she call you 'bubbie?'" he asked, smirking.

Betsy sneered at Ben's cheeky attempt at levity and abruptly tossed him the racket bag. "Tell your father I need to run an errand in the city center," she said, restarting the cart with an aggressive turn. "I'll be back in an hour."

Ben hopped out and stood flat-footed on the driveway. He heaved the racket bag over his shoulder as he watched his mother hastily reverse the cart and zip back down the narrow street. The gardeners stepped into their vehicle and drove away in the opposite direction. The low roar of the truck's motor gradually faded to an almost inaudible hum until Ben was left in silence. His focus was drawn upward to where a lone cloud had lazily shifted into place to block the sky's unrelenting blaze. He waited patiently with his eyes closed, motionless for as long as the tiny cloud would oblige, savoring the fleeting respite from shouts and sunshine.

Don't give up on her.

seven

Despite the agreeable blue skies, Ben would have preferred to stay inside, enjoying the cool dimness afforded by four walls and drape-drawn windows. But the house was just generically antiseptic enough for him to make an exception today. He rested his head against one of the pool's lounge chairs and breathed slowly, taking in the sweet smell of the jasmine vines scaling the wooden fence just off to his left. A buzzing pair of hummingbirds faithfully inspected each bloom with their needle-nosed heads. He thought about how much Jake would love this. His partner had always preferred warm-weather getaways: South Beach, Palm Springs, Tulum. Ben never protested, but never pined for them quite the way Jake did. It felt funny and a bit disappointing now, knowing the comfort of this serene poolside setting was somewhat lost on him.

He thumbed through the latest issue of *The Cypress Weekly*. Each Friday the club circulated its own periodical for the residents—seven or eight pages of local and national news, thrown together by a pair of young journalism students. His mother had left a copy on the small table next to his chair. He pictured Liza as he bypassed a piece with the morbid headline "The Widowed Wealthy," a how-to for wives who find themselves left with inordinate amounts of cash following the passing of their husbands.

He tossed the *Weekly* back onto the table and glanced at the cover again. Color photos of the two fledgling editors stood out next to what seemed like an unnecessary prediction of yet another week of perfect weather. They couldn't have been older than nineteen, Ben determined.

What an age. And what a thought to be back there again. Back to a stage in life where, whether burning for it or having it thrust upon them, most experience their first taste of true independence. In spite of its messiness and it often being filled with more misses than hits, we were adults(!), even if in legal terms only. There was an inherent thrill that simmered when met with these unknowns.

He'd thought he was so ready to leave for college. Ready for some distance, some newness. Ready to forge ahead, equipped just enough to seize any chance there was to shape a new history for himself. To develop into someone he sincerely liked, and whom he hoped others would love. What he wasn't ready for was the realization that he had absolutely no idea how to do that. As a teen, he'd worked tirelessly at stifling what came natural to him. After enough comments about how he stood with his hands on his hips ("Put your arms down, Benny"), or the way he pronounced certain words ("People will keep calling you names, sweetie"), he had learned to check anything that could possibly give him away. He guarded against these little idiosyncrasies with everything he had, as if his life depended on no one being able to immediately tell there was something different about him. And there was comfort in that anonymity, as artificial as it may have been.

The problem was he'd gotten too good at it. The hope he'd stored deep down that once he stepped on campus he'd no longer have to think about every single thing he did or said had sort of evaporated. This was him now. How could he go back? How could he stand returning to that exhausting state of hyperanalysis that had left him almost devoid of any real personality? The prospect of having to run each would-be friend's reactions through that "what do they think of me" filter was too much now. And it felt like the loneliest place on Earth.

And so it was one night freshman year when he found himself on the roof of his dorm. There was an amazing view of downtown from there, and after once spying a custodian accessing the necessary stairwell, he'd grown accustomed in recent weeks to ignoring the "Do Not Enter!" sign and sneaking a peek after sunset. That particular night felt different. He'd skipped his classes three days in a row. His roommate, whom he didn't particularly like but was at least someone familiar now, had left for the weekend, leaving behind the cheap bottle of whisky he'd scored from an older brother. The buzz left Ben a little off-balance on the roof's somewhat warped surface. This could be dangerous, he thought, if someone got too close to the edge up here. There were no railings, no barriers. One misstep and you could go plummeting nine stories to the concrete below. He looked up at the night sky and spotted the red blinking of a silent plane miles in the air, no idea of its destination. He imagined it never stopping, carrying its passengers farther and farther away from where he stood at that moment. It made his throat tighten, realizing just how badly he wished he were on it.

He'd called home earlier that day. In spite of everything, whenever he'd felt his most vulnerable—down, ill or afraid— Mom's was somehow the one voice he wanted to hear first. She had answered and quickly noticed that something seemed off.

Perhaps he'd disguised the anxiety and fear in his voice too well, as after insisting he was "fine" and was just calling to say hi, she rebuked him for his confessed truancy that week. She didn't need to remind him that school was expensive and that there were expectations he perform well. After making him promise he'd reapply himself to his studies, she'd explained that she was keeping her travel agent waiting on the other line and needed to get going.

If he stretched his neck, he could almost see the bottom. He wasn't exactly afraid of heights, but he was surprised how close he'd let himself inch to the roof's edge now. There was a chilly breeze, and he was forced to widen his stance against the swirling air's attempt to knock him off balance. How could they not be more careful about letting students access this area? he thought. He gripped the clunky cell phone his parents had issued him for "emergencies." There had been no answer at Abby's. Grandma would be fast asleep by now and he hated to wake her. He dialed home and was surprised to hear his father's hushed voice. Mom must have been in bed.

"Everything okay, Benny?" It was just late enough to warrant this question straight off.

There was a silence, until the tears started and Ben was unable to hide the muffled sounds of his uneven breathing. He didn't have an explanation. No tragedy or disaster to divulge. He wasn't homesick. Just...lost. The words erupted from his mouth like a geyser. Erratic fragments of sentences, and thoughts that must have sounded like the unhinged rant of an imbecile.

But there had apparently been no need for economy or clarity in his words for his father to recognize their desperation.

Jim waited until Ben had finished. Then, steady and with kindness, he simply said, "Come home, son."

It hadn't mattered that Ben didn't immediately know if his father had meant tonight or for good. He wasn't being instructed to "tough it out" or patronized with "it'll pass." In a fraction of a moment, his father's cue, a phrase so direct and uncluttered it seemed almost ridiculous now, had somehow been enough to make him consider the possibility that he was going to be okay. And it was therefore enough to nudge that feeling of isolation just outside the boundaries of hopelessness. He wiped his nose with the sleeve of his hooded sweatshirt, looked up at the glowing skyscrapers in the distance, and took one step backward toward the safety of the forbidden stairwell.

~~~

Decked out in a pair of boat shoes with a red polo tucked over his belly, Jim stepped out of the house and walked up to Ben's chair by the pool. Ben had slipped off his shirt but remained under the protection of a large umbrella.

"Where's your mother?" asked Jim.

"She said she had an errand to run and would be back in an hour."

"Huh." Jim scratched behind his ear, frowning. Then he said, "How 'bout a beer?"

Ben closed the book he had moved on to from the *Weekly*. "I'd love one."

His father returned a few moments later with a tray holding two Coronas and a small bowl filled with a pile of plump cashews. Each beer had a slice of lime wedged into its opening.

"Ahh, perfect," Ben sighed, grabbing one of the slippery bottles from the tray and forcing the lime through its spout. "Thanks, Dad."

They tapped their bottles together and enjoyed a long swig in the shade.

"Want some music?" Jim asked, reclining next to Ben now.

"Sure," Ben replied, a bit surprised. "Where are you going to play it?"

Jim held up his phone and pointed to a small shrub behind their chairs. "I had little speakers installed around the pool. They can sync up with my phone." He smirked, proud of his minor technological achievement.

Ben laughed and gave an almost pitying little fist pump.

Jim had to squint at his phone, but after a few exaggerated taps with his index finger, the low hum of string instruments came crooning from the speakers.

Ben grabbed Jim's phone from where he had set it on the table. He lowered his sunglasses to the tip of his nose and slowly read the title of the selection playing.

"The overture to Wagner's *Parsifal*?" Ben asked, raising an eyebrow. "Since when are you into classical stuff?"

"I don't know that I am," Jim said, a bit defensively. "It's just a relaxing playlist someone recommended. I can change it if you want."

"No, no," Ben assured him. "It's fine. I like it." He paused for a moment, as if listening more closely. "Kind of sounds like something from *Game of Thrones*."

"Never seen it," Jim said. He kicked off his shoes then and groaned, "Ugh, it was a rough morning on the greens."

"Oh yeah?"

"I was putting for par six times and bogeyed each one."

Ben had to smile. This was an area of the game with which his father had always seemed to struggle. Countless were the Sunday mornings Jim would come home grumbling about how many putts he'd missed. "We were there too early for the greens to be mowed," was a common excuse for his lack of success. Ben never found the nerve to suggest the course wasn't the problem.

"Well, there's always...tomorrow," Ben reminded him, and Jim's grimace softened a little at this simple realization. Then he asked, "How was Dan?"

"He didn't show, actually," Jim replied.

"Wait, what?"

"He wasn't there this morning."

"Really?" Ben asked, his expression tightening.

"Members of our group skip once in a while," Jim said, just a little too upbeat to be believable.

Ben grunted, unsatisfied. His mother's concern from last night had resurfaced in his mind now.

"I don't want you to get all stressed out about this, Benny. Nothing we can do about it now. If Dan doesn't want to come to the party, that's his own problem."

Ben appreciated his father's attempt at reassurance, but he knew this was more than "Dan's problem." He cast his eyes downward.

As if able to see the wheels turning in Ben's head, Jim snatched the *Weekly* from the table and tapped him playfully on the arm. "What did you think of Al and Liza?"

Ben glanced at Jim briefly. "If you're worried I had a similar run-in like last night, no. We got along just fine."

Jim grimaced a bit. "Aw, come on. That's not what I meant. I was just curious what you thought of them."

"They were both very nice and welcoming," Ben said after a pause. "Liza's a bit intense, I suppose."

"Yeah, she's a pistol, isn't she?" Jim chuckled. "At least she's been in a better mood these days."

"Why's that?"

"She tried giving up Coke and smoking at the same time recently. It almost killed her."

"*Cocaine?*"

"Good grief, no," Jim scoffed. "*Coca-Cola.*"

"Oh." Ben waited a few moments, carefully considering his next comment. "She and Mom seemed to have hit it off here."

"You could say that," Jim nodded, taking a sip. "Your mom's sort of gotten in with Liza's friend group." Ben leaned in a little now. He was fishing. Jim looked over each shoulder, as if needing to ensure no one was within earshot. "See, Liza has these fancy get-togethers a couple times a month for her lady friends where she kind of goes all-out. Not a lot of people get invited, I guess. So when your mom was, I think she thought it was quite the coup." Jim shot Ben a little wink and quipped, "She's always gravitated toward the exclusive. But don't tell her I said that."

"No worries." Ben smiled.

It felt strange. While admittedly a little disappointed not to be learning anything new regarding the whole Jewish nonsense, there was relief in seeing his father's apparent ignorance on the topic. Jim didn't like gossip or phoniness. And Betsy's little lie was the kind of thing he would be terribly embarrassed about.

"Don't get me wrong," Jim continued, "I'm glad she's settling in here well—*really* well—and finding some close friends. That hasn't always been easy."

"I'm glad too," Ben said. He took the book from his lap and placed it on the table between them. "What about you, Dad?"

"What *about* me?"

"How are you taking to this place?" Ben regretted he hadn't pushed his mother further on this question earlier, and didn't want to make the same mistake twice.

"They make it pretty easy to love it here," Jim said. "I get to golf every day on amazing courses, the restaurants are great, and there are plenty of activities to get involved in." Then gesturing toward the sky, "And my God, the weather."

"I thought you might miss the seasons."

"I can't say I miss the cold," Jim said, "but yes, I wouldn't mind having a little more variety sometimes."

"You guys did the whole snowbird thing the first two years at Citrus Hill," Ben said. He had leaned in further now. "Couldn't you do that here?"

"Well, I think if we were going to do half-and-half, we'd have purchased a smaller home here. I was the one who originally suggested we choose one place, actually. And when your mom agreed, this was the house she chose."

"Then why are you guys holding on to the house in Minnesota?"

"It's a bit of a sore spot between me and your mom," Jim admitted. "She's right that we shouldn't keep paying the property taxes if we're never there. I told her we could make up some of the cost with renters, but she doesn't want anyone living in the house."

"Mom kind of made it sound like she was the one who preferred you kept the place. I just assumed it was so she had somewhere to keep all her stuff."

"We could easily rent a storage space if that were her concern. No. She's just covering for me." Jim guzzled the last few swallows of his beer and set the bottle on Ben's book. "I don't know," he exhaled. "Something just doesn't feel right about getting rid of it."

Ben couldn't say he was surprised by his father's sentimentality. Jim had always tended a bit toward the nostalgic. But it was the first crack Ben had seen in the almost impenetrable reverence with which everyone seemed to describe this place.

"Too many memories?" Ben asked.

"I'm not sure it's that. But I do miss it."

Ben saw an opening. "Is it possible that some part of you is hoping you'll go back?"

Jim lowered his head in thought before answering. "Maybe. For so long, I couldn't wait to retire and just take it easy. No more long hours to keep or cranky patients to deal with. The schedule got pretty brutal."

"I can certainly understand that," Ben agreed. He also understood that his father's overwhelming caseload had partly been his own fault. Over the years, there had been occasional murmurs in the orthopedic community that Jim was too quick to recommend surgery for his patients. But Ben knew this tendency to forgo a trial of conservative treatment likely had more to do with his father's inability to say "no" than with any sort of abuse of practice. More and more, patients wanted what they thought would be a quick fix. Often, they found that in Jim.

"The club couldn't be more perfect for what I was looking for, really," Jim said. "Day to day, there are so few decisions I need to make. But after a while there's only so much time a guy can devote to leisure."

Ben's face was flat. "You mean you're bored."

"I wouldn't say that, necessarily," Jim cautioned. "There are tons of things to do around here. But it's a strange feeling when no one's counting on you for anything anymore. When people have relied upon you for almost forty years to show up and do a good job, to then all of a sudden have nothing expected of you? It can be unnerving."

Ben nodded and said, "I get it." But in fact, he couldn't think of anything better than living an expectation-free existence. No schedules or "have-tos." No need to field questions about when you're finally getting married, or if and when you'll have kids. No apologies for disappointing someone. What was unnerving to *him* was learning his father apparently had so few other interests, or perhaps had historically so little time to develop other interests, that his only avenue for self-fulfillment was when he had a task to complete for someone else. To think he had all the time in the world now, but wasn't sure about how to most happily go about spending it, sadly felt like a forfeited, and possibly unrecoverable, opportunity.

"It's different for your mom, you know?" Jim said. "Her day-to-day life isn't all that different down here."

"This morning she said she didn't miss traveling much. That really surprised me."

"Yeah," Jim sighed. "I've offered a few times to take her somewhere, but she hasn't been interested. She tells me I shouldn't feel like I have to do that. We moved to Florida because of me, so it feels strange being the one wanting a break from it."

Ben lowered his sunglasses from his eyes and turned to Jim. "Dad. No one can take a twenty-five-year vacation."

"Your mother could."

Ben had to chuckle. It was true, albeit a little sad if he were being honest. "But that's basically what you guys are doing here, isn't it?" he continued. "I think it's totally natural that you're itching to find something that keeps you interested."

Jim nodded slowly but said nothing.

Ben sensed his father holding back. "You want to go back to work, Dad?" he said, as if giving Jim permission to say it.

Jim grabbed his bottle and started to peel away the damp label. "I'm too old to start up something new down here," he said. "And I'm not going to go searching for some place that's looking to rehire a retired orthopedic surgeon."

"Would Sid have a spot for you back home?" Ben asked.

Years ago, when Ben had made it clear that he had no interest in working in a surgical setting with his father, Jim had coordinated a transition plan to have one of his partners, Sid Leary, eventually take over the practice when Jim retired. Although Sid was nearly fifteen years younger, the two had been friends since the late '80s, when Sid was finishing up his fellowship at the hospital where Jim usually performed surgery.

"In a heartbeat," Jim said. "He's overwhelmed the way it is."

"But you don't want to go back to working over forty hours a week, do you?"

"I wouldn't have to. I could maintain a small clinic schedule a couple of days a week and be in the OR one morning. Sid would be glad to have the extra help." Jim's voice grew excited. "And the dean of the medical school sent me an email last month, wondering if I'd have any interest in coming back to do a few lectures."

Ben smiled supportively. "Sounds like you've given this some thought."

"A bit," Jim said, managing to remove the beer label in one piece. "But I'm not sure how realistic it is."

"Why not?" Ben asked, pushing himself upright in his lounge chair.

Jim glanced at Ben. "Do you really have to ask that?" he said, smirking.

"Oh, come on," Ben urged. "What could it hurt to just talk to her about it?"

"It's not that I'm afraid to bring it up," Jim insisted. "I'm just not sure yet that I want to move is all. But I like the idea of it. That it's a possibility. Plus, I'd look forward to seeing you guys and Abby and the girls more often."

Regardless of the likelihood of Jim and Betsy ever returning to Minnesota for good, it made Ben smile to hear his father even implying that he missed his kids and grandkids. It was a bit ridiculous that it should feel so refreshing. "We'd like that too, Dad."

Jim paused a moment, then said, "I don't suppose you'd give it a shot?"

"Give what a shot?" Ben asked, nervous now.

"With your mother. About moving back."

He'd walked right into this. "Oh, Dad. I don't know if that's such a good idea."

"Why not? She listens to you."

"She does not!" Ben laughed.

"Well, she'll listen to you before she'll listen to me."

Ben tried not to change his posture too obviously, but he couldn't help slumping a bit in his chair. He liked to think he had little trouble saying no to others. It was a virtue, he thought, to be clear and direct in turning down requests he had no intention of fulfilling. The prospect of having to broach yet another sensitive subject with his mother, presumably before the trip was over, seemed like one responsibility too many for the weekend. It had been a shaky enough start to begin with; and now he was expected to persuade her into something she'd given him every impression she had no interest in doing? It didn't seem fair.

But something about the way his father had asked this, an almost childlike appeal to what he seemed to think was some kind of special sway Ben held with his mother, eclipsed the strong urge Ben felt to decline. "I'll see what I can do," he said.

Jim smiled again, brightly. After a brief silence, he swung his legs to the side of the chair and sat up tall, either proud or satisfied. "Ready for another one?" he asked, picking up Ben's empty bottle and giving it a little shake.

Ben looked up and hesitated for a moment, still distracted by the thought of his new assignment. "Sure. Thanks, Dad."

As Jim stood to head back toward the house, Betsy came zipping up the driveway in the golf cart.

"Speak of the devil," Jim said.

They watched her abruptly park in the garage. She acknowledged neither of them before entering the house.

Jim clenched his teeth. "This doesn't look good," he said, checking Ben's reaction. "I'll be back in a minute."

Agitated now, Ben stood and repositioned his chair from where the sun had begun creeping up on his toes. He had sent Jake a text as soon as he'd sat at the pool, asking how things were going at home. He wasn't too concerned that he hadn't received a response yet, their spat from yesterday afternoon notwithstanding; although it was a Saturday, Jake would probably be in the office for most of the weekend, attempting to make a dent in the huge pile of returns his company inevitably had flooding in this time every year.

When he sat back down, Ben's phone buzzed once, signaling his awaited response from Jake. He paused for a moment when reading the text, his mouth left open in confusion.

Things are coming together great! You should stop by and check it out!

"What the hell?" Ben whispered to himself. He fumbled with his phone a little. "Oh shit. Shit!"

In his attempt to inquire about Jake's work, Ben realized he had inadvertently responded to the message Dwayne had sent him yesterday afternoon. He resent the text to Jake as he had originally intended, and ignored Dwayne's offer. "Goddamn it," he griped, putting his phone on the table.

Jim returned from the house with a single bottle of beer and presented it to Ben. "What's the matter?" he asked.

"Nothing," Ben replied, flustered. "Just my phone's acting up." He took the beer from Jim's hand. "You're not having one?"

"Nah, I'm a bit worn out," Jim said. "Think I'm going to lie down for a bit. We've got a big night ahead of us."

"Is Mom okay?" Ben asked.

Jim looked back at the house. "We should probably give her some time," he said. "She's been running herself ragged the past few weeks worrying about this damn party. Probably just hashing out some last-minute details with the planner."

"How much is there to do?" Ben glowered.

"Your mom sent out invitations, but it's basically an open house for the entire club. There's a full buffet being privately catered, a live band, bartending services to coordinate, extra wait staff. The club has people for all this, of course, but your mom wanted things done a certain way. And she'll want us to get there early."

Ben closed his eyes briefly. "Okay," he said.

His father produced a smile so large it should have been enough to bolster anyone's spirits. "We'll have some fun tonight!"

Ben managed a smile too. "Looking forward to it," he said, trying to sound as convincing as possible.

Jim groaned as he straggled to the front door with the tray held at his side, a little unsteady. When he reached the top step, he peeked at the sky, then lowered his head and turned to face the pool again. "You should take a dip!" he shouted, wiping the back of his neck. "Even Satan's sweatin' today."

eight

Ben set out on the golf cart to explore the complex network of paths that linked The Cypress Club like a web. He'd needed a little space. Rather than looking forward to a potentially fun celebration with his parents tonight, he felt uneasy when considering how his mom might react if even the slightest element were mishandled. With all the work she'd put in, he could appreciate how she might be a little on edge as the day finally arrived. Throwing the perfect party may not have been a worthwhile endeavor to him, but it obviously was to Betsy. Still, he knew it wasn't going to be as easy as just cutting her some slack and vowing to enjoy it.

~~~

After Jim's official retirement, Betsy had insisted on throwing a party at their country club in Minnesota. The guest list was a virtual *Who's Who* of the Twin Cities orthopedic community, along with a crop of old friends the Apts had collected over the years. Most were fellow members of the club. With some apprehension, Betsy had entrusted a majority of the night's particulars to the club's event staff. Since they'd joined, she and Jim had attended numerous events there, and while she had occasionally recoiled at some of the planning selections for previous parties, after being satisfied with the food options and securing adequate wait staff, she was content to let the club handle the remaining details.

With the exception of Abby and her husband Terry, Ben and Jake spent most of that night trying to avoid talking to people. Periodically, one of Jim's tipsy colleagues would approach them and effectively manage to insult Ben or Abby by insinuating that anyone in the health field who was not a surgeon was essentially a peon. The constant parade of egos, however, serendipitously afforded the group ample joke material in their attempt to stave off boredom. The open bar helped too, of course.

The cake had been the first problem of the night. Betsy had ordered a large, double-layered sculpture in the shape of a doctor's bag and stethoscope. What was presented instead was a thin sheet cake which looked as if it could have been purchased pre-made at the local grocery store, the type of thing suitable for a high school graduation or routine office party. It was covered in icing depicting only images of the items, rather than the three-dimensional monster Betsy was expecting. The word "retirement" was misspelled "retirment."

Rumor had it that when Betsy saw the cake in the back, she swiped her fingers across the incorrect lettering and flicked the frosting in the caterer's face. She then proceeded to demand someone find her *light* blue buttercream icing and a pastry bag. She would fix the errors herself.

Not long after the frosted disaster had been brought out, someone complained that the only gin option at the bar was mid-shelf quality, rendering the martinis "barely drinkable." When the buffet ran out of the main dish before everyone had been through the line once—the cardinal sin of party-giving as far as Betsy was concerned—her attempt at a hands-off organizational approach yielded to an almost obsessive preoccupation with every remaining detail of the evening's activities.

If anyone had cause to be irritated by the night's blunders, it was Jim. It was his party, after all. But he only calmly reassured Betsy that the problems were minor and in no way affected the good time he was having. This seemed to matter little to her, as she continued to flutter about the room pointing fingers and directing staff in the most menial of tasks. From the speed of their service to the loudness of the DJ's music, she stuck her hand in everything. Ben and Abby had both attempted to intervene and reinforce Jim's insistence that everything was fine, but this only seemed to exacerbate Betsy's already agitated demeanor.

Ben had thought it was legitimate to get a bit irritated by the litany of issues the club seemed to be bumbling. But the extent to which his mother became unreasonably demanding suggested that her concern was more about how the attendees viewed *her* than it was about whether or not her husband was enjoying his night.

In the days and weeks following the party, club members who'd attended had largely positive things to say about the night, and openly regaled Jim and Betsy with stories about what a fun time everyone had. A few close friends of Betsy's did mention the cake, making offhanded comments like "you certainly didn't run out of that!" or "were you trying out a new patisserie?" But other than these harmless quips, few seemed to recall the oversights by the staff; or if they had, chose not to mention it.

Undeterred by Jim's urging to the contrary, Betsy lodged a written complaint with the club's manager, contending that the food bill should be halved, the cake completely comped, and a formal apology issued. Considering the Apts' long history of membership and their somewhat prominent position at the club, the manager sheepishly complied, for the most part appeasing Betsy. At least now she could feel justified at the bridge table in recounting every detail of how she felt slighted by the staff's apparent ineptitude. Any connection between the event and the professional legacy of its guest of honor, however, had by that point been seemingly lost.

~~~

The air was thick. Ben continued chugging along in the golf cart at a lively clip to maintain a breeze on his perspiring forehead. He felt himself cringe, recalling the aftermath of that silly retirement party back in Minnesota. Even though Betsy had received an apology in addition to the monetary compensation she'd demanded for the night's gaffes, she moped about it for what had felt like months. What would it take for a similar meltdown to ensue this time around? The bigger the stakes, the bigger the potential for madness, Ben worried. He would try not to think about it for now.

It was getting late in the afternoon, the hottest part of the day. But the energetic residents filling the club's grounds showed no signs of slowing down. An almost endless procession of smiling speed walkers passed Ben with a welcoming little wave. He spotted portly men in checkered polos at every tee box, fairway and green. Pickleball enthusiasts were out with

their paddles in full force, slow-moving figures in skirts and
hats, contesting doubles matches on any court now under shade.
In one of the smaller pools near the main entrance, he watched
a dozen or so withered women attempt to perfectly mimic every
arm movement demonstrated by their earnest Water Pilates
instructor. The level of activity was dizzying.

He considered for a moment if perhaps he'd been a bit quick
to judge the club and its residents. On the surface, it almost
seemed possible that this place truly was a paradise. Here was
a community of plucky seniors who, rather than skidding
into the stodgy twilight of their retirement years, chose to fill
their days with activities as vibrant as the ubiquitous sun that
watched it all from overhead. If no golf, there's tennis. If not
pickleball, shuffleboard. No Pilates offered today? Try Zumba!
Jazzercise, croquet, karaoke, bridge, backgammon, bocce ball.
A bona fide smorgasbord of experiences sure to mollify the
uncertainty of even the briefest stretch of unscheduled time
for any ambitious joiner.

And there would always be more. Tomorrow they would get
up and do it all over again, as if finally repaying themselves for a
life's work that sacrificed anything remotely resembling leisure.
An all-or-nothing payoff, of which those now lucky enough to
have reached their seventh or eighth decade of life were going
to take full advantage. Was this how it was supposed to work?
Toil away for forty years so that one day you pack up, abandon
your family and friends, just to learn how to line dance? What
a reward.

He grew restless when considering what it meant for his
parents. Despite the desirable energy of daily life at the club,
his father had already seemed to identify its trappings as

unfulfilling. A natural conclusion, Ben thought. But the more he saw of this place and its people, the more a discouraging barrier began to take shape in his mind, a suspicion he feared would make any attempt at broaching the subject a complete waste of his breath: She would never let them leave.

After passing the third of several enticing restaurants, Ben was tempted to stop. Back home, he tended to gravitate more to speakeasy-like basement bars, where he could sample any number of craft cocktails from the latest hipster mixologist Minneapolis had to offer. But it wasn't often he could enjoy a refreshing glass of rosé on a patio this time of year, and the conspicuous salmon-colored glimmer from each tabletop called to him now like an old friend.

He parked in a pre-designated spot along a series of nine or ten other golf carts. To his left sat a shiny red cart, a bit larger than his parents', with a double "R" insignia stitched into each leather seatback.

Rolls-Royce.

Ben stopped for a moment to inspect the posh vehicle. Its windshield, the broad white stripe down the front—*a bit ugly, actually*—which led to the "Spirit of Ecstasy" hood ornament he vaguely recognized from his time spent at the country club growing up. It had always reminded him of a silver version of the winged lady who triumphantly held an atom overhead on the Emmy statuette. He stepped out of his cart and, as he walked by, resisted the urge to ever so gently drag his key against the scarlet paint of this absurd status symbol.

The restaurant he'd chosen was the least busy. Still, the patio bustled with rollicking residents, which only made it easier for him to choose a seat inside. It was happy hour. Drink specials were *only* ten dollars for cocktails, eight for most wines and beer. Ben sat at the bar and ordered that rosé. In an attempt to drown out the drivel from the ten TVs vying for his attention from the walls, he strained to eavesdrop on a conversation from the table at his back. He'd only gathered a few sentences—something about the latest woman booted from what he assumed must be at least season eight hundred of *The Bachelor*—when the ladies' voices became hushed.

Ben could sense he'd become the new topic of conversation and couldn't resist turning his head to get a glimpse of the curious gossipers. A couple of muted gasps confirmed his suspicion. He wiggled a few fingers to acknowledge them, but instead of sheepishly demurring, the ladies all smiled as if they'd succeeded at something and waved him over.

Eh, what the hell, Ben thought. He scooped up his wine glass and ambled over to the buzzing table. An empty bottle of Moscato rested in the center. "Hello," he said.

The four women, almost in unison, responded with a protracted "Hiiiye."

For a few moments, Ben questioned whether they were actually club members. Several other women he'd seen this weekend had appeared a bit younger than his parents. These ladies, however, with their long, healthy-looking manes and lineless faces that still moved, seemed as though they could almost pass as former schoolmates of his.

"Join us!" offered one of the women. She was tall in her seat, and by the quiet nodding of the others had quickly demonstrated her position as queen bee.

"Okay," Ben agreed. He dragged a chair from the empty table next to theirs and sat directly across from the tall lady.

"What's your name?" she asked, her mouth remaining ever so slightly open.

"I'm Ben."

"Hi, Ben," she smiled. "I'm Debbie."

"Nice to meet you, Debbie."

Debbie proceeded to rattle off the names of her girlfriends. But as Ben had so often experienced, if he didn't immediately repeat a person's name out loud when being introduced, it was lost until he heard it again.

"We were just mentioning how you looked a little out of place," the woman to his right commented. *Was it Shannon? No, Shelley.*

"I don't live here," Ben replied, smirking a bit for having to state the obvious.

"We figured," said Debbie.

"What brings you to the club?" asked the woman probably named Shelley.

"Just visiting my parents."

"And where are *they* this afternoon?" Debbie asked.

"They're at their house, probably napping," Ben said. He tipped his head toward the entrance. "It's not far from here."

"Well, that's exciting," Debbie teased, taking a sip of her wine.

"Oh, stop," the woman to Ben's left nasally chided. He was even less confident in her name. *Pam?*

"Relax, Kate," Debbie scolded. "I'm just playing with him." *Way off.*

Ben laughed a little. "I know it sounds very 'retired' of them. But they're throwing a party tonight for their anniversary. That's why I'm here."

"I bet that's what all the bustle around the main house is," the fourth woman quietly said to Debbie. Ben hadn't needed to repeat her name. "Candy" was memorable enough, and seemingly fitting; her lips shone like one of those autumn apples coated in crimson toffee. She turned to Ben and said, "We saw some catering trucks heading that direction earlier."

"Are you ladies not on the guest list for tonight? Apparently it's going to be a big group."

"We don't live here either," said Debbie, combing her fingers through her chestnut locks.

"Oh. I guess I just assumed since you were here—"

"I don't mean we're from out of town," Debbie clarified. "We just don't live at the club."

Ben glanced at each lady. "How do you get past the security gate? I got the third degree even with my name on a list when I arrived."

"Shannon went to high school with one of the attendants," Kate announced proudly.

Damn it. Right the first time.

"So you're a townie, Shannon," Ben offered.

"Yeah, I suppose," said Shannon, as if she'd never thought of it.

"What's the rest of Palm Beach like?" Ben asked.

"Not like this," Debbie interjected. She held up the empty bottle from the table then and pointed to it after catching a waiter's eye.

Ben laughed a little. "Of course not," he said. "But why here? I imagine there are plenty of places that don't require knowing one of the security guards to get in."

The ladies all looked at Debbie. "It's a great place to meet people," she said after a short pause.

Ben raised an eyebrow. "People?" he asked.

"Men," said Debbie, pursing her lips.

"You come here to…meet men," Ben said, a hint of uncertainty in his voice.

"That's right," Debbie replied, unflinching. "We're all divorced, so…"

Ben only bobbed his head a few times, unsure of how to reply. The ladies eyed him closely, cheeky grins gradually widening on their faces.

Debbie dipped her chin slightly. "I know what you're thinking," she said.

"What am I thinking?"

"'Four women their age getting together for happy hour at a retirement community? They must have one thing on their minds.'"

Ben waited. The obvious answer seemed to be coming. But for unknown reasons, he had trouble assuming it just yet. Maybe, just maybe, he thought, there was something he was missing. Would Debbie be feeding into his natural suspicion that she and her friends were only there to land rich husbands, if that were not the case? She'd already admitted their purpose was to meet men. So, was it just that they all had a thing for older men? No, he decided quickly. It had to be a combination of older men who happen to have a lot of money. Or maybe married men. Or married *white* men? Maybe pudgy men with tan lines who always dress like they're either about to head to the fairway or have just stepped off one. Or perhaps it was just some niche fetish for seducing Cuban waiters on or around posh patios. Ben knew the ladies couldn't be into *him*, could they? He was the only man under the age of fifty who didn't work there; it'd be a waste of time if they expected to find others of his ilk at the club weekend after weekend.

Whatever the reason for their attendance, he was ready to be surprised. After a few tense moments of him staring like a kid about to learn a juicy secret, the ladies all burst into laughter. Ben sat back in his chair and folded his arms until they finished. "What?" he asked.

"Your face!" Debbie howled.

Shannon was holding her stomach. "What did you think we were going to say?" she teased.

"I don't know," Ben grumbled. "You haven't said anything yet."

"Well, there's no mystery," Kate finally revealed. "It's about the money."

Ben had to laugh a little at this unapologetic admission. "So, you're gold diggers?" he asked. He flinched immediately upon saying this. It sounded trite and a bit hurtful when he heard it out loud, and that wasn't his intention.

Debbie squirmed. "Oh, that's such an ugly term," she said. "We prefer 'forty-niners.'"

Ben scoffed at this. "You guys can't be almost fifty," he insisted.

"No, like those California guys during the Iron Age," squeaked Candy.

Debbie shot Candy a disapproving frown. Then she turned to Ben and clarified, "She means the Gold Rush."

"Got it," Ben smiled.

The waiter returned with a fresh bottle of wine and asked Ben if he'd like a refill on his rosé. Ben hesitated, and ultimately declined. As the waiter replenished the other glasses, Ben studied the ladies for a while. He felt a growing attraction to them. By most standards, yes, they were beautiful. But he was more curious as to why they'd be so willing to invite him over and open up about themselves in this way. He knew he had a welcoming, maybe even disarming face; when he and Jake traveled, strangers always seemed to be approaching him to ask for directions. Or had there been something about his posture or the fit of his clothes that had betrayed him, signaling to these ladies he could be trusted more like a girlfriend? To this day, he hadn't shaken the impulse to attenuate himself among strangers.

Might he instead simply be a useful prop for any acceptable passersby, so they could see that these ladies were still capable of wooing a man their own age? If so, he didn't begrudge them that. Theirs had to be a tricky age to be single, especially if dollars were what they were after. They were old enough to be called cougars, but still too young to believably look like they belonged arm-in-arm with someone who could claim full Social Security. The shame of that visible age gap would be, as it seemed to Ben, more than enough to deter most people from the subterfuge required to land such a man. Perhaps that was the real draw of these ladies for him: the open and remorseless admittance of who they were, and the unabashed vigor with which they chose to pursue their prize.

Ben reconsidered the refill, and after the waiter had finished topping off everyone else, he raised his glass to accept a modest pour. The ladies all smiled at this spontaneous change of heart.

Ben extended his arm toward the center of the table. "To the forty-niners," he said.

Each of the ladies gave a little cheer, as if toasting to some victory or pesky problem solved. They all clinked their glasses before tipping them back for a hefty taste. Ben's eyes tightened, taken off-guard by the Moscato's overly ripe sweetness.

Debbie lowered her glass quickly and elbowed Candy. "Incoming," she purred.

Ben checked the ladies, who had all followed Debbie's eyes toward a corner of the bar. At Ben's back, a single gentleman had stepped in from the patio to presumably settle his bill.

"Looks promising. From behind, anyway," Kate whispered, lifting her chin to size up the man.

Ben had suddenly become invisible. He watched as the women remained quiet, their gaze keenly focused on the man like a pride of lionesses waiting to pounce on their unsuspecting prey. By the intensity of their stares, Ben assumed the man was ticking several boxes for his tablemates. He appeared trim and had a really nice tan. From their distance of about fifty feet, he didn't seem to be balding much. When the bartender stepped toward the till, the man turned slightly, and Ben was able to catch a glimpse of his face. He'd seen that leathery profile recently. And after the man showed his teeth when smiling to accept his check, Ben recognized those blazing choppers as belonging to one Dan Gunderson.

Ben stood abruptly. "Excuse me, ladies," he said without looking at any of them. He darted in the direction of the bar.

"Wait, I want you to give him my number!" Debbie chirped after him, the rest of the table falling into laughter.

Ben slowed his pace when he realized Dan was taking his time signing the bill. Maintaining a safe distance, he stepped just close enough to catch Dan's attention when he spoke.

"Hi, Dan."

Dan looked up from his bill, his tightened face suggesting a reaction more of annoyed confusion than surprise. Ben didn't move any closer. "Hello, Ben," he said. He smiled but kept his lips pressed together.

Ben watched Dan for a moment. He had looked nervous at first, fumbling with his pen like he'd just been caught talking about someone who was within earshot the whole time. But Ben's hesitation to say anything had seemed to quickly bolster Dan's confidence. He had turned to face Ben now, his brow raised as if waiting for Ben to arrive at whatever reason he'd had for approaching him.

Ben swallowed hard and looked to the floor. "Say, Dan—"

"Yes?"

Ben's eyes were alerted forward again by this quick reply. He stuttered slightly in beginning again. "I wanted to apologize for last night."

"Okay."

Ben paused, having hoped what he'd just said was apology enough. "I was out of line," he added. "Your decisions about your knee are none of my business. And I'm sorry."

Dan maintained his tight-lipped grin but said nothing. No "that's okay" or a jovial "hey, don't worry about it." No nod of acceptance. Only a smug silence that was louder than had he just gone ahead and shouted a paternalistic reprimand straight in Ben's face. Ben could deal with that. He knew *how* to deal with that. But this non-reaction, with its moments of dead air where his admittance of wrong was just left hanging in space above their heads, felt increasingly more painful and dismissive as each wordless second passed.

"You know, I had a great round this morning," Dan finally said, ending the awkward silence. It was as if he hadn't heard any part of what Ben had just said.

"Oh," Ben replied. "I thought my dad had mentioned you didn't play this morning."

"No, I did," Dan said, squinting at the bill he'd signed. "Just with a different group."

"Dad sure likes those early tee times," Ben said, smiling.

"It had nothing to do with the start time."

"Oh?" said Ben, his smile fading.

Dan looked up from his bill and wrinkled his nose. "It's good to have some variety in company."

Ben paused to take a deep breath. "I see."

"In fact, I'm a bit surprised your dad had such a large group with him."

Another pause. "Why's that?"

"Well, I'm sure you know your dad's handicap isn't exactly what we'd consider low." Dan was grinning again and had lowered his voice slightly, almost sympathetically. "He tends to slow things down a bit too much sometimes. Folks get antsy waiting behind us."

"I usually just let people play through when that's the case," Ben suggested, biting the inside of his cheek. It was no secret Jim wasn't a great golfer. By the time Ben was fourteen, he'd outscored his father on a par-3 course. But Ben knew how much his dad enjoyed it—the leisure of it. To Jim, it was more an opportunity to relax with buddies than to square off in fierce competition.

"Yes, well, some people take it pretty seriously here," Dan informed him. He laughed then, adding, "I'd hate to see your dad relegated to playing by himself."

Unsmiling, Ben replied, "I expect that would be really disappointing for him."

Dan remained quiet for a stretch before changing the subject on a dime. "Say, I bet you know a thing or two about St. Paul."

"Um…yeah, a bit, I guess," Ben said, shaking his head in confusion.

"Ruth mentioned this morning that Eli's got a conference coming up there in May. You remember our son's moving to Rochester soon."

"I remember."

"It'd be great for him if he knew a little more about the city. Some good restaurants, maybe."

Ben's response came slowly. "I'd be happy to give him some recommendations."

"And maybe you could show him around a bit. My guess is he'll have to be up in the metro area pretty regularly. And he's a bit shy. Not one to really speak up, or out of turn."

This felt like a reprimand. Ben eyed Dan carefully. "Sure."

"Great," Dan smiled. He slipped the bar's pen into the breast pocket of his Hawaiian shirt, then glanced at his watch. "Wow, I better get a move on. Ruth will have my hide if I make us late for the party."

Ben's eyes lit up. "So, you *are* going tonight?"

"Of course we're going," Dan said, his tone betraying his plans only after having secured this petty restitution. It was a cross Ben was willing to bear.

Dan turned toward the exit, not before flashing a smile to the table of ladies he'd somehow known were watching from behind. Ben offered a modest wave to Debbie and her team, and followed Dan out the door.

On the top step at the restaurant's entrance, Dan gestured toward the line of parked golf carts. "Isn't she a beauty?" he beamed.

Ben stood in silence for a moment before realizing Dan was referencing the gaudy red cart parked next to his parents'. "That's yours?" he asked.

Dan continued grinning ear to ear. "Yep," he said proudly. "Little birthday gift I got for myself last month."

Ben tried to act impressed. "Wow," he said. "She's somethin' else."

Dan nodded, satisfied. He descended the three concrete steps then hopped into his cart. Ben stayed put, pretending he needed another minute to admire Dan's new toy.

"I guess we'll see you tonight," Dan said, before turning the ignition. The cart's low purr was barely detectable from Ben's short distance, but Dan raised his voice now, regardless. "And hey, I wouldn't worry too much about your dad's game. There are all kinds of pros who offer private lessons for members."

Ben offered a thumbs-up from the steps. Despite their awkward encounter, he felt an impish grin tugging at the corners of his mouth. In the few steps he'd observed Dan take while exiting the restaurant and reaching the cart, Ben's eyes had been drawn to his lower half. Something about his bare left leg had struck him, an asymmetry that at first glance didn't register as anything noteworthy. But as he watched that awful

Rolls-Royce being carefully backed away under the low sun's angled rays, Ben was left with a sly sense of vindication when he realized exactly what it was he'd detected in Dan's gait: a pronounced limp.

nine

Ben spotted his mother in the kitchen. She wore a one-shouldered pink dress partially concealed by the large metal clock she was holding. She was squinting, intently adjusting its hands. Ben whistled when he walked in.

"Oh!" Betsy gasped, fumbling the clock. "You scared me!"

Ben giggled at her startled reaction. "Mom, you look fantastic," he said.

While Betsy's facial alterations were still taking some getting used to, Ben couldn't deny that she'd kept herself in wonderful shape. She had chosen a snug dress, and it was flattering to her taut figure.

"Thank you, sweetie," Betsy said, blushing a little. "Where have you been?"

"I took the golf cart for a spin." He nodded once at the clock and asked, "What are you doing?"

"It's daylight savings time tonight."

"Oh, that's right," Ben said. "Well, good. We get an extra hour of sleep."

"Lose," Betsy corrected him. "We *lose* an hour. Remember? 'Spring forward?'"

"Damnit, I can never keep that straight."

Betsy delicately returned the clunky clock to its designated location on the wall next to the refrigerator. "Abby actually reminded me that we needed to reset the clocks tonight. Your father and I were FaceTiming with her and the girls." She took a few steps back to make sure the clock was straight. "I wanted to get it done before the party. Lord knows I probably won't remember when we get home."

"How's Abster doing?" Ben asked. He hadn't texted her yet today.

"She's doing well," Betsy replied, rinsing her hands under the tap. "Glad the morning sickness is over. I guess Terry has some business coming up in California next week. And the girls are busy as ever, of course."

Abby liked to joke with Ben, somewhat cynically, that the happiest she ever saw their mother was when she finally announced her engagement to Terry. He was a member of the uber-wealthy Creeger family, who'd made their fortune first in agricultural and livestock commodities, then mostly hedge funds. Her reaction to Abby finishing first in their high school class of three hundred—Ben was fourteenth—or the birth of her first grandchild, paled mightily in comparison to learning Abby would be a Creeger. And despite Betsy's disappointment in not being given free rein in the wedding planning, the fact that a photo including her and Jim made the front page of the Variety section of the *Minneapolis Tribune* kept her beaming for months.

"I'm sure she wishes she could be here."

Betsy only smiled thinly as she dried her hands on a dish towel. There was a long pause.

"So, anything you need me to help with tonight?" he asked, hoping to avoid surprises. He was perhaps more hoping his mother would provide him some sort of occupation during the party, so as to limit the amount of socializing he'd be expected to endure with other residents. Anything was likely to be an easier assignment than the one his father had dropped in his lap that afternoon.

"Nope. Everything should be set, Benny." Betsy placed a hand on his shoulder. "All you need to do is try to have a good time."

"Sounds good," he replied, as if disappointed.

"You'll have plenty of people to chat with, sweetie." Betsy started counting on her fingers. "Al and Liza of course will be there. The Gundersons. Oh, and did I mention Tim and Nancy Conway are coming?"

"Our old neighbors?" Ben asked, contorting his face.

"Yes!" Betsy said, delighted. "They winter in West Palm Beach, so I invited them."

This wasn't exactly an exciting piece of news for Ben. He'd recently run into the Conways' two adult sons, Greg and Charlie, while socializing with some friends at a pub in Minneapolis. Reminiscences of the old neighborhood had quickly given way to a booze-ladened shouting match. Ben had voiced his disapproval of the brothers' creation of a political action committee in support of a conservative gubernatorial candidate during the last election cycle. Despite insisting to Jake the next morning that he'd only had a couple drinks, the conversation had apparently been disruptive enough that Ben was asked by management to leave.

He forced a smile. "Well, it'll be nice to catch up with them," he said. So much for no surprises.

Betsy gave Ben's somewhat worn appearance a long look then. His hair was messy from the cart ride and his T-shirt wrinkled from where he'd been sweating. "You should think about getting ready, Benny."

"We're not leaving for almost an hour, right?"

"Yes, but—"

"Nope," Ben interjected, raising his hand in agreement. "You're right. I'll hop in the shower here." Then with a hopeful expression, "Dad thought it would be OK if I wore a polo and jeans?"

"Of course," Betsy replied, a little unconvincingly. "Wear whatever you want." She sneezed then, violently.

"*Gesundheit!*"

Three additional similarly charged sneezes followed.

"Whoa, Ma. You feeling all right?" Ben asked.

Betsy tore a paper towel from the roll on the counter. "Oh, it's just this stupid hay fever. All the pollen here," she explained, sniffling. "I should probably take something."

"Did you pick up something at the pharmacy?"

Betsy looked at Ben carefully for a moment. "How did you know I stopped at the pharmacy?"

Ben pulled a crumpled piece of white paper from his pocket and extended it toward Betsy. "There was a receipt from CVS left in the golf cart. Did you need it?"

She walked up to him and snagged the receipt from his hand. "Yes, I do," she said after a short pause. Then gently tapping the tip of his pink nose, "I picked up some better sunscreen for you, too. Make sure you use it tomorrow if you're around the pool, okay?"

Ben grinned with a single, obedient nod. He watched Betsy move to the living room where she grabbed a small clock from an end table. How had he never noticed how similar her walk was to Grandma Helen's? The tight dress she'd selected forced her into short, quick steps. Grandma had moved the same way—with an apron almost perpetually cinched around her tiny waist—abbreviating her steps, as if taking too long of a stride would somehow appear unladylike.

Betsy looked back to where Ben stood, motionless. "Now go get ready!"

~~~

Ben was still waiting to hear back from Jake. He shot off another quick text before stepping into his new favorite shower. *Did you get some work done?*

Toweling off, he leaned toward the mirror to examine the apparent sunburn his mother had pointed out. A sharp line, formed by the border of his shades, ran across the bridge of his nose and below his eyes. He glowered at his reflection, looking like a typical tourist whose singed face implied a foolish disregard for the Sunshine State's unyielding stream of ultraviolet rays.

A response from Jake finally flashed on Ben's phone. *Ugh long day but yes got a lot done.*

Ben sifted through his suitcase to slip into a fresh pair of briefs and sat on the bed. He grabbed his phone to reply. *Great! Hopefully you can just relax tonight.*

Jake's text came swiftly. *Tony and Scott want to do dinner.*

Oh that could be fun. Ben hiked his knee to slip on a sock before adding, *Say hi to the boys.*

Tony and Scott were softball teammates of Jake's who'd recently begun dating each other. Scott had been the one to come up with their team name, "The Best-Looking Team

Here." Ben always got a kick out of watching the roll call for their games. The umpire would verify the first group, calling out whatever clever name the team happened to come up with—usually something like "Nine Inch Males" or "Quit Your Pitching." When "The Best-Looking Team Here" was invariably announced as the opponent, shouts would immediately spring from Jake's bench with players hooting, "You got that right!" or "Preach, honey."

I'm not sure I want to go, read Jake's reply.

Too pooped?

Nah. They want to grab drinks after.

The texts came in such rapid succession that Ben was making little progress getting dressed. He sent off one more. *You can still call it a night after dinner if you want can't you?* He dropped his phone on the bed and stood to rummage for an appropriate shirt, groaning in regret at not having just emptied his clothes into the enormous white dresser when he'd arrived. The muffled buzz of another message alert could be heard from the plush comforter into which his phone had sunk.

It's not that, Jake had sent.

Ben sat pantless on the bed looking at his phone. It wasn't like Jake to be evasive. If anything, when something bothered him, he typically came right out with it—almost to a fault, Ben had found. He was about to reply with an obvious *why not* when the three telltale little bubbles indicating another pending reply began pulsing on his screen below Jake's latest message. Waiting for what seemed like minutes, Ben was expecting to see a long paragraph come through explaining Jake's hesitance about spending the evening with his buddies. When the text finally appeared, Ben was surprised at more than just its brevity.

Oliver's in town.

After a moment, another text followed. *He wants the four of us to meet up after dinner.*

Ben's spine stiffened on the edge of the bed. It took a while for this bit of info to fully sink in. Tony and Scott weren't aware of what had gone on with Oliver the night after last summer's banquet. Or if they were, they'd either forgotten about it or passed it off as unimportant. Jake certainly hadn't mentioned anything. And it was doubtful Oliver would have either. For all he knew, even Jake didn't know what really happened.

Oh.

It wasn't a helpful response. But Ben was at a loss for what to say. Tony and Scott certainly wouldn't care if Jake asked for a rain check; they could appreciate how crazy it was this time of year for an accountant. But how often was Oliver in town? It was a question Ben knew Jake would have to negotiate if he declined the invitation from his friends. Everyone knew Oliver and Jake had become close during the season. Skipping out would draw more suspicion than if Jake simply went along and had a few with the group. Ben also understood how unfairly awkward that would be for his partner. And yet, he couldn't help but breathe a selfish sigh of relief. Knowing he didn't have to participate in the uncomfortable scenario he'd been solely responsible for creating, he suddenly realized it was possibly the first moment all weekend he was happier to be in Florida.

Ben waited for Jake's simple reply. *Yeah.*

I'm sure Tony and Scott won't mind if you duck out after dinner. It was all Ben could offer.

I know. I might just stay home altogether.

Nothing wrong with that. You've had a long day. Ben stood to slide into his jeans before shooting off another quick text. *I better get going. Mom & dad are waiting.*

OK.

Don't forget to set the clocks ahead tonight.

Jake replied with one of those yellow-faced emoticons he was fond of using. Its wide-eyed look of surprise suggested he, too, had forgotten about the pending time change. A swift "thumbs-up" followed.

Ben cracked a half smile and texted a departing heart emoji.

Love you too. Good luck tonight, Jake replied, as if to concede Ben's posh evening in paradise was somehow going to be the greater hardship to endure.

~~~

When Betsy saw Ben stepping out of his room carrying a flat, gift-wrapped box, she stopped her anxious buzzing around the kitchen.

"We wanted to be the first to give you guys a gift," Ben said, holding the box out to Betsy over the kitchen island. On the invitations she'd sent out for the party, Betsy had insisted on no gifts, but confided in Ben earlier that the request was likely to be ignored by guests. "It's from me and Abby."

"Oh, Benny, you didn't have to do that," Betsy said, her voice bubbly. She turned the package around to inspect each side before hollering to the living room. "Jim, get in here!"

Jim staggered into the kitchen, irritated that he had to leave his program. "What's the matter?" he grumbled. Then realizing Betsy wasn't alone, he added, "Oh, hey Benny." He briefly inspected Ben from head to toe. "Lookin' sharp." Betsy gently shook the box to grab Jim's attention. "What do we have here?" he asked, rubbing his palms together.

"It's an anniversary gift from our children." She eyed Ben inquisitively.

"Go ahead," Ben chuckled, seeing his mother's eagerness.

She opened it slowly, careful not to tear the paper as if planning to save it for reuse. Inside was a beautiful antique frame with a photo of Ben and Abby. The two of them were standing in front of a wintery background of leafless birch trees, the branches covered in frost. Betsy bit her lower lip and held up the frame in front of her.

"We realized you don't have many pictures of just the two of us since high school," Ben said.

Betsy was quiet. Her eyes welled with tears as she handed the frame to Jim. He smiled broadly and held it at arm's length with both hands. "What a great pic," he said. Then turning to Ben, "Is this..."

"Yep. Your backyard," said Ben. "I got one of my friends who dabbles in photography to take it for us a few weeks ago. We sort of lucked out on the weather that day."

Jim handed the frame back to Betsy. She set it on the counter, oddly silent.

"You okay, Mom?" Ben asked.

"Yes, I'm fine, sweetheart," she sniffled. "Thank you for the beautiful photo. It's absolutely precious." She grabbed a hand towel from a drawer and began to gently dab the corners of her eyes.

He hadn't expected her to be this moved. The photo had been Abby's idea. He hadn't been planning to bring a gift, but

Abby wouldn't hear of it. "She'll never let me live it down," she'd said. "If I'm not going to be there, you *have* to bring a present from us. Just make sure to give it to her at the right time."

He knew Abby had meant at a time when the gift might serve as a tool in helping to manage Mom's mood. "Think of it as part of your survival kit," she'd unironically put it. It gave him a funny feeling thinking about how contrived that sounded, even manipulative. But he conceded there was likely to be a time where he'd welcome the option to employ any such tactic. After his father's request to have him gauge Mom's level of interest in returning to Minnesota, he'd thought the gift might just be the perfect segue into that inquiry. He tried to view it as a demonstration of his openness to seeing her more, another sign of his good intentions. Getting to her after she'd had a couple glasses of wine, however, ultimately felt like an additional and very necessary boon to navigate that particular minefield. Right before the party therefore felt like the best alternate window for delivering his little peace offering. And by his mother's touched reaction, he appeared to be right.

A little brighter now, Betsy inspected the photo more closely and said, "This frame is gorgeous. Where'd you find it?"

"At a little shop near my place."

"It's just darling." She neatly folded the wrapping and tissue paper. She fit the top back on the box and studied it for a moment. "*Infinit*," she said, pronouncing a hard 't' at the end.

"I think it's pronounced '*on feenee.*' It's a little boutique a couple blocks from my condo."

"I haven't heard of it," Betsy said, wide-eyed.

Ben felt like laughing. When all the Apts still lived in Minnesota, Betsy almost exclusively shopped at an upscale mall in another suburb near their home. Infinit had only opened in the last year. He grinned at how surprised she sounded when its name wasn't familiar. "It's pretty new," he said.

"I'd love to see it."

"You'll have to visit," Ben said, testing the waters a little. He was surprised how quick he'd been to make such a direct suggestion. He glanced at her, worried it may have sounded spiteful. But she only smiled and nodded, the way one would to indicate polite entertainment of an unlikely possibility. There was a long pause, and then Betsy suddenly stiffened her posture, as if met with a cold breeze or troubling image.

Jim and Ben exchanged concerned looks. She was wringing her hands now. Reaching out to softly touch Betsy's elbow, Jim lowered his voice and said, "Honey, everything will work out great."

"I know, I know," she said, trying to convince herself. She raised her fingertips to the corners of her eyes. "I need to touch up my makeup before we leave."

Ben looked at Jim with the eyes of a child who'd just been struck by some frightening premonition. He watched his mother head toward the bedroom, her heels clacking in quick succession on the tile floor.

"I'll meet you in the car," she said, her back to them.

Jim waited until the door closed behind her, then turned to Ben with a nervous smile.

"Here we go."

ten

"Holy shit," Ben uttered under his breath. Upon entering the grand hall yesterday, with its whitewashed columns, marble flooring and backdrop of Floridian flora, the room had quickly announced itself to him as an overwhelming expanse of decorative detail. Yet despite the ostentatious introduction, Ben was ill-prepared for the gaudy scene laid out before him now. In just over twenty-four hours, the already impressive space had been neatly transformed into a dazzling spectacle of glitz and color.

Scattered about the room, dozens of round, elaborately set tables reflected hues of blue and purple light. The fountain, which yesterday had blasted out roaring columns of water, was now set to a low ripple, providing a cool ambiance of ocean surf. Staff scurried like ants to fervently fill a long buffet table with silver containers, while young bartenders audited their inventories behind lit onyx bar tops rivaling the length of the buffet.

Ben pivoted to Betsy. "Mom, this is incredible."

"It's all Dwayne," she replied, matter-of-factly.

Ben and Jim stood in place for a few moments, taking in the room's opulence. Betsy had a look of concentration on her face. She separated from Ben and Jim, carefully assessing the work being done at the bars and buffet table. A broad stage had been assembled in front of the palm trees near the back, and she approached a man who looked to be setting up some sort of sound system.

"There's a band?" asked Ben, turning to Jim.

"Yep. A ten-piece big band. I told you your mom went all out."

Ben's face lit up when he caught the activity at one of the bars. They were ready for business. "Wanna grab a drink?" he asked.

"I better wait here until your mother gets back."

"I can grab you something. What do you want?"

Jim paused. "Well, if you're sure you don't mind," he said. "Old Fashioned."

"You took the words right out of my mouth," Ben smiled. "Be right back."

A handsome young man greeted Ben at the bar with that now all too familiar Cheshire Cat grin. After placing his order, he waited as the bartender swiftly yet painstakingly began to concoct their drinks. There was something soothing about witnessing the preparation of a good cocktail. He watched the small lumps of sugar slightly dissolve under a splash of bitters before the bartender muddled them under an orange peel. A large, perfect sphere of ice was gently dropped into each glass, after which a generous shot of whiskey and a cherry garnish were stirred in to sweet perfection. Once again, Ben reached for his cashless wallet, but breathed a quiet sigh of relief when he noticed a small sign at the end of the bar which read, "No Tips, Please." He returned to Jim with both drinks in hand.

"Thanks, Benny," Jim said, accepting a glass. They both said "cheers" and enjoyed a long sip. "That's a damned good Old Fashioned," he continued, holding up his glass to study it.

Up to that point, almost everything at The Cypress Club, while no doubt expensive, had struck Ben as essentially devoid of any real taste. But he agreed with his father regarding the drinks. Booze was apparently something members took very seriously.

Betsy suddenly came stomping back from the podium to join them, her arms folded in exasperation. Jim and Ben braced themselves. "Apparently the band wasn't planning to go on stage until eight-thirty," she huffed. "I hired them to start at eight."

Jim and Ben exchanged a quick look, neither knowing quite what to say. This didn't sound like a particularly huge snag in the evening, but they both knew all it might take was something small to get Betsy going.

"Eh, it's just half an hour," Jim said, gently rubbing Betsy's shoulder. "Folks are going to want to visit for a while. Everything else seems in order, right?"

Taking a quick look around the room, Ben chimed in as well. "Yeah, look at this place. All the food's getting put out and the bars are set up. You've done a great job, Ma."

Betsy took a deep breath and cracked a smile. She threw her hands up, seeming to concede the smallness of this infraction from the band. "You're right," she said. "I need a glass of wine."

"I'll get you one," said Ben, relieved that the mini crisis appeared to be diffused for the time being. He was about to hop back to the bar before Jim interjected.

"No, let me. You two stay here and chat," he said. "Here." Jim handed Betsy his drink before scuttling up to the bar.

The move was a little obvious. Ben immediately considered saying something about his father's interest in moving back to Minnesota. Why not just get it out of the way? There hadn't been any major problems to tick Betsy off yet, and she had seemed to relax a little bit after the slight snag with the band's start time. Maybe this would be the best chance he had all weekend. Keep it casual, like it had just occurred to him.

Before Ben could say a word, however, Betsy quickly explained that people would be arriving soon, and that she and Jim would start the evening perched at the main entrance, welcoming guests in a sort of receiving line. She pointed to the tall stools the staff had set out. Ben counted them.

"Why are there three?" he asked, slightly panicked.

Betsy frowned in confusion. "Because there are three of us."

Ben had to resist the urge to instantly say no. He nodded slowly and waited, deciding how best to go about telling her that he didn't think this was a very good idea. Being given something to do was supposed to feel like a welcome benefit, an assignment that would provide the opportunity to do the exact opposite of the phony gladhanding his mother was now expecting him to undertake.

"Mom, do you think that's necessary?"

"Well, you'll want a chair, won't you?"

"No," Ben replied, carefully. "I mean, do you really want me sitting there with you and Dad? Tonight is more about the two of you as a couple, isn't it?"

Betsy flicked her fingers in the air to dismiss Ben's question. "Nonsense," she uttered. "It's about our family."

Ben's angle didn't work. He had hoped to imply that his presence may draw attention away from the couple—namely Betsy—and therefore persuade her to reconsider her decision to include him. He lowered his head slightly and exhaled. "Okay," he said, defeated.

"It'll be fine," Betsy reassured him, as if castigating a small child for pouting about something trivial. "We'll keep the line moving fast."

Ben scratched his neck and turned to hide his eyeroll. "How many people are you expecting?" he asked, taking a healthy swig of his drink.

"About five hundred RSVP'd."

"What?!" Ben exclaimed. He had to wipe a bit of whiskey from his chin.

"Is that a lot?" Betsy asked, blinking innocently.

Ben took a half step back. "Mom, you've got to be kidding. We're going to be stuck on those stools all night."

"Why?" Betsy demanded.

"Because it's a party. People will be trickling in slowly for hours."

Betsy's eyes widened then, and she shook her finger like a scolding schoolteacher. "Oh no they won't," she announced. "You list a start time on an invitation in this place and that's the *latest* anyone will show up."

Ben eyed her carefully but said nothing, still skeptical.

"Just you watch," Betsy said confidently. "We'll whip through that line in thirty minutes."

The two of them collected Jim from the bar and they made their way to the start of the receiving line. Betsy directed Ben and Jim to sit on either side of her. Insisting the guests would be arriving any moment, it took only one stern look for her to quash Ben's attempt at standing to refresh his drink. She turned around momentarily to set her glass of chardonnay on a small table behind them, then exaggerated her already excellent posture. She crossed her tan legs, gently rested her folded hands over her knee and produced the widest smile her taut face would allow, as if readying herself for a barrage of close-up photos. Jim looked cheerful, but maintained a somewhat slouched position, cradling his drink in his lap.

Ben had reached for his phone nonchalantly, when on the dot, as his mother had predicted, guests began filing into the hall in droves. He pictured the stream of well-wishers having been lined up around the block for hours, like in one of those old photos of folks waiting to get tickets to a new movie only playing in one theater. He quickly withdrew his hand from his pocket and bolstered himself for the inevitable onslaught of overzealous handshakes and pretentious rounds of small talk.

Ben was immediately impressed by how effortlessly Betsy kept everyone moving along. She had clearly prepared a script. With the swiftness of a conveyor belt, she never allowed anyone to stop his or her forward progress in the line, saying, "Thank you so much for coming," then quickly gesturing toward Ben and adding, "Have you met our son Benjamin?" Ben decided to take her lead and offered his hand to each guest, making eye contact of course, but always being sure to quickly transition his gaze to the next person, thwarting the initiation of any real conversation.

The women were impeccably dressed, much fancier than Ben had expected for a party like this. Accents of gaudy jewelry bedecked their wrinkled necks and wrists to excess. In such close proximity, he felt trapped inside the powerful cloud of perfume with which they'd all seemed to have perfunctorily doused themselves. And their new faces, despite the room's dim lighting, struck him as even more disturbingly unnatural than he had previously observed from a distance.

One of the first couples through the line was Ruth and Dan Gunderson. Anticipating a cool reception from Ruth, Ben produced a little smile and stiffened his posture while she and Dan briefly congratulated Jim and Betsy. Ruth grabbed both of his hands, pulling Ben to his feet, then encircled him in a big bear hug. "It's so good to see you again, Ben," she gushed.

Ben slowly wrapped his arms around Ruth and looked in the direction of this mother, completely taken aback by the unexpected display of affection. "You too, Ruth."

They separated, but Ruth kept Ben's hands firmly grasped in hers. "We're just thrilled for your mom and dad," she said. "It's been an absolute joy having them here."

Ben didn't know what to say, so he just stood there, awkwardly smiling as Ruth shook him in a vise-like grip. "Well, thanks for coming," he stammered.

Ruth eventually released him and moved on. Somewhat surprisingly after their encounter at the restaurant, Dan offered a similarly earnest salutation. His shirt bore the same tropical pattern Ben had noted earlier in the day, only that tonight's version was blue instead of red. An irritating wink from Dan seemed to signal some sort of shared understanding between them now. It was the only explanation for the gushy reacquaintance with Ruth.

As Betsy had expected, the Apts' old neighbors, Tim and Nancy Conway, also made an appearance. Betsy detained the couple a little longer than most of the other folks whom she'd gently nudged through the line. Being the only two guests who weren't members of the club, as well as the lone friends from the old neighborhood, Betsy made sure to offer a particularly warm welcome.

When she reintroduced them to Ben, Nancy did her best to act casual. But it quickly became obvious that Greg and Charlie had filled her in on the trio's awkward brush last year. The way she sympathetically tipped her head when addressing him, as if he were suffering from some sort of affliction—alcoholism, perhaps, or liberalism—gave her away. Her insistence on a hug felt more like a condolence than a greeting.

When Nancy embraced Ben, Betsy clutched Tim, saying, "I told Ben you'd give him the details about the boys' new company."

"Their PAC?" Tim clarified. Then looking at Ben with a gratified smile, "Of course! Is that something you're interested in, Ben? I'm sure Greg and Charlie would be happy to connect with you about it."

"What a fun idea!" Nancy squealed, apparently seeing hope for Ben's redemption. "Getting the three of you together again. You're on LinkedIn, aren't you, Ben?"

Ben squirmed a little. "Well, I'm not sure I'm interested in formally getting into politics," he said, quickly bursting everyone's bubble. He was pressed to think of anything more repugnant than initiating a networking session with the conservative Conway boys. "But you'll have to catch me up on how Greg and Charlie are doing."

Nancy opened her mouth to speak but Ben promptly cut her off. "Let's talk at dinner," he urged, then eagerly returned his attention to the fast-moving line.

The last few guests made their way through the line, offering additional congratulations and complimenting Betsy on her beautiful dress. It suddenly dawned on Ben that he'd barely noticed how Nancy Conway had been the only guest to address his mother as *Betty*. This would have been natural for Nancy, of course, likely unaware that her old neighbor had recently adopted a slightly different moniker for her new digs. In recalling Betsy's proclaimed reason of avoiding confusion among other members with the same name, Ben was struck now that of the four hundred or so guests they had already greeted in the receiving line, not one of the women had introduced herself as "Betty."

Liza and Al straggled in together toward the end, insisting they weren't on a date. Although reserved, Al looked happy to be there. Liza elbowed Ben and reminded him that she'd be tracking him down for that dance she'd made him promise her. Normally, Ben would cringe at the very thought of Liza's suggestion, but all he could think about was whether or not he would see any sparks between her and Ruth, if and when the two happened to cross paths. For the sake of his mother, he hoped there wouldn't be. For the sake of his own entertainment, however, he secretly longed for it.

Wrapping up the whirlwind welcome, rather than being exhausted, Betsy looked more refreshed than when they'd started. She checked her watch, then energetically slapped her thighs with both hands. "What did I tell you?" she said with a proud smirk. "Just a little over half an hour."

"Gotta admit, Ma, I'm impressed. And grateful." There was a short moment of quiet as Betsy collected her purse from the small table behind them. She rummaged for a compact and quickly touched up her makeup. Ben sat frozen, unsure if it was okay to move. "Now what?" he asked.

Peering into her small mirror, Betsy tipped her head a little and lifted her chin, as if searching for imperfections in a windowpane that had just been wiped clean. When satisfied, she gently clicked the compact closed between her fingers and turned to Ben with a mischievous grin. "Now we have some fun."

Ben paused, realizing he had no idea what that meant for his mother tonight. "Does this mean I can go back to the bar now?"

"Oh, for heaven's sake, yes," Betsy laughed. "Yes, you can go to the bar now." Then tapping his hand, "As long as you bring your mother back another chardonnay."

"You got it." Ben stood and pulled his shoulders back firmly to stretch, a bit stiff from his time on the stool. "How 'bout you, Pops?"

"I'm gonna wait a bit, Benny," said Jim. "Lot of night left."

"Suit yourself," Ben replied. He started to the bar but checked himself. "Where should I find you guys?"

"We'll be out there somewhere, mingling," said Betsy, fluttering her fingers toward the sea of guests who'd congregated among the dinner tables.

Ben scampered to the closer of the two bars. He was able to wiggle his way through the crowded line a bit, sneaking past members who were too busy gabbing to be bothered by his somewhat impolite intrusion.

He accepted his drinks then stepped away from the bar slightly, once again struggling to resist leaving a bit of gratuity for the dapper barkeep. He lifted his cold gin and tonic to his lips and cautiously surveyed the crowds swarming around the dinner tables. Grandma would have abhorred a sight like this. Even choosing a seat for dinner had seemed to turn into a competition. Folks staked their claims to what were apparently preferred spots by throwing a sport coat over a chair or an enormous Louis Vuitton purse beside a place setting. Near the stage, Ben noticed a woman simply tip each chair forward against the table to render it fully occupied. An elderly resident, bulldozing his way through the crowd to the same table with his head pointed like a Labrador, was met by an unsympathetic shrug from the woman, indicating he was too late. Disappointed, the hunched man turned his walker around and sheepishly sought the closest alternative.

Ben shook his head. Why his mother was so intent on impressing these people he would probably never know.

She'd been right about the receiving line, he conceded. Without it, he would have faced an entire night of repeating the same few sentences in a tedious loop. At least now he wouldn't feel obligated to seek people out to thank them for coming, nor would guests feel pressure to track down the hosts to offer congratulations. Things were going too well.

Through the mobs, Ben spotted Betsy surrounded by four or five women, all attending to her like a spoiled queen's doting clutch of ladies-in-waiting. Their eyes followed Ben as he crossed the room, Betsy's chardonnay in hand. When he neared their posse, they separated to either side of Betsy, opening an almost ceremonious semicircle around her.

"You all remember, Ben," Betsy simpered, pulling him next to her.

Ben gave a bashful little wave. "Hello, ladies."

Like debutantes, the women all rotated slightly sideways to narrow their shape. A few batted their fake eyelashes and produced flirtatious smiles. Each appeared to be around Betsy's age, although Ben was quickly learning that after a certain point, it was anyone's guess which decade of life most of the women at the club were actually in.

"Ben's a prominent physician's assistant in Minneapolis," announced Betsy.

Here we go again. Always starting with a résumé. He smirked and resisted another eyeroll. "I'm not sure about the prominent part," he said, "but I do work as a PA."

The ladies all cooed, overly fascinated.

"Everyone enjoying themselves so far?" Ben added, side-stepping any attempts at diving into the particulars of his job.

"It's wonderful," said one of the ladies.

"Yes," said another, observing the tables. "It's just breathtaking what they've done with the room."

"Well, the night's only getting started," Betsy quipped, shimmying her shoulders a little. "Dinner will get underway very soon. And then there's the music, of course."

A third woman shook her finger toward the stage. "You know, now that you mention it, I thought it looked like there was going to be live entertainment."

"You guessed right," said Betsy. "We've hired a big band."

"My goodness, how big?" asked the same woman, frowning slightly. "The stage doesn't look like it'll fit more than—"

"No, no, dear," Betsy interrupted, gently clasping the woman's forearm. "A band that plays *big band* music."

"Oh. Of course," said the woman, giving a nervous giggle.

There was a short silence. "Well, we should probably get ourselves settled at a table," Betsy said, linking her arm under Ben's and looking up at him. "Let's go collect your father."

As Betsy proceeded to cart him away, Ben strained his neck to offer a parting smile at the women. "It was nice seeing you, ladies."

They found Jim similarly surrounded by a group of guys, shooting the shit and elbowing each other like members of a high school football team in the locker room after a big game. When Ben and Betsy approached, the men all ceased their clowning long enough to scan Betsy's dress, each of their faces burgeoning into a ridiculous, boyish grin.

"Darling?" Betsy said, wrapping her arm around Jim's waist. "We should think about taking our seats. People are getting anxious for dinner to start."

Jim examined the crowd briefly. "I think everyone's doing okay, right?" he said, nodding as if he were trying to get her to agree. "Why don't we give it another ten minutes?"

Betsy turned up one side of her mouth, then said in a slightly hushed, but serious tone, "The food is ready, sweetheart." Wide-eyed, she held Jim's gaze for a moment. Jim frowned in disagreement but didn't bother to argue.

As the men continued to ogle her, Betsy, unable to mask her enjoyment of their attention, refreshed her broad smile. "Hello, fellas," she said, pulling her shoulders back slightly. They all just stood there, drooling like a pack of hungry hounds.

One of the more gumptious men, grey hair poofed off his scalp like a billowy helmet, nudged Jim. "You're a lucky guy," the man said. The lot of them rumbled in crass agreement with their buddy's comment.

"Easy there," Jim jokingly scolded. This pretend admonishment only emboldened the men further, prompting whistles and dopey catcalls.

Betsy seemed to relish every moment of it. "Behave yourselves!" she squawked, feigning offense.

"All right," Ben finally snarled, protectively taking a half step between Betsy and the men. Then he said to Jim, "Why don't we take our seats, Dad. I'm hungry."

After Ben and his parents settled themselves at a table, Betsy took to the stage to announce over a microphone that dinner was about to begin. She mapped out a convoluted order she expected each table to follow for taking turns. Ultimately, however, once the Apts had begun dishing up, everyone just ignored Betsy's instructions and hopped in line at the same time.

Aside from a small comment made under her breath, Betsy thankfully didn't belabor the fact that the guests overlooked her suggestion as to which table should enter the line after which. Ruth made it known that she didn't much care for the meat selections at the buffet. This prompted Nancy to describe how much easier she's found it to keep herself trim since becoming a vegetarian, which drew an evil eye from plump Ruth and a muffled snort from Liza.

When Dan inevitably launched into his second bureaucratic tirade in as many days—this time about the tragically unfair state of the income tax rates outside Florida for folks in his elevated bracket—Ben surprised himself by interrupting to ask Nancy about Greg and Charlie's PAC. It was his only tactic to shut him up. Within moments, Nancy had Dan transfixed with the possibility of his son Eli connecting with the Conway boys about their involvement in Minnesota politics. Pleased with himself, Ben worked on his chicken skewers and grinned slyly at the potentially serendipitous connection he'd just managed to broker.

On cue, the band started up at eight-thirty with a lively rendition of "In the Mood." Ben was still thankful for how loudly they were playing. While the conversation hadn't exactly been unbearable, not wanting to communicate by means of shouting was a reasonable excuse for him to withdraw.

Betsy bounced along to the band's beat in her chair, her palms facing forward, ready to break out into jazz hands. She stood up and grabbed Jim's hand, pulling him onto the dance floor to an uproarious round of applause. Multiple guests stood and did a little jig at their tables, chomping at the bit to run out there and presumably show off their best moves. Somehow, though, the crowd collectively knew to wait until the first song was over before making any attempt at joining their lively hosts on the floor.

To delighted gasps, Jim surprised Betsy by dipping her during the song's final, boisterous chord. She looked irritated at first, straightening her tousled hair after he carefully helped her upright. Realizing everyone was impressed with Jim's impromptu maneuver, however, Betsy beamed and raised her hand in appreciation, as if to signal the move had been planned. Ben laughed and slowly joined in the clapping.

A member of the band stood at one of the microphones and urged the crowd to recognize the happy couple, resulting in an even larger round of applause. Jim and Betsy faced the guests joyfully, his arm around her waist, holding her close. When the band started up again with "Chattanooga Choo Choo," Betsy waved in their patiently waiting friends, and the entire dance floor was rapidly inundated with a sea of eager seniors.

Ben hadn't seen anything like it since junior high. It brought back memories of his first Sadie Hawkins dance, before everyone seemed to develop that paralyzing "coolness" that all too often accompanies one's ascendance into high school. That dreaded first slow dance—one of those awkward baby steps toward formalized social coupling—would mercifully be interrupted by an upbeat song, and everyone would be so relieved just to have survived it without spontaneously combusting that all inhibitions eventually dissolved and the dance floor became a flailing tapestry of pubescent self-expression.

Unable to take his eyes off the wacky display unfolding before him, Ben resisted the urge to refresh his drink. Technically, the ladies were doing most of the dancing, in that they actually moved their feet instead of just their torsos and arms like most of the men. A few of the more garish women seductively circled their much older partners, not unlike an exotic dancer enticing her seated client when hired for a stag party or cheeky birthday surprise. One or two couples caught Ben's eye when they'd pull off a twirl or any real semblance of a synchronized move as partners. Still, knowing the preponderance of ballroom classes likely available to club members, Ben was a little surprised that this was the best they could do.

～～～

After finally refreshing his drink, Ben returned to the table and decided to update Abby on how the night was going. He was about to grab his phone from his pocket when he felt a hand gently press the top of his shoulder.

"Hello there," said a woman in a low voice. Ben swung his head around to see who it was. "May I sit?" asked the stranger, smiling politely. She walked around Ben's chair and stopped next to him.

Ben couldn't quite remember her from the receiving line. He sat up a little straighter to adjust the open chair at his side. "Of course," he said quickly, watching as she arranged herself in the seat, smoothing the folds in her white silk blouse. She was small, but alluringly elegant.

Much to his relief, she reached out her hand to reintroduce herself. "Francine," she said. "It's nice to meet you again."

By the way she had offered her hand to Ben, palm down, he wondered if she expected him to kiss it. Instead, he placed his own palm under hers to shake, and was pleased when she firmly reciprocated the gesture. "Yes, of course," he said, remembering. "Nice to see you again as well."

"I think we're the only two people not out there," Francine said, motioning toward the dance floor.

"Don't like dancing?" Ben asked. He took a sip of his cocktail from the table.

"I like it," replied Francine. Then with a sly grin, added, "But it's been fun watching, too."

Ben winked, acknowledging the shared sense of comedy radiating from the dance floor. The two watched together for a few moments, contentedly.

"Your husband was with you in line, wasn't he?" Ben asked, recalling more of his meeting with the couple now.

"He was," Francine confirmed, nodding cheerfully. "Richard's chatting with some buddies at the bar. I needed to give my feet a rest." She uncrossed her legs and extended her right knee, showing off a painful-looking stiletto.

Ben leaned forward a little to get a closer look. "Whew," he said, raising his brow. "I can imagine." He sat up and paused briefly before adding, "Great shoes, though."

Francine glanced at Ben and responded with a simple, "Thank you." She held his gaze for a few moments then continued watching the crowd, grinning, as if she had just learned something.

With the lively dance floor constantly changing shape, Ben found himself staring at Francine while she watched. She looked different from the other women he'd encountered that weekend. While similarly trim and put together, her face—with its high cheekbones and strong, dignified jawline—moved freely and with refreshing expression. Long auburn hair struck a contrast with her fair skin which, while not necessarily pale, stood out when compared to the multitude of bronzed mugs he'd observed floating around the club. Her voice was measured, and she spoke with a calm sophistication that seemed foreign there.

"Have you lived in Florida long?" Ben asked.

"Richard and I have wintered here for about five years," Francine explained, keeping her eyes on the dance floor. "We live in New York otherwise. Richard likes to say he's retired, but he's kept a hand in his companies."

"And where are you from originally?"

"I was born in Montreal."

From the few sentences they'd shared, Ben had detected what sounded like the hint of an accent in Francine's speech. Her omission of the "t" in her pronunciation of "Mon-real" not only confirmed this now, but managed to momentarily transport Ben out of the flashy pretension of Palm Beach and into the cultured commotion on Rue Crescent.

"I've never been," he said. "But I've heard it's lovely."

"Oh, you must go," Francine urged. "It's a spectacular city to visit, especially for Americans. It's unlike any place you'll find in the U.S."

"Consider it on my list," Ben replied with a bewitched smile.

Francine nodded once in approval. "I imagine you don't live in Florida, Ben?"

"Nope. Minneapolis."

"Oh, that's right," Francine said, pointing a finger in the air. "I remember your mother mentioning a while back your family was from Minnesota." She delicately sipped her rosé before continuing. "Minneapolis. Another wonderful city."

"You've been?" Ben asked, somewhat surprised.

"The Athens of America? Many times."

"*Athens of America*?" Ben slowly repeated.

"Yes!" Francine exclaimed. "I once heard a composer accurately compare Minneapolis to Athens due to its ever-burgeoning arts community."

Ben's jaw slacked. He and Jake had occasionally attended theater productions back home, but never considered their city a hotbed of artistic achievement. "I guess I didn't realize it was that prestigious," he admitted.

"Absolutely," Francine asserted. "Richard's done a lot of business there over the years. We've been fortunate to take in multiple outstanding performances. You've got one of the best orchestras in the world."

"When they're not on strike," Ben said, which made Francine wink in acknowledgement. He decided to shift his chair a little closer. "So, is Richard Canadian as well then?"

"No. He was born and raised on Staten Island. We met in New York when I first moved there." Francine stopped and tilted her head back in disbelief. "My goodness, can that really be thirty years ago?"

"And what brought the girl from Montreal to the States?"

"Work," Francine answered plainly. "I sort of got a promotion and ended up relocating."

Ben was disarmed by Francine's easy, confident demeanor, and without fully understanding why, found himself growing increasingly fascinated with her. He enjoyed watching how she held her short frame perfectly upright on the end of her chair, yet somehow continued to appear completely relaxed. She remained alert to their conversation as she almost imperceptibly tapped her now shoeless heel in time with the music. With no concern that he'd accidentally incite a twenty-minute political diatribe, Ben felt prepared to answer any manner of question she posed to him.

"A promotion in Richard's company?" Ben made himself ask, realizing he was staring.

"No, darling," Francine chuckled. "It wasn't quite that serendipitous. No, I was hired into the chorus of the Metropolitan Opera."

"Wow!" Ben exclaimed. "You're an opera singer?"

"Well, I was," said Francine. "I had been part of the chorus of Opéra de Montréal since its start in 1980, but it wasn't enough to make ends meet. I got by giving private voice lessons." She sighed before continuing. "Teaching was never really a passion of mine, though. So, when I was able to secure an audition, I left for New York. Fortunately, I was offered a spot."

"And then you met your husband."

"And then I met my husband," Francine confirmed. "Richard was a friend of one of the board members for the Met Opera Guild. We met at a fundraiser where the chorus performed."

Thoroughly amused, Ben leaned back in his chair. "*Donc,*" he said. "*Vous* êtes *une chanteuse.*"

Francine whipped her head around, as if she hadn't heard her first language spoken aloud in decades. "*Mon Dieu,*" she said, astonished. "*Parlez-vous français?*"

Ben laughed, a little embarrassed. "*Un petit peu.* I took French in high school, but I don't really remember much anymore."

"You never stuck with it?"

"No," he said, almost apologetically. "A language wasn't required for my major in college, and there's not a lot of opportunity to speak it regularly in Minnesota, so…"

"That's a shame," Francine said, raising her brow. "You speak it well."

Ben blushed then, like a child who'd just impressed his teacher.

Folks all around them clapped as the band finished another rousing number. When the first leisurely notes of "Begin the Beguine" were played, everyone on the dance floor coupled up. Tired of having to shout over the large brass ensemble, Ben was happy to finally hear a more subdued song.

Pivoting to Ben, Francine said, "So, Ben. Tell me what you do in Minneapolis."

"I'm a physician's assistant."

"Oh, that's a wonderful profession," Francine gushed.

"Yeah?"

"Yes," she said, scoffing a little at Ben's surprised reaction. "My primary care provider in Manhattan is a PA. She's fantastic." Ben said nothing. "What?" she asked, leaning toward him a little. "You're not convinced?"

"No, I am," Ben said, hurriedly. "It's just that that's not usually the response I get from…" He hesitated.

"From *old* people?" Francine urged.

"I was going to say people my parents' age." Even this sounded a bit insulting when Ben heard it come out of his mouth.

"Or maybe just those who happen to be your parents' friends?" Francine suggested, smiling.

"Yes, maybe," Ben conceded, relieved that she hadn't seemed offended.

"What kind of setting do you work in?"

"I'm in primary care, too."

Francine crossed her arms. "Splendid," she said. "That really is the way to go if you're interested in medicine, isn't it? Less school. Less debt."

"Can you tell my mom that?" Ben laughed.

"She doesn't think so?"

Ben shrugged and looked out onto the floor. He spotted Jim and Betsy in the center of the crowd, proudly participating in the night's first slow dance. He kept his focus on them when responding to Francine. "She'd *really* prefer to be able to tell her friends I'm an MD."

"Oh, I see," Francine said with a sympathetic smile. She paused then and sighed. "And so it goes here."

Ben averted his eyes from the dance floor and studied Francine's expression for a moment. "What do you mean?" he asked.

"Just that it's always a rat race to impress people here. Whether it's your own accomplishments or those of your children. Everyone is always sizing you up from the moment you open your mouth."

Ben laughed a little to himself then, tickled by how Francine could almost read his mind.

"You learn pretty quickly just to keep certain things to yourself," she continued. "Most people only ask about you for superficial reasons, anyway." She uncrossed her arms and took another sip of her wine. "I suppose it helps that I don't live here year-round."

"The competition would be tiresome," said Ben.

"Entirely," Francine nodded. "And it's the women who are the worst."

"Yeah, I kind of noticed that," Ben hesitatingly agreed.

"There is nothing in this place worthy of getting upset about," Francine said. "Nothing. It really is a paradise." Shifting her gaze back to the dance floor, she added, "But they tend to perpetuate these unnecessary conflicts. Comparing husbands, children, houses."

Or religion. Ben was reminded of Liza and Ruth's dislike of each other. Without question, Liza had a legitimate reason to be upset over Ruth's preposterous "Jewish conversion" charade. But the picture Francine painted of the club somehow made it even more bizarre to Ben that Ruth would ever think to bother with such a ridiculous undertaking. He scanned the room quickly, but when unable to locate either of them, he turned to Francine. "Why do you think that is?" he asked.

Francine exhaled and sat on the backs of her hands, pausing to carefully consider her response. "Because they're all the same," she eventually said. Ben studied her keenly.

"I'm sure this party is lovely," Francine continued, "and your mother no doubt went to a lot of trouble in putting it together. But it's pretty much what people do here every day, just tonight on a somewhat larger scale. They have to invent ways to stand out. Like rich little schoolgirls required to wear the same uniform as their less fortunate classmates. There has to be some way to set themselves apart. A ribbon or barrette in the hair. A fancy necklace. Fine shoes. These little additions that say, 'I'm better.' Most of the men manage to let go of that competitive streak a bit, if you can believe that. I think they're just exhausted, frankly, from all their years of corporate climbing." She was looking down now. "But with the women...it's drastically heightened. And a waste of time, if I'm being honest."

"They're bored," Ben said.

"Without question," Francine quickly confirmed. "And without even realizing it. Most think, 'As long as I have my day filled with activities, I'm busy.'" She glanced at Ben. "But it's not enough to just *do* things, you know? Just to be occupied each day." Ben slowly blinked once in agreement. "I don't care how ready for retirement you are," she insisted. "No one can take a 25-year vacation."

Ben chuckled to himself.

"What's funny?"

"It's just that I said the exact same thing to my dad earlier today."

"Well, you're right."

The band finished their latest number and Ben and Francine both clapped softly in polite recognition. Dancing couples broke their embraces to collectively face the stage and show their appreciation with enthusiastic applause. A rumble of small talk resumed among the guests as the musicians briefly stretched their necks in preparation for the next tune.

"I hope I'm not being rude when I say this," Ben ventured. "But you don't really seem to fit in here."

Francine produced a sonorous, almost melodic laugh, and gently slapped Ben's knee in a playful reprimand. "I'm not offended. And I realize I've been saying 'they' a lot. As if I'm not part of this sort of..." She hesitated briefly, searching for the right word. Then, catching a glint of the colorful fiber optic strands dangling from the chandelier above them, she lifted her eyes and said, "...*curious* community."

A kind word for her to use, Ben thought.

"But I am part of it too, I suppose," Francine conceded.

"You're only here for a few months each year, though, right?"

"Yes. Just for the winter."

"I imagine that makes it a bit tougher to build friendships."

Francine squinted. "Not really. I can't say I have any extremely close friends down here, but it's been fairly easy for us to pick up where we leave off each spring. Things don't change all that much." She grabbed her nearly empty wine glass from the table. "And like everyone says," she added, smirking, "you can't beat the amenities."

With even noisier gusto than in their previous numbers, a startling clang signaled the band was ready to resume. Everyone on the dance floor cheered upon hearing the first few bars, evidently a crowd favorite. Ben didn't recognize the song. Continuing his conversation with Francine seemed impossible against this new loudness, so the pair of them held their thoughts and waited for any sign of a lull. Within a few seconds, Ben spotted Liza emerging from the crowd, having found him sequestered off to the side of the dance floor with Francine.

Oh shit.

She was brandishing an unsettlingly large grin and steadily making her way over to him in a sort of dance-walk, pointing at him to the beat of the music. Ben grimaced at Francine, who only smiled back at him sympathetically. "Benny boy!" Liza hollered as she reached the table.

"Hi, Liza," Ben said, sighing a little.

"I made you promise you'd dance with me!"

"I remember."

Liza continued her little jig, completely ignoring Francine. "Well? Let's go, partner!" she egged on, reaching out a hand.

Ben waffled for a moment, then began to reluctantly stand. Liza kept her arm extended, waiting. "I guess I'm dancing," Ben shouted to Francine, disappointed.

Francine remained seated and reached out her hand to shake, palm up this time. "*Enchanté*, Ben," she said.

Ben accepted Francine's shake and rotated her forearm slightly to gently kiss the back of her hand. "I really enjoyed chatting with you, Francine," he said.

"The pleasure was mine." Before letting go, Francine drew Ben in close, as if to divulge a secret. The sweet scent of her hair reminded him of the lilac trees that had populated a neighbor's yard in his youth. "Ask her to tell you about her gun collection," she slyly whispered. Then removing her grip, she took her empty wine glass from the table and raised it in recognition of Liza, who only faintly turned up the corners of her mouth before hauling Ben away like a captive princess.

They'd barely reached the dance floor before Liza spun herself under Ben's arm and locked him into a rigid frame with her bony hands. Yanking him back and forth like a rag doll, the evening chainmail with which she'd chosen to adorn her neck clattered as furiously as it had that morning on the court. Ben measured how sharply the odor of tobacco from her hair contrasted with the lush fragrance he'd enjoyed only moments ago when parting ways with Francine. And while he wasn't exactly thrilled about how frenetically he was being handled, the band's upbeat song made him emphatically grateful not to be stuck in a slow dance. He reminded himself that the dance would be brief, so he steadied his frame, ready to endure the tortuous two or three minutes that likely remained before the next break.

When they bumped into Betsy and Jim, Ben felt simultaneously relieved and a little embarrassed. Both of his parents were beaming, and Liza illuminated an expression which screamed "I told you I would get him to dance!" Jim was perspiring rather heavily, the hair just above his ears soaked. Betsy glowed fresh as a daisy. With her mouth agape, she could scarcely contain her excitement at the sight of Ben with Liza.

"Well, hey!" Betsy squealed, turning Jim abruptly to align herself side by side with the newly formed couple.

Ben managed to slow Liza's pace just long enough to reply through slightly gnashed teeth, "Hey, Mom."

Jim shouted a little louder than necessary, "How you holding up?!"

"Never better!" Ben lied, mockingly matching Jim's volume. "You guys look like you've been enjoying yourselves."

"Oh, we have!" gushed Betsy. "Isn't the band wonderful?!" She nudged Jim a little then, causing him to nod jovially in agreement.

"Yeah, they've been fantastic," Ben said. "Everyone I've talked to has been really impressed with them."

In truth, Ben had no idea what the other guests thought of the band, other than the fact that most were enthusiastically participating on the dance floor. And although it was perhaps transparent that Betsy was looking for affirmation on her selection of entertainment for the evening, it was easy to agree with the high quality of their performance. Aside from the occasional tendency to overwhelm with the sheer size of their sound, Ben had really enjoyed the music.

Liza raised Ben's arms to indicate some level of ability she'd noticed. "Say," she announced to Jim and Betsy, "he's not half bad."

"Yeah, imagine that," Ben deadpanned, "a gay guy who can dance."

Their smiling expressions unchanging, Jim, Betsy and Liza either hadn't heard Ben's comment, or chose to awkwardly ignore it.

Jim broke the brief silence. "Well, carry on!" he said, then whisked Betsy away, weaving through the throng of aged couples peppering the marbled floor.

Liza continued her raucous leading and Ben did his best to keep up. As he'd observed that morning on the court, Liza seemed the last to show any signs of fatigue, her penchant for cigarettes notwithstanding. He caught approving glances from many of the other guests and just smiled politely in return, recognizing their amusement in his reluctant participation. When the song reached its merciful end, Liza encircled Ben in an exuberant embrace, his smile giving her the false impression that her partner had experienced an equal level of fun. Rather, Ben was just glad to have gotten through it without anyone injuring themselves.

The cursory applause from the crowd slowly faded, and the first frightful notes of another slow song could be heard under the din of chatter and clapping. Ben stiffened, dreading the possibility of being forced into a contrived moment of closeness with Liza. She stood bug-eyed and unmoving, eagerly waiting for him to decide. He would have to think quickly.

"I could really use a drink," he blurted. "Do you want to grab a drink?"

"Okay," Liza chirped, taken somewhat off-guard. "Sure!"

What Ben really wanted was to just get away. He would have grabbed a drink regardless, but standing at the bar with Liza for ten minutes sharing a cocktail was an easy exchange for the tedious five he'd otherwise have to suffer squeezed torso-to-torso with her skeletal frame on the dance floor. He escorted her over to his favorite bartender, where the two were promptly greeted with a warm smile.

Ben motioned toward Liza. "For the lady…" he said, politely indicating that she be served first.

The charming barkeep rested his hands on the bar with his arms extended, maintaining eye contact with Ben as long as possible before Liza ordered.

"Rum and *Pepsi*," she impatiently demanded.

"Comin' right up," said the bartender. Then he pointed at Ben. "Gin and tonic?"

"Good memory," Ben said, impressed. "Thanks."

Ben and Liza stood with their backs against the bar, surveying the crowd. It had noticeably thinned, though not nearly to the level Ben had expected by that point in the night. Liza tucked her chin to examine the jumbled web of metal hanging from her neck. Ben held back giggles, watching her clumsily attempt to piece apart the tangled mess.

"Aw, the hell with it," she yipped. Then with a resigned exhale, she asked, "So, you like the band?"

"Sure. They're great."

"I suppose you were hoping they'd be playing newer stuff. Like maybe that Canadian kid, Justin Beaver?"

Ben raised an eyebrow.

"Or what's that black lady's name with the blonde hair who's so popular nowadays? She married a rapper." Liza tapped her chin a few times. "Bounce?"

Ben roared with laughter. "You mean *Beyoncé.*"

"Yeah, that's it."

"And it's pronounced *Bee-ber*," Ben instructed, catching his breath. "With a 'B.'"

Liza was grinning now, apparently proud of herself. "Yeah, whatever," she scoffed good-naturedly. She paused then, pointing to Ben's neck and the thin metal chain that had popped out from under his shirt while they were dancing. A small red ornament with the faint silhouette of a bird crookedly dangled over the edge of his collar. "That's pretty," she offered, eyeing the conspicuous piece of metal.

It took Ben a moment to realize what Liza was talking about. He looked down and clasped the small disc between two fingers, neatly tucking the chain back inside his shirt.

Liza continued to gawk at his neck. "Does it mean something?" she asked, expecting a closer look.

"No. Well, I don't know. I think it just means 'peace.'"

Liza only furrowed her brow and nodded. "Well, it's lovely," she said softly.

"Thanks."

What Liza hadn't seen was the underside of the piece, on which was inscribed in tiny letters, *Thomas*. Ben's confirmation name. The chain had been a gift from his grandmother, and after her passing last fall, he began wearing it again as a sort of homage to her memory.

While Betsy had always purported to maintain some level of connection with the church, Ben and the rest of their immediate family had almost completely disassociated themselves from anything resembling faith or an adherence to doctrine. Having zero interest in perpetuating for his mother the absurd charade that the Apts were anything but a stereotypical lapsed Catholic family, it took every shred of restraint he could muster now to avoid asking Liza about her exclusive luncheons, or her "feud" with Ruth Gunderson.

But there remained an instinctive reflex in him to protect his mom. He didn't want to blow her cover, a fact which his quick reaction to hide his necklace from Liza had plainly reminded him. The alleged firearm collection Francine had alluded to now seemed an appropriate subject to end the void of silence.

"I was surprised to see a sign for a shooting range this afternoon," Ben said with feigned innocence. "Is there really one on the club grounds?"

Liza was resting her elbows behind her on the bar. "Yep. It's very popular."

"And they just have guns you can borrow there?"

Liza was unphased. "Most members have their own guns. For protection."

"People must think this is a pretty dangerous place then, huh?" Ben jokingly suggested.

Liza had produced her vaporizer by this point and was closely observing the activity on the dance floor. "Well, some of us have a lot to protect," she shrugged, blowing out a large cloud of fog. "Besides, when you're a little old lady living alone, it's nice to know you've got some extra insurance."

"I'd hardly call you a little old lady."

"Well, whatever I am," Liza grumbled, "I'm glad I'm prepared. Got a purse gun stashed in each room of the house."

"Seriously?"

Liza gave Ben a once-over. "Serious as a heart attack, Benji."

Benji? No one had called him Benji since high school. It wasn't a nickname to which he was necessarily averse; many of his classmates had begun addressing him that way as early as middle school, and it had never bothered him. It felt strange, though, hearing Liza say it after all these years.

"But why so many?" Ben asked.

"Think of it," Liza challenged. "If you're in your house and you need your gun, are you really going to run upstairs to your bedroom nightstand to grab it when you notice an intruder downstairs in the kitchen? It makes no sense. Just like smoke alarms."

"Smoke alarms?"

"Yes."

"No one has a smoke alarm in every room of their home."

"Well, they should," Liza asserted.

"The bathroom?" Ben was laughing as he said this, stirring his drink. The idea of needing a smoke detector in a room full of tile and water sounded like overkill to him.

"*Especially* in the bathroom," Liza added. "Some idiots keep candles burning all the frickin' time in there." She held a finger in the air now. "It's the most common room after the kitchen where something accidentally catches fire."

Ben wasn't convinced this was true, but admittedly had never thought about it, so decided to leave it alone. Liza turned around to face the bar then, her drink already finished. Ben assumed she wanted him to order her another and was about to ask the bartender for a refill when something caught Liza's attention. She glared toward the main entrance. "Oh, you've got to be kidding me," she sneered. "What the hell is *he* doing here?"

Ben followed Liza's eyes to see who had drawn her ire. He spotted several people hovering in front of the door, mostly women. "Who?" he asked.

"Speaking of fire, I'd like to light a big one under his ass."

"*Who?*" Ben repeated, chuckling a little now at Liza's crankiness.

"Bud Gillespie."

Ben squinted. Standing among the women at the entrance, he identified a tall man in a white collared shirt with the top three or four buttons undone. A gold chain caught just enough light for Ben to see it shine against his exposed, copper chest. "Bedroom Bud?" he asked.

"Yep."

"The guy who—"

"*Yep.*"

On the surface, Ben could sort of understand the guy's appeal. He looked fit and tan—but not leathery—with a passably handsome face, and was better dressed than most of the other men there. His full head of salt-and-pepper hair stood out in sharp contrast to the club's overabundance of glossy, mottled scalps.

Ben put his back to the bar. "Not bad," he said, shaking the ice in his glass.

Liza closed her eyes tightly. "Oh, hell," she snapped. "Not you too."

Ben giggled like an incorrigible teenager. "What?"

"It's not funny," Liza scolded, chiding him with one of the whacks she normally reserved for Al.

"Hey!" Ben yelped, covering his arm where she'd hit him. "What's the big deal?"

"He's not supposed to be here," Liza complained. "The party was by invitation only."

"He doesn't seem to be bothering anybody."

"Just you wait." Liza motioned toward the circle of ladies which had coalesced around Bud by the entrance. "Look at him. He's already beginning to pester them."

Ben leaned away from Liza slightly. From what he could see, Bud seemed to be enjoying the attention. But it was the women who were doing most of the talking. "Are you sure it's not the other way around?" he asked.

"Oh, please. That guy showed up for one reason and one reason only. He's on the prowl. Just looking to sow his horny seed."

Ben laughed at this; but in reality, he was struggling to understand what the problem was. Yes, Bud's party crashing may have been a bit rude. And while Ben certainly didn't advocate his apparent unsafe sexual practices, he didn't begrudge Bud looking for a little honest action.

"Why don't we just make sure we find him a condom?" Ben cracked.

Another wallop. "*Ow!*" Ben howled, clutching the same arm.

Liza ignored his cry and paused, cocking her head slightly to one side. "Come to think of it," she said, "that's actually not a bad idea."

Ben continued rubbing his arm. "Well, I'm thrilled you came to that realization *after* assaulting me."

"Oh, knock it off," Liza said, swatting at the air. "You're fine."

Perhaps reminded of Al by the mild brutality she'd levied on Ben's arm, Liza explained it was time for her to find out where her "non-date" had run off to. With his limited mobility, Ben couldn't imagine Al was ever far off, much less running anywhere. He spotted Al slumped at a table just a few paces from the bar, monitoring the shenanigans of the crowd.

Liza made a beeline for the dance floor, whizzing past Al with scarcely a glimpse of recognition, and found Jim fanning Betsy's forehead in a break from their latest bit of boogieing. Between each exchange of whispers, the two ladies shot a series of astonished glances in Bud's direction. Ben could only dip his head and groan from his vantage at the bar, wondering which was more ridiculous: Liza's pressing need to divulge the latest Bud Gillespie gossip with Betsy, or his mother's likely insatiable desire to hear it. He watched as the two ladies maneuvered behind the stage, almost conspicuously concealing themselves from Bud and the rest of the crowd.

Ben said a silent goodbye to the night's peace.

eleven

Get out of my head you freak!

Ben had to tease his sister after she texted for an update on the night's events. At an abandoned table far from the dance floor, he gave his legs a rest and thumbed whatever insights he could. Betsy's little tiff about the band starting late was customary, as far as Ben was concerned. The receiving line had been less tedious than expected. He'd even survived dancing with Liza. Nothing had really gone wrong.

But Abby could see past Ben's benign assessment of the evening and had texted an eerie reply: *You're freaking the fuck out right now, aren't you.*

She was right. No one understood Ben's pessimistic leanings better than his twin sister. Despite describing his enjoyment of the few testy comments at dinner, or his refreshing chat with an elegant Canadian, Abby accurately sensed an underlying pensiveness. It didn't matter if all signs pointed to relative harmony. When it came to Mom, Ben couldn't just relax. He took a few deep breaths and tried to follow Abby's advice to "cool it." Just lie low for another hour. Everything's fine.

A message finally came through from Jake, letting Ben know he'd decided to join Tony and Scott for dinner after all. He offered no hint as to whether or not he planned to follow up on Oliver's suggestion that they all grab drinks as well. Ben didn't want to seem too eager to know if his partner would be running into Oliver. Even asking about it, he feared, might somehow be too powerful a suggestion, and therefore tip the scale in favor of Jake deciding to stay out. Instead, he simply texted *Have a good time*. A cryptic "wink" emoticon was the only response Jake apparently thought necessary to provide. So, Ben would just have to white-knuckle until his phone blinked with any additional details.

Slumped on the front of his chair, Ben lifted his head briefly to see if he might find Francine to continue their conversation, but he didn't see her anywhere. He tuned out for a while on his phone. Tapping a news app, he scrolled past a catalogue of depressing headlines and stopped eventually at a series of close-up photos that NASA's spacecraft Juno had recently captured of Jupiter and its moons. Ever since seeing a poster in Mr. Elliot's fifth grade science class comparing the size of all the planets in scale to each other, the enormity of the gas giant had always been a sobering reminder to him of the relative minuteness of Earth.

At first glance on his phone, the blurry photos' thin pastel waves of pink and orange more resembled the strokes of an exquisite Impressionist painting than the string of violent, unending storms he knew them to be. And the longer he studied them, the more it felt like trying to find the hidden image in one of those once-popular 3D picture books, which his young eyes had always been determined to see but could never quite fully decipher. He had to laugh, thinking how the lack of clarity wasn't much different from what he'd felt for most of the weekend up to that point.

He let out a wide yawn. He'd already had a fair amount to drink, but balked at the possibility of ducking out early. Asking permission would no doubt strike another prickly exchange with his mother, which he frankly wasn't sure he had the energy to brave. A tall glass of water and a cup of black coffee might do the trick, he decided. He would hit the restroom then make his way over to the dessert table, where earlier, positioned between plates offering drying crusts of lemon and red velvet cake, he'd spied a pair of large coffee dispensers.

He groaned when he was met with a long line outside the door of the men's room. In his experience so far in life, the need to queue before peeing had been an almost exclusively female burden. While normally a fan of shifts in gender convention, this present reversal was decidedly not to his liking—an inconvenience he could only assume resulted from the pressing urgency of a population stricken with ever-ballooning prostates. Hoping to avoid the wait, he opted to zip across the room to a smaller bathroom he remembered seeing when arriving yesterday.

The band was showing no signs of slowing. Their latest raucous song blared so brightly behind him that Ben could scarcely detect the sound of his own footsteps on the stone floor. When he neared the substitute bathroom, the area thankfully looked deserted. He wouldn't have to wait. He rounded the corner but stopped abruptly when he found two people standing partially concealed behind a large pillar, apparently arguing. It was dim, but just light enough from his distance for Ben to eventually identify that the couple wasn't a random pair of guests involved in a spat. It was his mom and Bud.

Ben's first instinct was to remain hidden, ready to witness Betsy hand Bud what promised to be an epic dressing-down for his audacious decision to crash the party. Within moments, however, it became clear that the purpose of their encounter had nothing to do with Bud's unexpected attendance. Unable to pick up what was being said, Ben watched as Betsy, her back to him, slowly shook her sinking head with her arms wrapped around herself tightly. Bud's hands waved in what looked like a desperate attempt to explain something. When Betsy's shoulders began to shudder uncontrollably, Bud stopped his intense gesturing and slumped a bit, as if defeated. Her head lifted eventually, and she pointed both of her hands toward her chest, still shaking. Bud moved to touch her exposed shoulder but she pushed him away firmly, then wiped her cheeks.

Ben slowly backed away from the corner and stood against the wall, frozen. The clamor from the band was hushed by the deafening drum of his own pulse in his ears. His breathing grew shallow and labored. His neck tingled. What he'd just witnessed looked nothing like the haughty rebuke of an offended hostess, more the scorn of a jilted lover.

With short, languid steps, Ben's feet gradually propelled him forward. His vision tunneled as his wide eyes zeroed in on a narrow path back toward the dance floor, struggling to process what he'd seen, what it meant. His already pounding heart thumped faster now. The pace of his gait increased, and he raised his head then with a renewed focus on his destination. Short of running, he moved as quickly as his legs would carry him back to where he'd sat with his parents at dinner. There, he spotted Betsy's bulky handbag resting on the table and snatched it up. Feverishly rummaging through its contents, he was about to withdraw his hand when his fingers unearthed a small, plastic container hidden under a wadded mound of tissues. He paused for a moment and closed his eyes tightly before slowly removing what his fingers had already identified as a prescription medication bottle. Almost afraid to look at it, Ben held up the vial between his thumb and index finger. He felt the blood drain from his face when he finally opened his eyes and read the label: *Zithromax, 250 mg.*

Ben had prescribed the same antibiotic hundreds of times for his patients. With the exception of treating ear infections in children, its most common use in his practice was to fight bacteria which had been transmitted sexually. He squeezed the bottle in his hand, the foggy enormity of what he'd observed in the past two minutes slowly coming into focus. Before he could consider it further, his attention was grabbed by the brisk clatter of a pair of high heels steadily approaching him from behind. He turned around sharply, drawing his mother's purse to his chest like a teenager caught with one of his dad's dirty magazines.

Betsy identified her handbag then peered at Ben. "What's going on?" she demanded.

Ben held up the pill bottle and shook it in Betsy's face like a miniature maraca. "Tell me these aren't what I think they are," he insisted. He could see mascara slightly smeared under her right eye.

Betsy studied Ben's expression briefly. "What are you doing?" she sneered, snatching the bottle from his hand. "You're digging in my purse?!"

"Answer me, Mom."

Betsy seized her bag from Ben and tossed the pills inside, pointing an angry finger at him. "These are none of your business, Benny."

"The hell they aren't," Ben hissed. "I know where you were just now."

Betsy fumbled through her bag. "What are you talking about?"

"I saw you with Bud."

She glared at Ben momentarily, then lowered her head to continue sifting through her purse, as if to inspect the rest of its contents. "How dare you," she muttered, refusing to look up. Then more firmly, her voice cracking slightly, "How dare you!"

Ben took a step back. "How dare *me?*" he said, in awe of her apparent lack of shame. "This is what you went to the pharmacy for after brunch this morning, isn't it? The 'errands' you had to run? After you found out Bud was the one who infected Sue, you rushed off to that minute clinic. Didn't you?!"

Betsy denied nothing in repeating, "This is *none* of your business."

It was clear to Ben that his mom's plan would be to simply ignore the allegations. As if in muzzling the topic now, she could somehow make him unsee what he'd seen, or think something other than that she had cheated on his father. And as if in doing so, his perception of their family, now irretrievably altered, could somehow remain intact.

"How can it be none of my business?!" Ben growled. He stared at Betsy coldly as she arranged her bag over her shoulder and crossed her arms in defiance. "Where's Dad?" he asked then, warily surveying the room. Jim was off at one of the bars, laughing as he and a group of buddies joked with unlit cigars bobbing from their mouths. "Give me one good reason I shouldn't go tell him right now," he scowled, puffing his chest out slightly. "Don't think I won't."

"You will do *no* such thing," Betsy instructed, reaching for Ben's forearm. He recoiled, swatting at her hand. She paused then and eyed him intensely before continuing. "Now you listen here. I am not discussing this with you any further."

"That seems to be your answer for everything these days," Ben said. "Tell me now."

"Leave it alone," Betsy replied, tensing her jaw. "This is private."

From behind them on stage, the booming of the band's brass instruments forced Ben to reluctantly lean in a bit, unable to hear her. He fixed his hands on his waist. "That's not good enough, Mom."

"Well, it's going to have to be," Betsy said, unblinking.

"Jesus Christ, it's your fortieth fucking anniversary."

"Watch your mouth."

"I'm not going to watch my fucking mouth, Mom. This is insane!"

"Keep your voice down!" Betsy snarled, glancing over each shoulder.

But shouting was the only way to be heard over the ear-splitting music, as Ben ignored her hollow chastisement. "So this is what you do down here, huh?" he hollered.

"What do you mean, *do?*"

"You play tennis, go to parties, lie to your friends. Fuck around on Dad."

"What did you just say?"

"Which part would you like me to repeat? The 'fucking around on Dad' part?"

Betsy's mouth froze, half open.

"How many other boyfriends do you have in this hellscape, Ma?"

"I will not be spoken to like that."

"Is this the first time?" Ben said, pushing. "I'd really like to believe it's the first time. That it's this place, and these..." He looked around the room quickly. "...these *people* that would make you want to do something like this."

Betsy raised her fingers to her temples. "I'm not having this conversation with you," she repeated. "I am not."

"Is that what this is, Mom? You just need to feel *liked*? Are you really that starved for attention?"

"No, I—"

"What then?!" Ben interrupted. "You're unhappy? You told me you love it here."

"I do love it here."

"Then why the hell would you risk your marriage to have a fling with some smarmy guy who's probably made it with half the ladies in this joint?"

"Stop."

"I can't believe you'd do this to Dad."

"*Stop* it, Ben."

"If you don't tell him I swear to God I will."

"I said STOP!" Betsy put her hands up, her cheeks red with fury. She took a few deep breaths and swallowed hard before lowering her arms. "You don't realize how it can get, Benny."

"How what can get, Ma?" Ben asked, straining to hear her.

"Complicated. When you've been together as long as your father and I have—"

"Oh, don't give me that bullshit. You're making excuses."

Ben's own recent infidelity popped into his mind. Yet, he was convinced his situation had been entirely different. He hadn't gone all the way. There had been no planned deception on his part, no feelings behind it. He'd made the choice to tell his partner, even though Jake may never have found out. And despite their mutual understanding of monogamy, they weren't married. This made what he did less awful, he'd told himself. More forgivable.

"Why am I even having to explain myself to you?" Betsy said, indignantly, refolding her arms. "I should hardly expect someone like you to understand."

"What the hell is that supposed to mean?"

"Never mind."

"No, Mom. Tell me. Who is 'someone like me?'"

Betsy bit the inside of her cheek. Her shoulders raised with a deep inhale. "Someone who's never been married, that's all," she said. "Who has no interest in it."

Ben's face tightened. "How would you know if I have any interest in marriage?"

"Well, you're in a different relationship every few years."

"Bullshit. Jake and I have been together for almost six."

"Yes, and most people your age would've married by now!"

Ben was reeling at what he saw as his mother's attempt to turn this around on him. He could feel the tops of his ears burning. "What the fuck does that have to do with anything?!"

"It just means take a look at yourself before you start pointing fingers at me, mister. Take a look at your own relationships. It's different when it's a real—"

Betsy stopped herself. One last, dissonant chord thundered the end to the band's number and the remaining crowd members erupted in another rapturous round of applause. The room quieted to a low rumble, leaving Ben and Betsy silently staring at each other.

"*What?*" Ben finally managed.

"Never mind," Betsy answered, softly.

"A real what, Ma?"

"Nothing."

"No, tell me."

"*Nothing.*"

Ben slowly backed away. "Oh, no," he said under his breath, a look of disbelief on his face. "No, no, no, no, no."

"Benny, I—"

"Tell me that's not what you really think."

Betsy didn't move, offering only a blank stare.

"Okay," Ben said, folding his hands together calmly. "No, I get it. At least now we know. Now we know how you really see me. What you think of my relationships. Of Jake." He narrowed his eyes then and leaned in slightly. "*Frivolous.*"

"I didn't say that."

"You were going to."

"But I didn't!"

"Why didn't you just say it's *unnatural*, Mom?"

"Stop! It's not what I meant!"

Ben shook his head, slowly at first, then increasingly more rapidly. "I'm so stupid. This is so *stupid.*"

"Benny—"

"I can't believe I was stupid enough to think coming down here would just smooth things over." He paused, breathing through his teeth. *Don't be ugly*, Grandma would have urged. But it was too much. His cheeks flushed as he leaned in farther to get in Betsy's face. "What a fucking joke."

Before Betsy could react to this, as if out of nowhere Liza appeared and poked her head between the feuding pair. With an impish grin brandished across her rugged face, she squeezed Betsy's arm. "Oh my God. What did he say?"

Flustered, Betsy could only shake her head and reply, "Who?"

"Bud!" Liza yipped. "You said you were going to really give it to him."

Her mouth agape, Betsy briefly made eye contact with Ben.

"Yeah, Mom. Go ahead," he taunted. "Tell her how you *gave it to him.*"

Liza repeatedly eyed them both, her head darting back and forth as if watching a tennis match.

"He...he said he was sorry," said Betsy. She dipped her head and covered her mouth with her fingers.

"That's it?" Liza groaned, disappointed.

Ben's nostrils flared watching Betsy. "Unbelievable," he laughed. He made a move then as if to leave, but hesitated. Reaching under the collar of his shirt, he pulled out the chain from around his neck and held it up so Liza could get a good look. "By the way," he announced, glancing at Betsy before turning back to Liza. "It was a confirmation gift."

Liza only grimaced in confusion while Betsy, her head still down, collapsed her face into her hands. Ben charged toward the exit, sweeping past the reception desk before slamming his way through the double glass doors. He was already outside when the perky concierge leaned over the counter and hollered cheerfully after him.

"Have a wonderful evening!"

twelve

Ben had never really been fond of gay bars. If all he desired were a few drinks, he'd just as soon stay home, sheltered from the inevitable pestering by a slew of desperately horny strangers. In an era prior to the dawn of endless hookup apps, however, regular attendance in his twenties had become something of a basic necessity. Scoring a casual tryst required one to bide his time, filtering the masses in the few tedious hours prior to bar close on weekends.

Sure, he'd made some friends along the way. Even a few boyfriends. When a boyfriend had ever insisted on going out, at least it was easier to navigate the crowds together than when flying solo. But ultimately for him, those old haunts along Hennepin Avenue, which ostensibly served as a safe place to rendezvous with like-minded buddies, were really nothing more than a hunting ground for his unwavering libido.

Each of the five men Ben had called "boyfriend" had started out as what he figured would be a one-night stand. When anyone insisted on getting his number, he would tend to casually comply. It was easier to say "yes" at the time, and then ignore any unwanted attempts at contact later. For whatever reason, though, he gravitated toward partnership. Perhaps it was less work than the never-ending siege of seduction required just to get laid, as long-term coupling eventually became a welcome furlough from the banality of his Saturday night clubbing routine. What would be the point of going out to the bars then anyway? He already knew who he'd be going home with.

Ben's prevailing distaste for the *scene* made finding himself now plopped on a stool at a gay bar just a few miles from The Cypress Club all the more confounding. After storming out of the party, he'd hopped in a cab and when asked "Where to?" had hesitated only slightly in instructing the driver on a preferred destination. The cabbie had dropped him off under a sign glowing with the name *Slip*, and Ben handed the bouncer his ID along with the fifteen-dollar cover before darting to the restroom.

Bellying up, he had immediately flagged a bartender and held up two fingers when ordering. Trance music thumped from multiple speakers of indiscernible location, and the fatigue that had begun to envelop him only an hour prior was somehow gone. He was jittery now and, with a double gin and tonic in his hands, found desperate refuge in the welcome burn of each swallow.

Within a few minutes, the booze streaming through Ben's system effectively mellowed his racing brain enough to review what had just transpired between him and his mother. He rested his elbows on the bar, ruminating over what his next step should be—if there even were a next step. His ire over her infidelity was only compounded by her insistence that he remain silent about it. It seemed impossible for him to envision a scenario where he didn't tell his dad, or at least convinced Betsy to confess.

But how would he persuade her to do that, exactly? Guilt? Blackmail? Invoking reason? None of these options jumped out as particularly worthwhile strategies at the moment. All Ben knew was that Jim didn't deserve this, and he anguished over how the news might affect him. His neck tensed when he considered the possibility that they'd all be better off if he simply did nothing—if he actually relented and just kept quiet as he was told. Maybe having to deal with the aftermath of his petty revelation to Liza would serve as penance enough for Betsy and her exposed iniquities.

The weight of the awful scenario in which Ben now found himself entwined with his parents was further intensified by a single word he kept repeating in his mind: Real. A real relationship. It's different when it's a *real* relationship, his mother had nearly said to him. He wondered how far this word was from *normal*. She and his dad had a normal relationship. A real, normal relationship—insinuating that what he and Jake shared must be unreal and abnormal. Artificial in some way. Not necessarily wrong, perhaps, but expendable in her view, which convinced Ben now that any suggestion of Betsy caring about him ever getting married, much less being in favor of it, was a wild and disingenuous diversion.

Downing his drink, Ben watched for the bartender to circle back. He checked his phone for any sign of Jake. Still nothing. Dinner had to be over by now. He would have let Ben know if he'd decided to hit the bar afterward, or if he'd seen Oliver. Maybe he was in bed already. While Jake had always been a bit of a night owl, he'd had a busy day, Ben tried to tell himself. He wanted so badly to text him again and tell him everything that had happened. But after he revealed the fact that he'd stormed out of his parents' party, he wasn't sure how he'd go about explaining his current whereabouts, which Jake was certain to ask. It was likely too late to try calling Abby. She'd no doubt be terribly anxious to hear every juicy detail, but he recalled her self-reported struggle with exhaustion during her previous two pregnancies, and decided to wait until morning.

In the meantime, Ben would do his best to enjoy the view. The place was packed with attractive guys. Lean, serious-faced figures were stationed around the bar like mannequins, all purposefully striking their thirsty poses. But like most other nights out in his experience, while it was easy to appreciate how clean and coiffed most of his fellow clubgoers were, he could identify only two or three men in the room whom he'd ever actually consider sleeping with.

To his amusement, one of those select, handsome gentlemen just happened to be cruising him from across the bar. Ben had looked up to find a keen pair of eyes analyzing him, and he automatically calculated the duration of the man's stare. He was convinced of his interest when the man met what Ben privately considered his "two second rule." If a guy made eye contact for more than two seconds, it was an unequivocal sign of sexual interest. And this man had just held his focus for at least five.

The guy rested his tattooed forearms against the bar's edge, eventually turning his head bashfully when Ben caught him staring. Demonstrating no such sign of discretion, Ben fixed an unsmiling gaze on his strapping admirer and waited intently for the rebound of attention he knew would come. His view was suddenly blocked when the bartender stepped in front of him to set down another gin and tonic. While thrilled for the refill, Ben didn't recall ordering it. He cleared his throat and peered up at the bartender.

"This one's on the gentleman," explained the burly barkeep.

Ben leaned in his seat to see around the bartender. Just when he was about to extend a thank-you to the cute guy who'd been eyeing him, he watched the bartender instead point to his right, where at the end of the counter, Ben noticed someone staring in his direction. He squinted as the beaming gentleman raised his hand in recognition.

"Oh, you've got to be fucking kidding me," Ben muttered to himself. He lowered his head and exhaled, glowering at his fresh drink. It took a few seconds before he could return his eyes to Dwayne and offer a tense smile.

Mistaking this as a cue to join him, Dwayne promptly bounded up to Ben. He had ditched his suit and bowtie for tight jeans and a button-up with a busy, floral pattern.

"Well, hi there," Dwayne said, blasting his almost offensively white smile. He stood close enough that his knee brushed Ben's thigh. "Is it over already?"

Ben shifted in his seat. "Hi, Dwayne," he said, flatly. "No. I, uh...I'd just had enough."

There was a long pause. "Was the party that bad?" Dwayne asked, delicately.

"The *party* was fine. It was the people I needed a break from."

"Oh," Dwayne laughed. "Yeah, I know what you mean." He pursed his lips over his straw.

Ben looked up at him and smirked. "You do?"

"Sure. A lot of the events I do are at places like The Cypress Club. I've spent enough time around similar folks. There's definitely a vibe you get from certain members. That's partly why I've made it sort of a rule to sneak out after everything is set up." Dwayne stopped for a moment and shrugged before taking another quick sip. "I suppose I don't really notice it much anymore."

"Mmm," Ben grunted, now quietly pulling apart pieces of a damp napkin from the bar. The weight of Dwayne's ogling eyes was suffocating.

"Don't get me wrong," Dwayne hastily added, lightly touching Ben's shoulder, "your mother's wonderful. But yeah, they definitely like things a certain way there." Dwayne removed his hand and ducked then slightly, studying Ben's expression. He waited a few seconds before laughing nervously. "I guess that's retirement!"

Ben only stared at his glass. He reached for the straw and began stirring.

There was another long pause. "Thanks for the drink," Ben said eventually, not looking up, to which Dwayne fired back, "You're welcome!" Ben resented the pressure of having to engage in small talk as some sort of repayment for accepting the drink. He finally made brief eye contact and forced himself to find a few words. "The club looked great tonight," he said. "My mom seemed really pleased with how everything turned out."

"I'm glad," Dwayne beamed. The heavy concealer under his eyes was less obvious in the bar's low lighting. "But that's my job, after all."

Ben nodded slowly, already out of things to say. Then, in a brief boost of energy, he sat up straight on his stool and squared himself toward Dwayne. "Look, Dwayne, that text I responded to this afternoon was by accident. I appreciate the gesture, but—"

"No worries," Dwayne interrupted, raising a hand and laughing a little. "It seemed pretty clear where you stood yesterday afternoon when you arrived. But I thought it wouldn't hurt to find out for sure."

Ben exhaled in relief. "Nothing personal," he said, apologetically. This was a lie, of course. It was completely personal. Ben had no interest in speaking with Dwayne, much less going home with him.

Dwayne waved him off. "Don't worry about it," he said, taking up the stool next to Ben. "You're certainly in the right place though, if you're interested in finding a hookup. There are a lot of cute guys here tonight."

"I'm not here to find a hookup," Ben corrected him. He rescued his phone from the damp bar. "I've actually been waiting two hours for my boyfriend to text me back."

Dwayne's shiny forehead almost furrowed. "I didn't know you had a boyfriend."

"Why would you?"

"I don't know. Just the way your mom talked about it, I guess."

Ben shot Dwayne a look. "What do you mean?"

Dwayne hesitated, seeing Ben's reaction. "Oh, well..." he stuttered. "I just...got the impression that you were single."

"What did she say that gave you that impression?"

"I might not be remembering right."

"What did she say? *Exactly*," Ben insisted.

Dwayne waited a moment before carefully continuing. "I don't even know how it came up, to be honest," he said. "But she alluded to the fact that you were gay, too. She insisted on showing me your picture." He scanned Ben up and down briefly. "Needless to say, I thought you were really cute."

"And she said I was single."

"Not in so many words," Dwayne said. "But she—"

"What?" Ben jabbed, his eyes narrowing. He crossed his arms slowly then, waiting.

Dwayne squirmed in his seat a little, attempting to delay his response before finally relenting. "She said you were 'always looking.'"

Ben stared at Dwayne blankly, as if he had just uttered something in Chinese. The cold look made Dwayne stiffen, unable to say or do anything but stare back. Ben gradually swiveled in his chair to face the bar again. He let out a caustic chuckle, then reached to guzzle his gin and tonic.

"I didn't really understand what she meant," Dwayne tried to explain. "But I sort of assumed by her tone that you weren't in a relationship. I apologize if that made things awkward yesterday."

"You didn't do anything wrong, Dwayne," Ben said, his eyes focused on the glass of ice in his hand.

"Well, as I said, I might have heard incorrectly."

"No. I don't think you did." Ben rested his forearms on the bar, then raised his folded hands to his mouth and bit down gently on his knuckle.

"Look, I didn't mean to upset you."

"You didn't," Ben again lied.

"It's totally possible I'm wrong about what I heard."

Ben repeated a slow nod, then turned to Dwayne with a final look of dismissal. "Thanks again for the drink."

Dwayne waited a moment, then slowly stood and adjusted his crisp collar, offering an uncharacteristically narrow smile. "It was nice to see you again, Ben," he said courteously. "I hope you enjoy the rest of your time in Florida."

Through the corner of his eye, Ben watched Dwayne walk away and disappear into the crowd. The restlessness from which he'd briefly escaped resurfaced with a noticeable itch in his legs. He put pressure on his thigh to quiet his bouncing knee while he flagged the bartender to serve up a whiskey. He snatched his phone again to check for any messages, and when he found none, immediately shot off a frustrated text to Jake:

Are you fucking alive?

He slammed the phone down, drawing a concerned glance from the bartender. The cute guy from across the bar was long gone. Irritated, Ben forced down the shot, his face contorting as the acrid spirit traveled to his stomach with a biting punch. He startled when standing proved more challenging than expected, requiring one hand on the bar to catch his balance. After the first few shuffled steps, however, he steadied himself enough to cut a path to the restroom, all under the bartender's increasingly watchful eye.

A cool splash of water to his face offered modest revival, and Ben studied himself in the mirror. Black lighting forgivingly mellowed the shiny redness outlining the bridge of his burnt nose. In an unfortunate trade-off, however, the dark circles that looped under his eyes, ever more noticeable and frequent, were acutely magnified. It was an unfamiliar image from the one stamped in his memory. A memory collectively shaped by the thousand previous last-minute rechecks he'd performed before returning to the sweaty playground of a dance floor. It had been easy for him to dismiss Dwayne's earnest attempts at masking his age as ridiculous, even pitiful. Now, mulling over his own worn reflection, he wondered how soon it would be when he too lacked the confidence to step foot in a gay bar without the aid of Botox, fillers or foundation.

Ben stood up and ran his damp fingers through his hair, hoping to freshen his look. Leaving the bar was on his mind until he stepped out of the bathroom to find his same buff suitor from the bar gawking from the other end of the room. The man stood with his back against the wall, biceps bulging over his crossed arms. Ben stopped to consider this. A minute ago, he was prepared to hop back in a cab and return to the dreadful mess he knew waited for him at his parents' place. But with this renewed distraction in front of him now, he was prepared to let that wait.

Ben stared back, abandoning any illusion of coyness. The patient fellow shyly dipped his head and bit his lower lip. Normally, Ben would consider this move a contrived turnoff. But tonight, for whatever reason, it seemed to be working. He watched the man uncross his arms and stuff his hands in his front pockets, his shoulders elevating with a boyish innocence that almost seemed to belie the obvious appeal for sex.

Summoning enough resolve, Ben started across the room, keeping his gait slow but purposeful. It took work to control his breathing. Despite their slippery overflows of vodka and soda, the clusters of pushy bodies in his path weren't enough to disrupt his eye contact. He stopped about a foot in front of his alluring tempter, who immediately straightened his spine against the wall. Ben sized himself as the taller of the two, affording an implicit sense of control, which he liked. The guy was even more attractive up close, a pleasant reversal from Ben's expectation. Green eyes, set deep like peridots, gleamed against the man's chestnut complexion. His shadowed jawline popped out slightly when he clenched his back teeth with a satisfied smile.

Ben looked to his left slowly, eyeing the dance floor thumping in a deep section of the bar. Kaleidoscopic strobes intermittently outlined a field of bopping silhouettes in the foreground. He returned his eyes forward and had only to tip his head slightly then, hinting in the direction of the action. A short nod signaled agreement, and Ben took his quarry by the hand, weaving him through the maze-like crowd.

The fury of the music surged with each determined step. Frenetic strobes of bright and dark somewhat disoriented him at first, but Ben didn't stop until they were firmly established in the center of the dance floor. Finding his focus, he slipped his fingers just inside the front waistband of his dance partner's jeans, drawing him closer. The two embraced and slowly synced their movements with the beat.

It wasn't long before Ben's polo was being peeled over his head. Grateful not to have to initiate the disrobing, Ben showed no objection, promptly acquiescing by raising his arms. While not in perfect shape, he kept himself reasonably fit and didn't feel bashful going shirtless. A brief reluctance about the appearance of sunburn lines around his neck and upper arms faded after realizing they were likely imperceptible under this lighting.

Ben reciprocated by removing the man's white V-neck, revealing an additional smattering of small tattoos across his pecs and shoulders. His small nipples, resembling fleshy stalactites, aimed downward slightly from his overdeveloped chest. Ben barely resisted the impulse to roll their swollen tips between his thumbs and index fingers.

When his neck was kissed, Ben pulled back slightly and danced more energetically, as if the music demanded more serious focus on their moves. If only he could just keep it like this. Everything was still okay if it just stayed like this. Drunk, shirtless and sweaty, and wrapped in a stranger's wanting arms, he was only dancing. But as he felt that silky pair of lips return to his neck, it was becoming increasingly more difficult to ignore the growing arousal below his waist. A small nibble to his earlobe became too much. With the pounding music precluding all verbal communication, Ben could only pleadingly shake his head. Hoping that in spite of this man's roguish, I've-got-you-now smile, he could somehow convey that he wanted to stop. That while he relished the touch, he *needed* to stop, for fear of losing control.

After a few beats at arm's length, Ben paused and squinted. He pointed with two fingers to his partner's enormous pupils, which had become dilated since joining the dance floor, nearly overlapping the piercing green irises Ben had earlier admired. Almost guiltily, the guy grinned and glanced down at his left pocket, out of which he drew a small plastic bag containing a single pill. He dangled it in front of Ben's nose, giving the packet a little shake. It had been years since Ben had partaken in club drugs, an occasional indulgence he'd since left behind with his twenties. He watched the guy gingerly drop the pill into his own palm, then examine it between two fingers. When he teasingly gestured the pill toward Ben's face, Ben instinctively opened his mouth to accept it, only to watch its playful owner quickly withdraw his hand and deposit it onto his own tongue. Ben barely had time to register his surprise before being pulled forward and kissed deeply, the pill effectively transferred into his mouth. He swallowed it quickly, extinguishing the bitter tang of the chalky tablet's residue, until all that was left was the inviting warmth of this man's lips, and the exhilarating cocktail of chemical messengers exchanged by their wet exterior.

Ben succumbed with a vigor and dedication that betrayed any pretense of resisting. He positioned himself securely behind his partner, encircling his smooth, taut abdomen as they swayed in unison to the music. Fully hard now, Ben pressed himself against that firm ass, which with every arch of the man's tattooed back signaled its obliging desire. All Ben need do was say the word and it would be his; a simple tilt of the head to show his readiness to get out of there and off his feet, but certainly not to rest.

He was content not to decide in the moment, however. Soon enough, the decision would be made for him, when under this hazy canopy of multicolored lights, that tiny little pill in his belly, and the exquisite euphoria it so graciously granted, began to stage its inexorable assault on what was left of his already groggy inhibitions.

thirteen

Ben had it timed at exactly fourteen seconds. He'd been trying to summon enough strength to flip onto his back. Hindered by a searing pain in his temples with even the smallest attempt at repositioning his head on the pillow, he had no choice but to remain motionless, eyes firmly closed, as he counted the interval between each charitable wave of air that passed over his sweaty legs. Not until the pain was outmatched by an intense feeling of overheating did he manage to roll over and expose his burning chest to the predictable breeze from the oscillating fan nearby. He closed his eyes more tightly and waited for the spike of pressure in his head to subside. All he wanted was to be able to sit up and survey what he'd accurately suspected were entirely unfamiliar surroundings.

The air's cooling effect was most prominent over Ben's naked groin. He reached down and adjusted himself, detecting a slippery residue which he quickly identified as some sort of lubricant. Ignoring the pain in his head, he opened his eyes and looked to the left to see a nude figure lying face down next to him, the man's ribs expanding and contracting in a slow, sleepy rhythm. Ben pushed himself up and sat with his legs crossed under him, inspecting the stark bedroom. A dark blanket over the window dampened the overpowering daylight. He paused briefly to study the door, over which hung some sort of hybrid of a rainbow-Cuban flag. On the floor, various articles of clothing seemed strewn at random around the bed's perimeter. There, next to a pair of lavender briefs that were not his, lay a spent condom, slumped over the toe of his shoe like a lazy snake sunning itself on a rock.

He peeked over at his unconscious, naked trick. The sheet was pulled down to the backs of the man's thighs, accentuating the slope of his impressively bubbled backside. A surge of excitement momentarily rushed through Ben as he traced the man's smooth outline with his eyes. He couldn't help but imagine what it would feel like to be inside him. That warm, silky acceptance around his cock, which after enough earnest thrusts possessed the power to make him lose all sense of place and time.

A rising tension in Ben's chest forced him to avert his gaze. With the realization that he had already fucked this gorgeous body, but would probably never remember it, any thrill he enjoyed from his unexpected bit of voyeurism quickly waned, until all that was left was the dreadful emptiness of his own shame.

Somehow both Ben's phone and watch had neatly found their way to the nightstand. He reached for his phone to check the time, but the screen was black. He hastily pressed a few buttons, relieved to learn it wasn't out of battery, only turned off. While he waited for the phone to boot back up, he drew his watch close to his face and could only blink repeatedly with his jaw lowered in a stupefied droop.

12:01

He jolted to the side of the bed, tapping the watch's face with his nail as if it would miraculously set back the hands. His parents were expecting him for brunch at ten o'clock.

As quietly as he could, Ben rummaged around the floor in search of his scattered clothing. His shoulder screamed as he strained to pull his polo over his sweaty back, a painful reminder of his inauspicious return to the tennis court only a morning ago. Lowering each leg into his jeans, he monitored any signs of rousing from the bed. With the man still lying on his stomach and facing away, if not for the recognizable tattoos on his forearms, Ben couldn't say with confidence whether or not this was the same person he'd shared an intoxicating dance with last night. He tried and failed to remember if they had exchanged words at all, much less gotten around to names.

After tiptoeing out of the apartment and scurrying down the gloomy stairwell, Ben opened the door to the street only to be blasted by a force of sunlight nearly brutal enough to drop him to his knees. He immediately turned his back and bent over to shadow his phone, navigating through the murky screen in a desperate attempt to find the Lyft app. Its signature square of deep magenta was faded to a light pink under the sun's brilliance. Ben thumbed the app aggressively, then exhaled in relief after the GPS found his pickup location and indicated only a three-minute wait for the closest driver. When the confirmation came through, Ben squinted in confusion as he rechecked the time displayed at the top of his screen. "What the *fuck*?" he gasped.

1:04.

Spring forward. It began trickling back to his foggy brain. A faint recollection of his mother systematically adjusting the clocks yesterday evening before they left for the party. His steadfast watch had remained an hour behind of course, requiring a manual correction, which he'd been far too altered last night to remember to do. Before he was able to properly gauge the stress this apparent time travel had caused, his phone began spitting out an almost endless barrage of message alerts. Dozens of texts and at least ten voicemails, all cast into the cellular network while both he and his phone had slept away the morning, were finally landing at their destination.

The Lyft arrived. Hopping into the back seat, Ben barely looked up from his uncharacteristically hyperactive phone. The driver politely confirmed the destination, then frowned as he watched Ben in the rearview mirror guzzle all three of the tiny complimentary bottles of water tucked on the inside of the door. Rather than trying to go through all the messages from the beginning, Ben opened the most recent voicemail. Oddly, it was from his sister. His parents, trying unsuccessfully to get ahold of him, must have enlisted Abby for help. With one hand screening his bloodshot eyes and the other holding the phone to his ear, he waited for the message to start.

Within a few seconds of hearing Abby's voice, Ben could feel his stomach violently tightening. She sounded eerily calm but exhausted, wholly unlike the bossy "big" sister he was expecting to hear scold him for needlessly worrying Mom and Dad on their anniversary weekend. He uncovered his eyes, then noticed the periphery of his vision begin to narrow when he realized Abby was in Florida, and that she was waiting at the Palm Beach Gardens Medical Center with Betsy. He didn't wait for the message to finish before leaning forward and shouting to his driver, "I need you to take me to the hospital!"

Without asking questions, the startled driver whipped the steering wheel at the next turn and reversed directions.

Ben immediately dialed Abby's cell. She answered before the second ring.

"Ben? You need to get here right away."

~~~

In the twenty or so minutes it took to get to the hospital, Ben learned from his sister that sometime after midnight their father had collapsed on the dance floor and badly injured his head in the fall. The doctors had attributed the loss of consciousness to atrial fibrillation, a condition for which Ben knew his dad took medication but had thought was under control. When Betsy had been unable to track down Ben, she called Abby in a panic and evidently sounded so distraught that Abby felt she had no choice but to hop on the earliest flight she could find to Palm Beach. Vague when pressed for more details on Jim's current condition, Abby simply told Ben that it would be best if they discussed everything in person when he got there. She assured him that Jim was in no pain and that he was being very well cared for, but calmly reiterated the importance of arriving as quickly as possible.

At a red light three blocks from the hospital, Ben snatched the driver's pack of gum from one of the beverage holders and darted out of the Lyft. Any trace of his headache or shoulder pain had vanished with the startling news about his father. The physiology of the fight-or-flight response had always been fascinating to him. The cascade of epinephrine, norepinephrine and cortisol now surging through his system made his hectic legs, only minutes ago weary and stiff, feel fully capable of leaping over a fence in a single bound. His pupils autonomically dilated, and the omnipresent effect of the sky's brightness was harshly intensified. Yet he resisted the urge to run, hoping that moderating his speed would somehow steel his nerves enough to adequately process what he was about to see. So instead, he shaded his eyes under his forearm and deliberately negotiated the last block at a non-frenzied clip.

Once inside the main entrance of the hospital, Ben dipped into the first restroom he found. Perhaps not surprisingly, considering the tacky dryness that persisted in his mouth, he hadn't felt even the slightest urge to relieve his bladder since waking. But he wanted to check his appearance briefly. Questions were sure to be swirling about where the hell he'd been or what he'd been doing since leaving the party last night. Showing up looking a little less disheveled than he felt might temper these concerns.

He washed his hands thoroughly then splashed his face a few times. He sucked up the pool of water he'd collected in his cupped hands, his cheeks puffing alternately as he swished it around a few times like mouthwash. The three pieces of the green gum he'd pilfered from the driver would hopefully be enough to mask any detectable offense his breath was otherwise sure to deliver. An Alfalfa-like tuft persisted in sticking up at the back of his head, so he combed his fingernails through his hair in an only partially successful attempt at taming it. It would have to do.

The neuro ICU was on the third floor. Ben shot up the stairs, hoping to make up some time by avoiding any wait at the elevators. As he approached the nurses' station, he slowed his pace to catch his breath. A singular whiff of air moved over him when he entered the unit. Each section of a hospital, as he easily recalled from his PA rotations, had its own distinct, often repellent odor. It didn't matter the facility. In the intensive care unit, it was the paired stench of hand sanitizer and feces, mixed with the crusty foul of semi-dried sputum caked to the disposable tubes which jutted out from the swollen windpipes of its hapless inhabitants.

Ben swallowed hard, pushing back the contents of his uneasy stomach. He didn't want to turn green in front of the nurses, as if his barfy complexion under the sun-tinged redness of his nose would make his face resemble some kind of bizarre Christmas ornament.

Just as he was about to ask someone where he could find his father, Ben spotted Betsy through the sliding glass door of Jim's room. She was standing with her back to the door, her arms wrapped around herself. Under what looked like a blue scrubs jacket presumably borrowed from one of the staff, he could see she was still wearing the pink dress from last night. A large curtain was pulled, masking the contents of the remainder of the room.

Every instinct Ben felt urged him to join his family. To check on his dad. To give his sister a recess from consoling their likely hysterical mother. But his legs chose otherwise. Fixed to the invisibly filthy floor like a fly to sticky tape, he was unable to move. He bent forward at the waist, enticing gravity to take over and force his heavy feet to step forward and catch his balance. A few more lethargic paces and he'd be at the room. His heart sped when he saw Betsy turn around just before he reached her. *My head hurts*, went a fleeting thought, which accompanied the return of pain to his temples. He could only manage an inquisitive whisper as he tried to peek around the curtain. "Hey."

Betsy stopped him gently and collected his hands in hers. Ben could see his father in the bed, an explosion of wires and tubes exiting his face and arms. The recognizable gasping of a beeping ventilator was the only discernible sound in the otherwise deafened space. He identified an enormous contusion on the right side of Jim's distended forehead, the grim herald of what must have been a tremendous insult to the delicate brain tissue whose swelling had nowhere to safely expand within the confines of that rigid skull.

Abby stood up from her chair and met Ben's eyes. Her cheeks were pale and drawn, exhibiting an expression that read as both disappointed and sympathetic. Ruth Gunderson was there as well, slumped in the corner with a glossy-eyed stare. Betsy blinked several times as she looked at Ben, sniffing loudly then producing a painful smile from her tired, tear-stained face.

"It's time to say goodbye now, sweetie," she said.

Pulling his eyes from the pathetic state of his father, Ben squinted at Betsy, unprepared to believe her. He reexamined the trauma to Jim's head and somehow it quickly became obvious. There was too much damage. Could a functioning mind possibly survive such a gruesome disfigurement? And if so, to what end? If Jim were ever to resume breathing on his own, what chance was there that the trillions of series of synapses cramped into that inflated space could have continued with even a remote level of vitality?

He was dead. Or brain-dead at least, which Ben understood as the same thing. He'd been kept "alive" only the way one would keep an organ to be transplanted alive. A ventilator pumped air into his lungs. Fluid nutrients dripped from a plastic bag into his wrist like a leaky faucet. The independent pacemaking tissue of his heart, now back in step with the aid of medications, continued to perfuse blood through his veins. But his brain, the all-important command center for every pump, twitch and thought, was gone. A total and irreversible loss of function which, once the equipment was turned off, would issue death by any definition.

Ben drew his hands to his forehead, then slid them down his face to cover his quivering chin. He inched the few steps to Jim's bedside. Up close, he looked like a different person, and not just from where the impact had taken place. His skin shone with a firmness more resembling a made-up dummy. The only hint of familiarity was in the upturned corners of his swollen mouth. Even in death he smiled.

Ben reached for his father's hand and whispered to no one, "Oh, Dad."

Jim's lifeless arm was heavy and unwieldy, requiring a careful grip from Ben as he drew it closer, to press his father's fingers against his unshaven cheek. He turned his head slightly to gently kiss Jim's knuckles. His hand felt unexpectedly warm. This once strong hand, which had taught him how to properly grip a tennis racket to produce topspin, which had secured his own small fingers to the handle of the lawnmower the summer he turned twelve, and which, through the careful guidance of an arthroscope, had offered hope to suffering seniors over the years, was now as useless as those countless arthritic hips that had ached for Jim to fix them.

Behind him, Ben could hear the muffled whimpering of his mother and sister, their vigil finally ending with the somber revelation of his father's passing. A churning knot began to arrest his abdomen again, a tightening ordinarily felt when trying to control either laughter or a wailing sob. In this case it was neither. Ben dropped his father's hand suddenly and darted past Abby to the bathroom, where he fell to his knees and violently emptied the watery contents of his stomach. Tears squeezed out the corners of his eyes with each involuntary spasm. He remained still for a few moments when finished, repeatedly spitting the last acidic remnants from his lips.

Betsy stepped in and leaned over to rest a consoling hand on his back, lullingly whispering over and over, "It's all right, sweetie."

Ben breathed slowly, the weight of his mother's hand ebbing on his ribs with each careful, purse-lipped exhale. "I'm okay," he murmured, rolling his shoulder to squirm out of contact with her. He expected that she, Abby and Ruth would assume the shock of Jim's condition had incited this uncontrollable bout of sickness. It would have been natural, after all, seeing his father like that. But Ben knew that had had nothing to do with it. He'd endured shocking news before—terrible sights of ill or injured patients, his dying grandmother—and never reacted physically the way he just had. No. He was simply hungover. And like any other morning-after, where his body labored to metabolize the toxins from the previous night's overindulgence, a pungent odor was all it took, this time care of a standard hospital room, to spark the reflex of regurgitation that so often eased his looming queasiness. The physical relief had come. But in doing so, Ben had yet to realize, it had also inadvertently cut short the final tender moments he was ever to have with that now broken, lifeless body in the next room, which for nearly forty years he'd not unproudly called "Dad."

~~~

It would be a while before Betsy finished coordinating everything in the room. With her signed consent, the nursing staff had begun turning off the machines and preparing Jim's body for cleaning. Ben and Abby stepped out and it was then that Abby finally relayed the sequence of events Betsy had chronicled, detailing their father's injury.

Somewhat to Ben's surprise, Abby didn't ask him where he'd been all morning, which he took to mean either she didn't care, or that the answer was already clear. Maybe both. It was rare for Abby to need explanation when it came to Ben's feelings or actions—some kind of sixth sense you hear talked about between twins—just as she'd surmised his angst from a single text the night before. Ben wasn't always sure this was a plus, as it made it almost impossible for him to ever put anything over on his sister. And he never quite achieved the same level of uncanny perception about her that she did for him, another tiny failure which constantly reminded him that she was and always would be the "big" sister. Regardless, at least he wasn't getting the third degree, so he chose not to volunteer his whereabouts from last night. He wasn't so sure Betsy would be as equally uninterested.

Following his mother's advice that he get some air, Ben walked downstairs to the pharmacy to secure himself a toothbrush and a small tube of toothpaste. He cringed in front of the cashier woman when he swiped his card and caught a whiff of the embarrassingly rancid bouquet emitted by his armpit. He promptly added a travel-sized stick of antiperspirant to his purchases.

In the same first-floor restroom he'd stopped in when arriving at the hospital, Ben took his time brushing his teeth, trying to eradicate the coppery aftertaste left over from his lost battle with nausea upstairs. He dabbed under his arms with a wet paper towel, then lathered on a healthy layer of the deodorant to each side. Having something to do with his hands was a helpful distraction, he found, and it felt good to be even a little bit more freshened up. When he finished the makeshift sponge bath, he grabbed a large coffee and a sports drink from the cafeteria. Walking seemed to ward off the achy stiffness in his still somewhat dehydrated legs, and he began to wander the floors of the hospital, alternating sips as he double-fisted his two beverages.

The changing scenes of busy staff from unit to unit provided a soothing effect. Ben appreciated how the intertwining roles and duties somehow came together to create a functioning wellspring of human recovery. Organization had always been attractive to him. From the perfectly stacked columns of organic soup at the grocery store to the lengthy list of folders into which he'd categorized his work emails, he often longed for the comfort of knowing everything had its place.

But the coordinated tableau of nurses wasn't enough to reset the chaotic swirl of thoughts running through his head. He couldn't fight the need to manically retrace the steps his sister had described that led to his father's passing. As if perfectly understanding every minute detail would somehow reveal a clear picture of how Jim's death had been unpreventable, maybe even inevitable, and that it therefore didn't matter that he had disappeared for over twelve hours while the macabre events unfolded.

Abby had begun with the fall. A few younger women who were not members of the club had reportedly crashed the party and livened up the pace on the dance floor. Shortly before midnight, during what the band had announced would be their final song, multiple people witnessed Jim collapse just in front of the stage. Evidently, he'd fallen straight forward like a board, arms at his side, with his forehead absorbing the entire brunt of contact with the unforgiving marble floor. With a restricted airway rendering CPR useless, the technicians, no doubt flustered under Betsy's frenzied finger-pointing, were forced to intubate Jim in the ambulance. They rushed him to the hospital, where it was quickly determined the trauma to his head had caused a massive stroke. Subsequent tests confirmed an absence of all cerebral activity, resulting in the devastating prognosis that the best-case scenario would leave Jim in a perpetual vegetative state.

As Abby had alluded to over the phone, the doctor assigned to their father's care had attributed Jim's fainting to a temporary lack of blood flow, most likely caused by his irregular heartbeat. By 2:15 a.m., despite Betsy's reluctance, all efforts to sustain high-level brain function were ceased. Abby had barely been able to decipher her mother's distraught mumblings. She called Terry in California to secure a private jet, called his parents over to stay with the girls, and was in the air a dazed ninety minutes later. After she arrived, the best the doctors could do was to maintain Jim's breathing, preserving life in legal terms only, until Ben could get there to say his goodbyes.

In a futile attempt to clear his head, Ben continued his random wandering. He passed the maternity ward and was surprised to see what appeared to be an old-fashioned observation window down the hall. He'd assumed these viewing galleries had become obsolete, with newer hospitals now trying to promote bonding and breastfeeding by having newborns room with their mothers around the clock. Curious, he walked by. Six or seven newborns were resting peacefully, while a nurse facing away at a standing workstation completed the day's documentation. A single bassinet sat empty directly in front of the window.

Ben's thoughts quickly betrayed him again as he was drawn back to the details his sister had recounted. Based on her explanation of the events, he'd been left with as many questions as answers. These *younger* women she'd mentioned—could he have unwittingly exposed his father to danger by casually inviting Debbie and her trio of trespassers to the party? Why hadn't Betsy joined Jim during the band's final song? Didn't anyone at the club perform CPR? For Christ's sake, half of them were retired doctors. Was Jim taking his atrial fib medications; and if so, was the correct medication prescribed in the first place? Had the EMTs intubated too early? This last thought reminded him of a former patient, who had survived a similar stroke after paramedics failed to check her blood pressure before inserting a breathing tube. The error had only worsened the constriction of blood vessels in the patient's brain, leaving her profoundly disabled for life.

This whirlwind of confusion was temporarily halted when a door opened inside the nursery, and out walked another nurse. She held an infant so small it could've passed as a doll. Ben felt himself grinning as he watched the baby being carefully placed into its clear crib, its tiny pink face wrinkled up like a cranky prune. The nurse flashed him a smile and mouthed "yours?" through the window. Ben shook his head, then squinted to read the name card pasted over the baby's head: Leo.

He did a bit of a double-take after noting the birth time listed on the crib next to Leo's. "Larry" had been born at 1:58 a.m., Leo at 3:01. Practically twins. Ben closed his eyes then. "Wait," he whispered to himself, alerted once again to the nettlesome time change. He realized that while the boys' birth times were listed as over an hour apart, their actual deliveries were in fact separated by a mere three minutes—coincidentally occurring around the 2:00 a.m. jump.

This made Ben think about what Abby had told him regarding the decision to discontinue attempts at preserving Jim's brain function. It couldn't have taken place at 2:15 a.m. That time had not existed today. The moment at which the clock was to turn over from 1:59, it would become 3:00. Betsy must have simply given Abby the time she noted on her watch. Ben couldn't help but wonder what would have happened if all this had occurred during the autumn daylight saving time instead. It was bizarre to consider a circumstance where the timestamp of his father's death could conceivably have been listed as taking place *before* his injury. And what of little Leo and Larry here? Had they actually been twins and born during the November time change, with one twin at 1:58 a.m. and the other three minutes later, their birth order would effectively be reversed. Watching their swaddled forms sleep, Ben speculated for a moment whether that had ever happened. In the last century of childbirth, he quickly decided, how could it have not? But which of the two would the parents then consider the elder? Growing up, would the kids argue about who was the true big brother or big sister, or who might have rightful claim to being the "baby" in the family? Whatever the outcome, it would make for an interesting anecdote for the twins to eventually tell when fielding the inevitable inquiries so often associated with multiples.

Ben had once teased his sister by insisting that he remembered her giving him an elbow to the forehead to position herself for first delivery in the womb. Initially, it didn't seem like it should make much difference. But with him and Abby, their birth orders had become inextricably linked to their interactions as siblings and children: the first to crawl, the first to walk, the first to talk. It had always been Abby. She always blew out her candles first at every birthday party. She was the first to answer if a question had been posed to them as a pair. And so it went with their mother's expectations and encouragement of who would and should meet every milestone *first*. Even into adulthood, as it seemed. Maybe it had always felt safer for him to just wait. If Abby couldn't do it or reach it, the pressure was off to even try. Had he really let himself succumb to this self-fulfilling prophecy, unable to assert his own interests and personality in light of Mom's unwitting benchmarks for her children? And to think it all might have been the reverse, but for a few inches in utero.

Ben caught himself again. None of these questions were of any consequence, merely the hectic distractions of a worried mind desperate to numb itself into disbelief. But it wasn't working. He did believe. He was alert and painfully aware of the reality before him. A reality that may hurt less from the actual loss of his father than the gnawing guilt of having been notably absent for it. Or even partly *responsible* for it. Perhaps the two pains could somehow merge eventually, relieving him from the constant impulse to rank and classify every reaction. In this moment, however, the typically trusty strategy of neatly boxing his emotions was giving him nothing but fits.

He looked down again and envied the two helpless newborns. With the years they had before an onslaught of expectations would be thrust upon them, they were blissfully unaware of the thankless drudgery they were about to inflict on their likely ill-prepared parents. *How could it possibly be worth it?* he wondered, glowering with his head cynically tipped to one side.

There was one thing, however, about which Ben felt no confusion. In a situation like he'd experienced this morning, one would normally expect a son to feel only sadness or a deep empathy for his mother and their shared loss. But as he spaced out in front of the observation window, Ben could find these feelings nowhere. Instead, an almost comforting certainty was beginning to take shape: a feeling which, fairly, could only be described as contempt. An unequivocal scorn, borne not solely out of the discovery of his mother's infidelity and his belief that the revelation of it had made him flee last night. Rather, perhaps curiously, it was the understanding that his father's death might forever shield her from having to answer for her deception.

He could see it. She would use her grief to ward off any attempt he made at confronting her about her betrayal of his father. And by the time things came around to showing some sense of normalcy again, what good would it do to unpack those feelings and resentments? The one person who would care to know about it, who *should* know about it, was gone.

A buzzing in Ben's pocket subdued his ire for a moment. He closed his eyes, anticipating the call from Betsy, as if she could hear his meandering thoughts and had to intervene before he talked himself into confronting her. He pulled the vibrating phone out of his snug jeans and paused with it in his hand. His heart sank when he realized the caller was Jake, somehow the last person from his mind. Ben watched the screen until his partner's name gave way to a missed call alert. There was no way he could face him.

Slowly placing the phone back in his pocket, Ben attempted to return his focus to forming a first sentence for the inevitable encounter he would initiate with his mother. He knew letting it wait would only soften the urgency; and with tempers sure to flare, broaching the subject would no doubt require a delicate hand, so he needed to be prepared. To his annoyance, however, nothing cogent was coming to him. He patted his chest, suddenly realizing he must have lost something back in that dark apartment, and a new distraction overwhelmed him—a powerful appetite, which only an hour ago would have been sheer anathema to his brutalized system.

Ben lowered his eyes for a final time. And as he dragged his fingers across the bare patch of skin where his grandmother's missing necklace should be, his heart only sank further, unable to fathom poor Leo and Larry here having to wait twenty-one years before they could legally partake in what his recovering body was so desperately craving. What he wouldn't give right now for a stiff drink.

fourteen

"It's only two hundred dollars more for non-members," Betsy had explained. Her decision not to hold Jim's funeral at their own parish church came as a bit of a surprise to Ben. The space likely would have been large enough to accommodate anyone wishing to attend. But Betsy insisted it was going to be too tight, opting instead to wait an additional ten days and pay the upcharge for non-members to ensure a slot at the Basilica Cathedral in Minneapolis.

Jim had stipulated cremation in his will, something Ben wasn't sure would fly during their preparatory meeting with the presiding priest. "While the church encourages the burial of bodies," the pudgy pastor clarified, "cremation is a legitimate option when not chosen as a denial of Christian doctrine on resurrection."

Ben and Abby exchanged curious glances during this explanation. Betsy sat calmly, occasionally offering a slow, earnest nod as if none of this were news to her. Two weeks ago, she was doing all she could to pass the Apt family off as a devout clan of Orthodox Jews. Not exactly what most would consider a prime example of Christian faith in practice. Now, sitting in the sacristy of one of the largest Catholic churches in the country, Ben could only quietly sigh, bewildered as he watched his mother commune with a complete stranger about the intimacies of his father's memorial wishes.

He knew he could have had it worse. While Betsy's religious seesawing was perhaps a bit uncouth, his partner had been afforded no such wavering of familial faith identity in his upbringing. When Jake came out to his parents, his father—a seminary student before knocking up Jake's mother on a mission trip to Haiti—essentially disowned his son. Ben had never met him. He'd met his mom, Tephy, once over lunch. But Jake's father forbade including him at holidays—at least as long as he and Ben were together—and his mother quietly complied. Jake responded by refusing to participate in family events if his boyfriend weren't welcome.

Ben didn't have the heart to ever tell Jake that he sometimes envied the relationship, or lack thereof, he had with his parents. It was clear where they stood with each other, unlike with Ben and his own mother. There were no nebulous comments or behaviors Jake had to figure out. No exhausting analysis he had to launch to understand exactly how his father felt about him. For better or worse, he just knew, because his dad told him. The not knowing is what's so terrible. Like how Ben imagined it would be to wait for the results of a potentially bleak medical diagnosis. Or how once, years ago, he'd overheard a friend's parent ghoulishly comment that if her child were ever kidnapped, she'd rather know he was dead than not know at all. Even if the answer were awful, wasn't it better to just know?

It was perhaps this harsh reality of Jake's that made it possible for him to sit Ben down the very day he returned from Florida to explain they were breaking up. Ben hadn't needed to confess anything. After some tears bemoaning Jim's passing,

Jake had soberly offered Ben an opportunity to volunteer his whereabouts that night in Palm Beach. But Ben, fearing the loss of another person close to him—the closest—played dumb. Jake only tipped his head and reached for his phone, holding it up to display a screenshot from Google Maps. In case of emergency or an inability to contact one another, they'd always made a point of automatically sharing their location with each other on their phones. When Ben hadn't responded to Jake's texts, Jake had been able to narrow down Ben's whereabouts to a few-foot radius. Based on the blinking dot indicating Ben's location on the map, it suggested either a gay bar named Slip or an auto parts store next door. At 1:00 in the morning, Jake had little doubt as to which it was; and when pressed from there, Ben had decided to come clean.

Ben attempted to explain that his behavior had resulted from his fear of Jake possibly hooking up with Oliver to spite him. As if his own indiscretion last summer may have subliminally signaled a green light for Jake to do the same. They would have been *even* in some bizarre way then, and Ben could finally be washed from the stain of his own original betrayal. But when he'd considered the real possibility of his partner being with someone else, something in him had "flipped," he said. He'd wanted both scenarios, yet he'd wanted neither. Vacillating between the two, rather than waiting, he'd opted for a sort of self-sabotage instead. It was perhaps the only means of control he had over the situation, notwithstanding the recklessness of the action required to actually seize that control.

While this may have been an honest answer, under the circumstances it was received as nothing but a hurtful excuse. Ben urged Jake to reconsider, citing some vague statistic about how important it was not to make any major life decisions for at least six months after a tragedy. But Jake couldn't do it. Not this time. Not even now, when after Jim's death Ben would need him most. He just wouldn't feel right about staying, he'd told Ben—he didn't know how he could respect himself if he just let this slide. What could Ben say to that? He couldn't very well tell Jake how to feel. He couldn't expect him to look the other way, to forget, or to ever really trust him again.

What hurt most was how explicit Jake had been in insisting they no longer *could* be together. "Not with you like this," Jake had said. Not if when anytime Ben was met with a threat to his happiness, there would be some profound void to fill. And certainly not if his mode of coping, his self-medication, his drug, would be to lose himself in the arms of another man. Jake couldn't have foreseen this, and it was a vice he wasn't prepared to accept—at least not in his partner.

The desiring of others wasn't the issue. Jake accepted that as natural, and a distraction that would never go away, in either of them. So, one is left with the option to either cheat, have an open relationship, or learn to live with the temptations. Ben had apparently chosen his path. It felt like a harsh indictment of his character after Jake had pointed this out. Suggesting, perhaps rightfully or even accurately, that Ben was innately flawed in some way, and had shown it, which now required his relegation to the sidelines of the relationship field. Jake had therefore insisted on a fourth and far more frightening option for them: simply splitting.

~~~

Two hours before the funeral, Ben found himself enduring a tedious receiving line for the second time in as many weeks. To think he had put up a fuss in Florida—sitting for half an hour of greeting smiling well-wishers with a drink in his hand—when today, he was faced with standing through ninety painful minutes of overwrought condolences, unsure of how to contain his own grief while feeling obligated to participate in the awkward mourning of others. By the time the actual service began, he was effectively drained of all real feeling.

Reminiscent of his Catholic schoolboy days, Ben reacted to each ritualistic phrase during the Mass like a stone-faced Pavlovian dog, robotically performing the repetitive transitions between sit, stand and kneel. His mother, apparently in no need of consoling, sat in an alert posture with keen interest in the officiant. Ben struggled to curb his distaste for the fact that her behavior that gray morning had seemed to revert back to that of an invigorated hostess, rather than the bereaved widow of a devoted husband and father. From the methodical handing-off of each attendee in line before the service, to her triple-checking for the correct shade of lilies set in front of the pulpit, she may as well once again have been neurotically crossing off items for a party to-do list. It was a far cry from the ho-hum service a few months ago for his grandmother, which he had watched Betsy quickly delegate to her brothers.

Ben cracked a smile thinking about Grandma Helen. She would have abhorred all the fuss Betsy was going through to stage such an ostentatious production. He patted his chest, feeling the small bump under his tie where her confirmation gift had been rightly restored. A few days after returning from

Florida, a small package had arrived at his work. Inside was the necklace from his grandmother, along with a brief note from his up-to-that-point nameless one-night stand. Turns out they'd gotten around to more than names after all. In this case, Google had been his ally, as "Diego" managed to track Ben down with a quick search combining his name, occupation and city. While a little unnerved at first by the ease with which he could be located, Ben was grateful for this simple act of kindness. It was something he could picture Jake doing.

He turned slightly then to glance at the rows behind him. Before he'd taken his seat with his family, he noticed Jake had sneaked in at the back of the church. He was easy to single out, sitting alone with several empty pews between him and the next closest attendants. Watching Abby and Terry together, and envying them having each other to lean on, Ben regretted not coming right out to Jake with his most recent infidelity. Had he summoned the nerve, maybe Jake would be sitting next to him now up front, instead of consigned to where mere acquaintances or women with fussy children usually sat themselves at things like this. And while Ben found it incredibly admirable, even characteristic of Jake—himself now familyless—to still show up and pay his respects, thinking of how they had broken up without either of them truly wanting it, his presence, which should have provided Ben with a much-needed sense of support, somehow made the morning feel exponentially more difficult.

The priest slogged on through the eulogy, reciting a banal litany of Jim's professional accolades. Ben could only cross his arms and look up, pretending to admire the ornate ceiling. Betsy maintained her sanctimonious disposition throughout.

With each listed accomplishment, she beamed and nodded like an astute piano teacher, approving her pupil's execution of an intricate finger sequence. Similarly to the obituary she had almost single-handedly dictated, Jim's life had been encapsulated into a succinct package of predetermined milestones, sprinkled with a handful of envious travel destinations. The fact that it was being delivered in a church that his father had never attended, and by a man he'd never met, seemed sadly impersonal to Ben. And wrong.

Nowhere was it mentioned how much Jim enjoyed spoiling his two granddaughters, or how he'd reluctantly indulge them when they'd ask him to play a round of Candy Land or insist on painting his toenails. How bad he was at bridge despite years of card-playing—he was always too busy chatting to place accurate bids. Or the anxious looks he'd get from other parents when he'd cheer too loudly during Ben's tennis matches in high school. Apart from a brief reference to Ben and Abby attending the same undergraduate university as Jim, a stranger sitting in the church that morning might well have wondered if the man had ever had children.

With the service drawing to a merciful conclusion, Ben stood with his family to begin their exit out of the church. A trio of hockey-haired altar boys, each holding what looked like long broomsticks with a crucifix at the top, led the lethargic procession down the center aisle. An oppressive cloud of incense repeatedly wafted up from the golden thurible hanging from a long chain in the priest's hands. It had been some time since Ben had stepped foot in a church that employed this ostensibly meditative tool, and he'd forgotten how much he disliked its woody stench.

Against the backdrop of an enormous stained-glass window magnificently fixed above the front end of the church, a hushed "ooing" cooed from the robed figures in the choir loft. One of the "perks," as Betsy had described it, of holding the service in the Basilica was being able to employ their 90-voice choir for the liturgical music. Over the group's harmonized humming, a solo voice began performing what Ben recognized as the first verse of "Beautiful Savior." He lowered his eyes and pictured Francine, imagining if this is what she may have sounded like, her warm, mezzo tones soothingly invoking an appeal to something he had long ago renounced. Ben listened closely to the words of the choir's a cappella notes as they masterfully crescendoed to a dramatic climax in the final verse. Gone for a moment was the cynicism he would typically reserve for such mystic phrases as "Light of my soul, my joy, my crown," and he felt his tired eyes welling for the first time since standing in his father's hospital room in Palm Beach. Perhaps he was less immune than he thought to the pathos conjured by a large group of voices raised together in song. And whether it was a lack of desire to fight the tears, or simply his growing inability to do so, he gave himself permission to feel the sadness.

Ben's self-allowance was brief, however, as nearing the end of the church he again noticed Jake, slumped forward with his elbows resting on his knees. Although Jake's head was down, the sob-like pulsing of his shoulders easily gave him away. In what had always been a peculiar reaction for Ben when seeing another person cry, his own tears quickly dried, as if there were some kind of unspoken requirement that someone keep it together, therefore compelling him to gather his composure. Was this to be the last time they'd ever see each other? With the choir now exiting to quiet organ music, all Ben could think about was how much he wanted to step into that empty pew and cradle Jake's bawling head in his lap. To tell him that the coming weeks would be impossible without him. That maybe they should consider giving things another shot. That he would always love him.

Wiping his cheeks with the back of his hand, Ben exhaled slowly. He fought back the re-welling in his eyes that had uncharacteristically resurfaced from the sad sight of his grieving, now former, partner. His attention was abruptly torn from Jake, however, when he felt a tugging on the cuff of his suit jacket. He tipped his head slightly toward his mother to listen, expecting her to urge him to walk up and offer his support to an obviously struggling Jake. Instead Ben was left expressionless, unable to produce a response, as Betsy lifted a critical eye to the emptying choir loft.

"That soloist sounded flat," she said.

~~~

One week after Jim's funeral, Betsy surprised both her children by putting their childhood home on the market. The property's plum location in an affluent suburb had offers rolling in within minutes of submitting the online listing. Aided by her realtor, Betsy had shrewdly orchestrated a three-family bidding war, which ended in her acceptance of an offer twenty percent higher than her already hefty asking price. With the healthy check she received from the sale, combined with Jim's life insurance policy, his 403b, IRA, and a remaining stake in the orthopedic business he'd kept a hand in after retiring, she suddenly found herself the charmed dowager of an enormous estate.

It was perhaps this substantial nest egg that made it easier for her kids to understand why Betsy had decided she would return to Palm Beach and keep the now even more unnecessary-seeming five-bedroom house to herself. By the deliberate way she'd voiced her sacrifice in moving away from home and traveling less, Ben and Abby had originally guessed she'd be anxious to move back to Minnesota. Her third grandchild was on the way, after all. But as Ben had sorely learned recently, it was a fool's errand to attempt predicting his mother's behavior with any accuracy these days.

Things moved quickly from there. As soon as a buyer had been found, Betsy immediately designated multiple areas of the home as "off limits," so as not to disrupt the orderliness with which she would arrange everything for the movers. Ben was glad he'd made a point of asking to sift through his parents' old photo albums before they were packed away. He holed up for hours in their family room, boxes stacked in each corner like columns, carefully considering the most meaningful snapshots he remembered of his dad.

He stopped when he came across a photo from the first time his parents ever took him skiing. It was in kindergarten—first grade at the latest. Betsy had captured an action shot of Ben on the bunny hill. Jim was behind him with his hand securely gripping the back of the young Ben's coat. A huge smile beamed across Jim's face in the faded photo, his eyes closed in laughter. Peeling it out from its clingy position under the photo sheet, Ben could only laugh at his own panicked expression, as his wobbly legs tried to keep him upright on the crisscrossed skis.

After several falls and some frustrated tears, he'd made it down the hill on his own that day with Jim close by, shouting and clapping encouragement all the while. His eyes watered a little thinking back on that bright day on the slopes, and the cheerful protection so carefully provided by his father.

Although Ben had repeatedly reminded himself that there was likely nothing he could've done to change the course of events leading up to Jim's death, a painful doubt lingered: that because of his early departure from the party that night, he somehow shared in the responsibility.

If only he could have been there when it happened. If he could just have been one of the first at his father's side when he collapsed. What was worse, perhaps, was that he couldn't go back. He couldn't undo it. Even with the best of intentions, there was no longer any action he could take, or words he could say, that would make it right again. Guilt was certainly one emotion he'd never struggled to find, and that powerlessness ate at him now like a cancer.

Ben recalled reading somewhere that after a bad experience, it could be therapeutic to think back and simply imagine what you would do or say differently if given the chance to relive the situation. Asking himself this question, he decided he would have approached Jim about his heart meds, and asked whether or not he had been taking them as prescribed. While himself an MD, his father had at times required reminders from Betsy to take his medication. Had there been a discrepancy, Ben could easily have adjusted the dosage, or even recommended trialing a completely different drug. Writing a new prescription would've been a cinch. And instead of his mother securing a prophylactic antibiotic after her extramarital sexual encounter, maybe the reason Betsy left for the pharmacy that afternoon could have been to pick up the new medication Ben had suggested for his father. Jim would have then taken it. And his heart would've been fine. And it wouldn't have mattered if Ben had left the stupid party or not.

The exercise sort of worked. In reassuring himself that his own hostile response to his mother that night wasn't the reason Jim was gone, Ben's worries somewhat mellowed for the time being. Yet he struggled to understand why he still felt so miserable. Why didn't his pain just fade equally alongside his supposedly waning guilt? Couldn't he just be content with the fact that he'd assuaged any true feelings of culpability? If it were true, he should feel better about it, and be able to get on with it. What was the next stage of grieving, anyway? Denial? Bargaining? Or was there to be a protracted phase of depression he got to look forward to in the near future? Acceptance, if there were to ever be such a thing, seemed impossibly far off. And if he did manage to reach that final stage, what the hell was he supposed to eventually accept?

It didn't matter at this point. All he knew was that he was stuck. Maybe he'd *been* stuck since he'd stood at his grandmother's bedside that awful morning last November. It dawned on him then that the torment he was experiencing was a direct result of that lack of forward progress, leaving him smack dab in the middle of a different stage of grieving. That all too familiar and wickedly persistent place he couldn't seem to leave: Anger.

Perhaps the pain hadn't simultaneously eased with his abating guilt because it had attached itself onto this new but possibly more useful emotion. Whether his gathering fury would be used as a weapon or a shield against his mother remained to be seen.

fifteen

It felt strange, boxing up items from his old room. For the most part, Betsy had converted both Ben and Abby's bedrooms into more standard guest rooms after they had graduated from college. All the posters of teen idols and sports heroes were long gone. The few remnants of his presence that remained—some trophies, old yearbooks, a wooden tennis racket probably left over from first grade—were thrown unorganized onto the shelves of his closet. Abby, having never really held sentimental attachments to objects the way Ben had, took only about fifteen minutes to consolidate similar items in her own room. With a small box resting on her pregnant belly, she stepped into the doorway of Ben's room and let out an exasperated sigh.

"I'm taking off," she said. Ben was standing in front of the closet, studying its scattered contents, as if devising a strategy. "You haven't even started?" she scowled.

"I know, I know," Ben grumbled, not turning to look at her. "What's Mom doing?"

Abby rolled her eyes. "Obsessing over the silverware. She's stuffing bits of it in with the Christmas decorations."

"What on earth for?"

"She's worried the movers will steal it." Ben nodded in tacit acknowledgment.

Abby watched him for a few moments. "Do you need help?" she asked.

"No," Ben replied, a little irritated.

There was a short silence. Abby set her box on a chair next to the door. "Listen, Ben," she said carefully, "there's something I've been meaning to talk to you about."

Great. "Okay," Ben said, finally pulling his eyes away from the closet.

Abby hesitated. "Terry's dad offered him a new role in San Francisco, and I think he's going to take it."

"A new role? Doing what?"

"Some kind of leadership position, overseeing the management of their salt ponds. I don't really understand it fully."

"So, what, you guys are thinking about moving?"

"No. We *are* moving."

Ben's jaw dropped a little. They'd never lived more than ten miles apart. Through college, job changes, and an array of romantic attachments, they could always be at one another's doorstep within minutes. He never really considered the possibility that she wouldn't be around. Now the first to move away, too. "Seriously?" he asked. Abby said nothing. He waited a moment, but she only stared at him. "So, just like that," he said.

"It's not 'just like that,'" Abby replied, scolding him. "It's been in the works for a few weeks. Things were finalized right before Dad died, and there just hasn't been a time when it felt right bringing it up."

"When would you leave?"

"Next month."

"Holy shit, Ab."

"Look, I know it must seem sudden. But it's a really important opportunity for Terry."

Ben slumped his shoulders, letting it all sink in. "And what are *you* going to do out there?"

"I'll be on leave in a few months anyway. Then I'll start looking for a new job, I suppose. I've checked it out a little already. There's plenty of need in the Bay Area."

"What about Mom?"

"She knows."

Ben raised an eyebrow, a bit irked that he was apparently the last to be let in on this bit of news. "And what'd she say?"

"She was excited. Anything that's a promotion, you know?"

"Right."

"She's already making a list of restaurants she wants to take us to when she visits."

"She didn't say anything about the distance?"

Abby reviewed the contents of the box on the chair. "What does she care?" she deadpanned. "It's only like two hours farther by plane. Not that I expect her to be making the trip that often. Oh, and she also hinted that I should consider being a stay-at-home mom after the baby comes."

"Please don't stop working."

"Oh, I couldn't. I think I'd go crazy."

Ben mustered a partially satisfied smile. Abby watched him for a few moments, then offered casually, "Why don't you come with us?"

"What?"

"Come with us," she shrugged.

"I can't, Ab."

"Why not?"

"Well, for one, I have a job here that I like."

"You don't like it that much." Ben recoiled a bit at this frank observation. She was right, of course. "Besides, couldn't you easily find something out west?"

"No, I probably could. I'd have to get licensed in Cali. It's just—"

"What?" Abby interjected, crossing her arms. She was being the pushy big sister Ben had always known, never allowing him a half or hesitant answer.

He paused, downcast. "I just don't know if I can take another big change right now."

With no clarification or explanation needed, Abby remained silent and only lowered her eyes in an earnest gesture of understanding. She held back tears and walked up to Ben, encircling her arms around his waist and burying her perfectly ponytailed head into his chest. He kept his arms at his side for a few seconds before lifting them to offer a similar embrace. "I love you," she sniffled.

"Love you too."

They held each other tightly for a while until Abby slowly began to peel herself away. Her cheeks were damp now and she tried to cover her face, as if Ben had never seen her cry.

"I'll let you know all the details soon," she said. She dabbed below her eye with her sleeve and collected the box from the chair.

Ben stuffed his hands in his pockets and slouched, but said nothing. ·

"I mean what I said."

"I know. Thanks, Ab," Ben assured her, smiling to himself. "I'll think about it."

And with that, he was alone.

~~~

Light snow had begun to fall outside the window, a regular, if not maddening, occurrence even in early April. Without a breath of wind, the thin flakes dropped like bundles of dangling kite strings from the silent sky. Ben had made a bit of progress on the closet, but it hadn't taken long for him to become sidetracked. He collected a couple of his yearbooks and sat on the edge of his old bed. The puffy new comforter looked like it had been nabbed from an upscale bed and breakfast, and once again he lost himself in the glossy pages of memory lane.

Image after image of student life—the overexposed faces of underclassmen randomly caught as they turned their heads in the direction of a sneaky editor's lens. Each black and white snapshot was captioned with a seventeen-year-old's cheeky attempt at cleverness. A few sophomore boys had grown in patchy beards, advertising their ascent into puberty as if it were some unique or grand achievement. All the girls wore baggy college sweatshirts. Sports rosters were terribly oversized. The hair!

And then there was Ben's unsmiling face. It featured heavily his senior year: math club, student council, honor society, the tennis team. He wasn't exactly frowning, he noted, just expressionless. Like one of those old portraits where the subjects were told not to smile, for fear the camera's slow shutter speed would render the faces a blurry, sepia-toned soup. It didn't seem to represent how he remembered those days. They weren't perfect, but engaging enough to have elicited at least some emotion, he thought. Not this militaristic posture he'd chosen to assume in each picture. That's how he imagined he'd pose if the photos had been taken today. It was as if his young self had somehow already sensed the impending melancholy of the next two decades, leaving his pale, vaguely pimpled face incapable of manufacturing so much as a smirk in its wake.

Wrapped in a knit shawl, Betsy stepped into the open doorway of Ben's room and gently knocked on its frame.

Ben kept his eyes on the book. "I'm just wrapping up."

Betsy crossed her arms to steady her shivering shoulders. "There's no rush, sweetie." Then turning to the window, she said, "In fact, maybe it's best you stay here tonight. It's coming down pretty good out there."

"Okay."

Betsy blinked twice at Ben's easy agreement. She uncrossed her arms and took a few steps closer, inquisitively tipping her head to the side. "What do you have there?" she asked.

"Just some of my yearbooks. I don't think I've looked at these since high school." Ben shifted up the bed slightly, making room for his mother to join. Betsy carefully approached and sat down next to him.

"Oh my goodness," she gasped, pointing to the open page. "Is that…"

"Yep," Ben confirmed, nodding. "Brian Lochner."

"Wow," Betsy exclaimed, covering her mouth.

Brian Lochner had moved with his family to the Apts' block when Ben was in junior high. The two became fast friends, and along with the Conway brothers formed a bit of a neighborhood posse. It got a little awkward shortly before graduation, however, when Ben decided to come out to Brian. While not unsupportive, Brian never quite figured out how he was supposed to act around Ben after that, and the two gradually found themselves spending less time together. This distance had actually ended up being a bit of a relief for Ben, as he found it harder and harder to withhold the fact that he'd developed a huge crush.

"I had forgotten what a little porker he was," Betsy said.

Ben frowned, insisting, "He wasn't that big."

"He was fat, Benny. Look!"

"All right," Ben conceded, turning the page. After a few moments he added, "He got a lot slimmer after joining the swim team sophomore year."

"Kind of a late bloomer, huh?"

"I guess so."

"He became rather handsome after that, though."

"I don't know," Ben said, evasively.

"He never married?"

"Not that I'm aware of. I suppose that would be tough moving around so much."

"I don't think I've spoken to his parents since Jane and Bob moved back to Chicago." Betsy drew a hand to her lips. "Gosh, can that really be ten years ago?"

"Time flies."

"Have you and Brian kept in contact at all?"

"No," Ben said. "We sort of lost touch after high school. Last I heard he moved to Virginia when the Navy transferred him again."

"You should call him up sometime."

Ben glanced at Betsy, then returned to the yearbook. "That'd be kind of weird, Ma."

"Why?"

"Because we haven't spoken in over fifteen years. I wouldn't even know how to get a hold of him."

"Oh, I'm sure that would be easy enough. You two were really close for a while."

Ben slouched. He closed the yearbook and tossed it over his shoulder onto the bed. "Can we talk about something else, please?"

There was a long pause. Finally breaking the silence, Betsy slapped her thighs with both hands and pushed herself to standing. "I suppose I should get back to my chores," she said. "I still have the kitchen to finish before the movers come on Monday."

"How long do you plan to keep your stuff in storage?"

"Until we can schedule an estate sale. I'll take a few things with me to Florida. There's room. But I don't need all the furniture and tools and appliances."

Ben nodded once, slowly. "Abby and I worry about you being lonely down there."

"Oh, I'll be fine, sweetie," Betsy scoffed, batting her hand as if shooing away a fly. "Liza and Al are already nagging me about when I'll be back for our next doubles match. They say hello, by the way."

Ben perked up a little on the bed. "So...everything's okay with Liza?"

"Of course," Betsy replied. She nudged Ben's leg a little with her knee and added, innocently, "Why wouldn't it be?"

Ben studied her for a moment, trying to decide if she was serious. Was it possible she didn't remember? With how shockingly the anniversary party had ended, he could understand how the rest of the night may have been a little foggy. Betsy had had her share of alcohol that night, too. Maybe she somehow convinced Liza that she'd misheard Ben when he'd so brazenly unveiled the confirmation gift from his grandmother. Or was it simply that Liza didn't care she'd been deceived by her friend? In the end, whatever the reason for the two ladies still being on speaking terms, he felt strangely relieved.

"No reason," Ben said, then quickly added, "Give her and Al my best."

Betsy flashed a satisfied smile. "You really don't need to worry about me, Benny. There are always new things to do and people to meet down there. It's the best place for me right now."

"Maybe you'll even find yourself a boyfriend."

Betsy's smile evaporated. She stood next to Ben, motionless. His eyes were fixed on his hands, either unable or unwilling to look at her.

"I couldn't possibly begin to think about things like that," Betsy said softly, her head lowered.

"Sure," Ben agreed, unconcerned if he'd hurt her. "But eventually you might want to." *Of course she would want to.* She already did and already had.

Able to sniff out the brewing fight, Betsy sat back down. "Look, Benny," she said, pausing to take a deep breath.

Ben was glaring at her now out the corner of his eye. *This ought to be good.* What excuse or ridiculous rationalization was she about to offer to explain herself? Some nonsense, he supposed, about how the past is in the past, or that it's time to move on, or that it won't do anyone any good discussing it now. Or maybe she'd drum up a sob story about how much she loved his father and how we all make mistakes. Whatever the bullshit answer his mother was about to give, Ben was prepared to come down on it with the full weight of an iron safe.

"You can't beat yourself up about this," Betsy continued. "I know you're probably feeling bad that you weren't there when your dad got hurt. And that he was already gone when you arrived at the hospital. But you have to know there was nothing you could have done. Okay? Nothing any of us could have done. And yes, I was worried sick about where you were or who you could be with that morning...but I don't hold it against you." She touched Ben's hand then. His eyes remained fixed on the closet in front of him. "We all make mistakes," she said. "I'm just sorry things didn't work out between you and Jake. I'm sure if you talked to him he would reconsider."

Thoughts rushed in and out of Ben's head like a sieve. Without saying as much, Betsy seemed to have put two and two together in assuming he'd spent the night with someone the day Jim died. Maybe Abby had helped fill in the blanks for her. Whatever the case, it didn't seem to be of much consequence now. And at the risk of giving his mother the impression she'd landed the final blow, he remained silent, as none of the elusive impulses scrambling his brain were able to land on his lips.

She'd upheld that there was nothing he could have done to save his dad. Fine. He'd already accepted that. What he heard, however, was that he still could have *been* there. As a son, he *should* have been there. And while his mother had ostensibly intended comfort in recognizing his painful regret, her words now felt more like a glowing spike being slowly driven into his side. She'd predictably insisted that "everyone makes mistakes." Just not her. The mistake was Ben's alone, and it was therefore only natural that he feel really bad about it. So bad, in fact, that Betsy could be absolved from the perception of any wrongdoing, because she had to play consoling mother to her grieving, yet culpable, child.

Ben sat inertly next to Betsy. Apart from his burning face, the rest of his body felt numb, barely able to sense his mother's palm gently patting the slump of his upper back. When he seemed to show no end to his silence, Betsy energetically snapped her fingers in the air, as if remembering something she'd forgotten to do. "I'm going to get you an extra blanket," she announced, and stood up to leave.

Ben stiffened his spine as Betsy was about to reach the door. "Mom?" he asked quietly from the edge of the bed.

Betsy turned around and shined a receptive smile. "Yes, sweetie?"

"Why did you tell Dwayne that I was 'always looking?'"

Betsy closed her eyes briefly and her face tightened in confusion. "What?" she asked.

"Dwayne. Your party planner."

"Yes, I realize who Dwayne is, Benny. I don't understand what you mean, though."

"I ran into him at a bar after I left the party. He said you told him before I arrived in Florida that I was 'always looking.'"

"What does 'always looking' mean?"

"I don't know. You tell me. You said it."

"If I don't even know what it means, how could I have said it?"

"Well, you said something."

"I think Dwayne may have been confused, honey. Was he drinking?"

"Of course he was drinking—we were at a bar. But he wasn't drunk, Ma. You two had a conversation about me earlier that weekend. He seemed to get the impression from you that I might be interested."

"Why are you asking about this, Benny?"

"Just tell me what you said."

"About what?"

"About *me*. To *Dwayne*."

Betsy fidgeted a little, then folded her arms. "That whole week is a blur, Benny. You can't expect me to remember every little conversation I had. I probably mentioned in passing that you were coming down."

"And that you thought he and I might hit it off."

"You were going to be there the whole weekend."

"So?"

"So, I thought he could show you around town."

"Why couldn't *you* just show me around town?"

"Because—oh, this is silly," Betsy sighed.

"It's not silly, Ma." Ben gave her an opportunity to respond before adding, "What made you think I'd be interested in Dwayne? Or anyone else for that matter?"

"Is that who you spent the night with?"

Ben was taken slightly off-guard by this. He'd already suspected Betsy knew he wasn't alone that night, but hearing it confirmed aloud was a bit of a jolt. "No," he scowled, a bit offended.

"Someone new, then?"

"I spent the night with a complete stranger, Ma. All right?"

Ben waited to enjoy his mother's uncomfortable reaction. Betsy, however, managed to hold back any signs of shock or disgust. Instead, she stood a little taller in the doorway, taking in a slow breath as if this admission had somehow vindicated her.

"And you wonder what could have given me the idea that you might be interested," she calmly replied.

"Ma, that doesn't make any sense!" Ben scolded. "You introduced me to Dwayne the day before the party."

"And this was the only time you'd ever cheated on Jake?"

Betsy's way of asking this sounded more like a statement than a question. Ben had never spoken to her about Oliver and couldn't imagine Jake would have ever said anything. He tried hard not to raise his voice. "What are you talking about?"

Betsy lowered her eyes to the floor. "I'm just saying that with how apparently natural it was for you to go home with a complete stranger, it's odd for you to think I was somehow in the wrong for wanting to introduce you to someone."

"So...what? You *wanted* me to cheat? Mom, that's nuts."

"Don't put words in my mouth."

"Then explain what you mean! What else am I supposed to think?"

"All I want is for you to be happy."

"And I can only be happy if I'm fucking someone else?"

Betsy winced. "Ben."

"I know you may not think that what Jake and I had was a *real* relationship, but we were together for six years."

"Oh, don't start with that again," Betsy said, pointing at him now. "That isn't what I think."

"I'm *asking* you what you think."

"You know I love you no matter what."

"What you're saying isn't matching what you've shown me."

"Don't yell at me."

"I'm NOT YELL—" Ben put his hands over his face and let out a riled breath. He waited a few moments to collect himself before finishing. "I'm not yelling. I'm just frustrated." *And sad,* but about what most, he wasn't sure.

Betsy was about to take a step toward him but stopped herself. "I wish you wouldn't upset yourself so much."

"It's not a choice, Ma," Ben quietly sneered.

"Maybe it's time you talked with someone."

Ben glared at her, a new fire in his eyes. "And what would I say, Mom? Huh? That I'm sad my mother has no regard for my relationships? That she keeps lying to me? Or how about that I'm confused and angry about the fact that she tried to create a situation where I'd sleep with someone else so she'd feel better about her own cheating?" He paused to emphasize his next words. "On my now *dead father.*"

Betsy stood frozen near the door, a wounded look on her face. The rapid rising and lowering of her shoulders signaled there was very little preventing her from gushing into a flat-out sob. "How can you be so cruel?" her cracked voice charged.

Ben stared, his eyes wide in disbelief. "Me? *Me?*" he asked, pointing to himself. "*I'm* the cruel one?"

"Not everything is always the way you think it is, Ben."

"Oh, I think I've got this figured out pretty damn well."

Betsy dabbed the inner corners of her eyes with her fingers. She held her breath for a moment before reluctantly murmuring, "I told myself I wasn't going to say this." Ben's attention on her was unwavering. She paused, her voice steadying a bit in indignation. "Your father wasn't perfect, you know."

"If you have something to say, just say it."

She paused again. There was no leaving it unsaid now. "He was seeing someone at the club, too."

As uncomfortable as it was, Ben had to ask. "What do you mean 'seeing?'"

"I think he was having an affair."

"You *think* he was?"

Betsy wrung her hands. "I'm almost positive he was," she said.

"Why? With who?" Ben asked impatiently.

"You really don't know?"

"What are you talking about? How the hell would *I* know?"

"It's just that you were chatting with her half the night. I thought maybe you'd have picked up on something."

There was long silence. Ben's expression had hardened in thought. He shook his lowered head in disbelief then looked up at his mother. "*Francine?*"

"Why do you think I sent Liza over to get you?"

"You're lying."

Betsy was completely calm. "She'd asked your father at some cocktail event about her sore hip. They got to chatting, and before I knew it, he was playing opera music around the house. You know she was a singer?"

Ben's stomach sank. "Yes."

Betsy only shrugged, as if she'd just offered irrefutable evidence of Jim's infidelity.

"That's it?" Ben asked.

"There are a few other small things I noticed that tell me I'm right. When you've been with someone as long as I've been with—" Betsy stopped herself. "—*was* with your father," she continued, "you know when there's a change."

"So, what, you're telling me that's all it took for you to cheat?"

"You know it's not as simple as that, Ben."

"Just a suspicion of Dad with another woman," he said, almost cutting her off, "and you had no other choice than to find Bud, huh?"

Betsy cringed at this accusation and put her hands up to shield herself from Ben's pointed question.

"I guess I shouldn't be surprised at this point," Ben added.

"Enough," Betsy said, more firmly. "Just...enough."

Ben lowered his head again.

"Why don't you just come out and say what you're really so mad about," Betsy added.

"Shit," Ben mockingly replied. "Where do I begin, Ma?"

"You know what I mean." There was another long silence. Betsy watched Ben thinking. "I wish it had been different with Grandma at the end," she finally said. Her face had softened slightly.

Ben couldn't look at her. His gut reaction was to immediately chastise her, having changed the subject just as he finally seemed to be getting to her. But she was right. There was a buried truth that hounded him, and either without knowledge or admission, he'd been directing his ire and energy at an alternate, more easily fought subject. After all the nonsense of the last month—the deceit, the scheming, the hurt feelings and disparagements— what had really stuck in his craw, what really left him unable to move on, to leave it alone, to call some sort of truce, even as he was making attempt after attempt to provoke some sign of hurt in her now, was the callous disregard he felt Betsy had shown for her own mother's last moments.

"It didn't need to be dragged out like that," Ben said quietly, glancing at Betsy.

"We wanted to be able to say our goodbyes," she replied. "I'm sure you can understand that. The way you had the chance to say goodbye to your dad."

"It's not the same, Ma. Grandma was struggling. They had to limit her pain medication because it kept dropping her blood pressure, remember?" Ben paused, lifting the back of his hand to his nose to avoid sniffling. The furnace had kicked on, producing a low hum from the floorboards, which offered cover for what felt like an unavoidable whimper. "Seeing her suffer like that—"

His speech was interrupted by the sound of his own quiet, involuntary groaning. There was a pressure in his stomach that reminded him of the time he'd gotten the wind knocked out of him in middle school, diving to catch a ball onto a mound of hardened snow.

"It just...*you* just...broke my heart," came his hushed response.

"Oh, Benny," Betsy said from the door. Her face was drawn now. "It breaks my heart too. Had I known it was going to be like that, you know we would have left earlier."

Ben had begun silently weeping by this point. Hearing his mother's reply, however, he quickly righted his posture and focused his rapidly blinking eyes on her. "*What?*" he asked.

"I said we would have hopped on an earlier flight had we known Grandma was struggling to that extent."

"But Uncle Phil said you guys were stuck due to storms."

Betsy wrinkled her nose a little. "What? No. I mean, I remember it raining. But I don't think there were bad storms."

"He said you told him it was borderline hurricane weather."

"Oh, that's silly," Betsy insisted. "You must not be remembering right."

"I'm remembering right, Ma."

Betsy raised two fingers to her right temple, trying to summon her recollection of that day last fall. "No. We were getting ready for our event when I got the call from Uncle Phil."

"What event?"

"Oh, there was this costume party I had helped coordinate for the club's Halloween activities," Betsy replied, waving her hands to imply it hadn't been important. "Had we known how quickly Grandma would deteriorate—"

Betsy stopped herself again and looked at Ben, as if hearing it out loud had finally revealed its ugliness to her. Ben's bloodshot eyes were wide now, like a feral cat, as he stared back at her. He waited, wanting to see if there was more, if there were some explanation or piece he was missing. But none came. She had said too much and she knew it. He knew it. And he could see by her guilty expression that she *knew* he knew it.

Ben thought of Grandma Helen in that bed. Her frail frame folded into the oversized mattress, rhythmically redistributing her weight to prevent pressure sores. The labored rising and lowering of her chest. Tiny muscles in her neck involuntarily straining to contribute whatever they could to maximize her intake of air. He shuddered at the thought of the awful gurgling sounds her throat had made.

And then he caught a glimpse in his mind of his mother in a costume. What would she have chosen for that party? A chambermaid? Nurse? Maybe an Oktoberfest beer girl donned in a gingham *dirndl*. One year she went to an event as a flamenco dancer. Or had it been a flapper? Whatever the character he pictured, it had to have been some low-cut, high-hemmed little number, sure to make the men at the club swoon and the other ladies envious.

"You stayed for a party," he said, no hint of interrogation in his words. Then he muttered to himself, "Another *fucking* party."

"Benny—"

"Grandma was on her deathbed, and you stayed down there so you wouldn't have to miss a party."

Betsy raised her voice slightly now, almost pleadingly, "I told you we didn't know!"

"What did you need to *know*, Ma? She was ninety-three and had already been in the hospital for two days. Wasn't that enough?!"

"Yes, but there was no way for us to—"

"Bullshit! You knew. And you didn't come."

"We did come."

"But you let her linger. In pain. And you could have prevented that. You could have let her go when she was ready. Given her some fucking dignity in her last moments. Instead you waited until *you* were ready."

"You're mischaracterizing it!" hollered Betsy, her shoulders trembling.

"What did you go as?"

"What?" she asked.

"You and Dad. What were your costumes?"

Betsy shook her head, caught off guard by the request for this seemingly unimportant detail. "Uh," she stammered, "the theme was The Jazz Age, so—"

"How original," Ben huffed, laughing a little at the accuracy of his suspicion. He could really see it now: Betsy decked out in a sequined, tiered-fringe halter with a long string of pearls and a feathered headband suitable for a tired, Roaring Twenties-themed bash. It seemed fitting for those cultureless fogies. Hearkening back to a period where their appetites for opulence and excess were not only actualized, but the aspired-to norm. He turned to face her. "Well, I hope your little party was worth it, Ma."

"Ben."

He stood and walked briskly to the closet. "Nothing like a daughter's love," he taunted.

Betsy gasped in horror. When Ben said nothing, she scowled at him and crossed her arms defiantly. "If this is what you really think of me, maybe it's best you don't stay here tonight."

"I'm not staying with you any night."

Betsy took a moment after hearing this. "What are you talking about?" she demanded. She watched Ben indiscriminately swipe the remaining items from the shelves into a box.

"You won't see me," he said, shaking the box to allow the jumbled items to settle. He didn't wait for a reaction. It hadn't been said to elicit one, only to inform.

"Look, I can't talk to you when you're being this obstinate."

Ben turned around then, slowly, to lock eyes with his mother. "Then let's *end* this."

Betsy flinched slightly at these words, hearing in them something painfully final. She shifted her gaze away from Ben's and glanced at the window. The snow was falling more heavily now. She walked over and gently pulled back the curtain to inspect what had accumulated, watching for a few moments as if to judge the snow's depth.

"The roads probably aren't too bad yet, actually," she said, looking down her nose at the whitened yard.

There wasn't much left to pack up in the closet, but Ben had turned his back, attempting to look too busy to acknowledge his mother. She took her time stepping back into the doorway, where she stopped and calmly folded her hands below her waist. She watched him again for a spell, her eyes reddening, her chin quivering. When it was evident he would not show himself to her, she dabbed her eyes, cleared her throat and said detachedly, "Drive safe."

~~~

It was the ache in his bicep that finally alerted Ben to how long he'd been standing there. How long does it take for pain to ensue if one attempts to hold something for any length of time? Depends on the strength and weight, he supposed. For Ben, with his strength and the weight of this box, he estimated ten minutes. There wasn't more for him to take than what two small boxes could carry. But he hadn't moved from the closet. After their encounter, he had stopped his rumblings and tilted his head to listen to Betsy's petulant sniffling slowly fade down the hallway.

Normally he'd be seething from an interaction like the one he'd just experienced. Another tiring disagreement with his mother, where afterward he'd be left more confused than when it started. More rattled and helpless than anything. But the confusion was somehow short-lived this time. All the mental drudgery he'd undertaken to proverbially unmask Betsy's marital deceit had been a waste of time, he began to realize. Any speech on it he'd planned, hoping he could force her to feel something if he just spoke it again, shone a spotlight on it, only seemed to have escaped him when the time came. It shouldn't be work to invoke remorse in someone for an act like that.

But there had been no sign of shame. No shred of humiliation on her part. He had felt it in himself instantly, and he hated any likeness to his mother that his own infidelity had forced him to consider. At least they were different in that regard; he was capable of feeling something regretful about it. Enough to take a sort of pathetic solace in that difference, anyway. And yet despite her lack, as it seemed, of any true sense of ownership, she was somehow still capable of identifying in him what was truly bothering him: the casting aside, as he saw it, of a woman who'd most helped shape the few things he liked about himself. A grandparent whose encouragements and affirmations somehow managed to sink in, despite the ever uncertain affections for which he'd hungered at home. Betsy could see that, and she'd plucked it from him like the bloom of a wilted flower when he didn't even have words for it himself.

A fragment of clarity festered its way into his rattled consciousness then. The question as to why his mother couldn't direct such high-powered perception at her own actions had rankled his mind before. But had he really never considered the possibility that, in fact, she *could*? It was one thing to possess the ability for self-awareness, even self-reflection. But what if those perceptions had no place to land? No space or level of consciousness that actually made one see or behave differently as a result of such inward thinking? It seemed too simple now to be true. That a person could go through a lifetime of experiences that were rich in almost every sense of the word, ponder them, share them, and yet not change. Not glean a new perspective. Not grow.

She didn't have it. Everything and everyone "close" to her was a mere extension of herself, Ben now realized. Recognizing this fully for the first time made him angry again. Maybe angry that it took a tragedy to finally see it, but somehow not angry at her. How can he be angry at someone for what they didn't have? Angry, yes, that if shown their shortcomings, a person chose apathy over improvement. But that was not Betsy. She was bereft. This change he wished in her could never be reached, and therefore made no sense to be worked on. He wondered then why he had been even slightly skeptical when his mother had told him Palm Beach was the best place for her. Any hesitancy to accept that seemed silly now in light of his new insight. She was right. In fact, it had probably always been the best place for her. Somewhere where the years she'd spent manufacturing an outwardly impressive facade might actually pay off. Where, instead of inevitably driving away those closest to her, her warped quest for attention would not only be welcomed with open arms, but faithfully nurtured and satisfied. She hadn't been ensnared by that place. She'd enlisted. There was to be no other option for her now but to return to

Florida and the desperate asylum afforded behind the cloistered gates of The Cypress Club.

And so his anger was that he couldn't be angry at her. Not even for the fact that after only two months of residence, she had already been so seduced by the empty splendors of that place that his grandmother's end-of-life care could only chart as an inconvenience. Rather, he felt thankful now. Thankful that Betsy had shown him, if perhaps unintentionally, what he was really looking for: to be finally unburdened of any lingering questions of who she was. And while there was perhaps minor discomfort in recognizing that this fresh knowledge made him sincerely dislike her, there was also something vaguely peaceful in it. Ultimately, it was more important that we love our families than like them, he told himself. Not unlike the way his mother had so lovingly attempted to make clear to him tonight. That she loved him *no matter what*. That despite who he was, she was willing to overlook it, in the name of love.

But was it possible to say that he still loved *her* if he chose to never be around her? Starting today, he would learn. Even if it meant severing ties with one of the last two people left in his life to whom he'd ever truly worked at being close. She was not being taken away from him by death, or a job, or his own inability to engender trust in a partner. He was simply letting her go.

"Yes," came the answer to his question. He would still love her. He may even miss her, and yet be grateful she was no longer a part of his life. Somehow this made missing his father hurt in a new way. Forget the guilt that would take time to truly extinguish completely. He missed Jim, of course. But strangely, he wished he were alive now so that it *could* be unmistakably true that he'd been with Francine. And there would therefore be a possibility that she and his father could be together now. And Ben could have reason to know her.

He caught a distracting glimpse of his shadow, cast from the closet's warm light. Dusk had fallen and his silhouette was sharper now against the dimness of the lamplit room. He stuffed his yearbooks on the inside edge of the box. Stacking it with a second, he paused in the doorway for one last, brief look before flipping the light switch with his elbow.

Outside the front door, the steps were already covered in nearly an inch of fluffy powder. The clean blanket of white in the street, quiet and beautiful, kept the air brighter than the twilit hour should have allowed. He arranged the boxes in the trunk of his car, feathery flakes thickening on his hair like ash. For the first time, he appreciated how tall the great oak trees on the block had grown, compared to what was stamped in his memory from childhood. It made him grimace a little when thinking of the fledgling greens their gnarled branches would begin to bud in just a few short weeks, forecasting the inevitable return to seemingly endless days of sun and sweat.

Closing the trunk, he removed his coat and tossed it in the front seat. He stepped over to where the sidewalk would be, its edges concealed, and pointed himself in the direction of the bare lilac bushes partially screening Brian Lochner's old house. Shallow footprints trailed him as he widened his arms and extended his tongue invitingly, delighting in the friendly chill of the snowy, spring air. Flushed with an anonymous surge of confidence, he reached into his pocket and thumbed a text to Jake.

Isn't Alcatraz on your bucket list?

sixteen

June had finally arrived. After two weeks of abnormally high temperatures in early May, the ground likely would have been safe by mid-month. But Ben didn't dare plant anything before now. "I don't care how warm we think the soil is," Grandma had once declared. "Never before June first."

It was always a bit of a guessing game, trying to gauge when it was time to begin the process indoors. Roughly six weeks prior to the last expected frost, Grandma would nurse a miniature forest of seedlings laid out in front of her picture window. When the ground signaled its readiness, it was time to move outside. Starting too early risked stunted growth, disease, or even the death of the precious plants. Waiting meant the bounty may be embarrassingly inadequate come fall. Grandma took great pride in her ability to accurately navigate these timelines—something of a badge of honor for gardeners grappling with a notoriously unpredictable northern climate.

One balmy spring, when Helen had been anxious to get gardening season underway, she paid the price for an uncharacteristic lack of patience. A cold snap, coupled with a mere quarter-inch cheat on planting depth, left her with half the harvest she typically enjoyed. Without the expected surplus, friends and family were left empty-handed that year. Their disappointed faces cemented a firm date in Grandma's mind moving forward, one she had passed on to her grandson: Never again before June first.

Ben had collected his seven-week-old seedling and arrived at the cemetery early that morning. Grandma had often started in the garden shortly after dawn. To do so in early June would've meant getting up before five, which Ben briefly considered, but ultimately decided was a bit excessive. Still, seven a.m. on a sunny Saturday was pretty good for him.

He had forgotten to bring a pad for his knees. Dew from the grass in front of Grandma's gravestone soaked through his worn jeans quickly. The hand spade he'd unearthed from a box of her belongings, however, made quick work of the damp soil.

"Who the heck plants a tomato in front of a grave?"

Ben laughed a little, knowing he was being teased. "It's not meant to produce some big harvest," he clarified. "It's just something I want to do." He shielded his eyes when turning around to face Jake. "Can you hand me the water bottle?"

Jake held out the bottle, a modest bouquet of pink daffodils cradled in his other arm. Ben patted the loose soil around the seedling and doused it with enough water to stabilize its base.

"There," he said, exhaling.

Jake knelt down next to Ben and gently laid the flowers in front of the headstone. With the sun already warm on their necks, they remained quiet for a few moments. Ben instinctively leaned against Jake's sturdy shoulder, and the two shared a heartfelt smile.

~~~

After Abby, Terry and the girls had left for California, Ben took up temporary residence in their home. The house wasn't selling as quickly as they'd expected, and with he and Jake having split up, it seemed a natural fit. It was also agreed that Jake could and would remain in their condo for the time being. Feeling there was no rush now to put it on the market, Ben was able to reach out one last time.

Some distance had helped. Jake hadn't wanted to separate in the first place, but felt he'd been left no alternative. Perhaps sympathetic to how utterly alone Ben was after his sister's move, Jake graciously agreed to meet for coffee. He was only doing it to be nice. There was no expectation to ever agree to getting back together. And surprisingly, it wasn't what Ben seemed to initially have in mind either.

Ben had arrived at the Caribou fifteen minutes early, only to find Jake already waiting for him at a corner table with two large lattes. "I got you the usual," he said. "Sorry, they were out of sugar-free vanilla."

"You didn't have to do that."

Jake only shrugged and slid the drink toward Ben.

"Thank you."

This was Ben's first relationship where he hadn't been the one who chose to end it. By the time he broke things off with his previous boyfriends—whatever the reason for his decision— he found he'd also invariably lost his attraction to them. That had always made it easier, to be able to coolly say "it's over." It shouldn't have come as such a surprise to him now that when he laid eyes on Jake, he still positively swooned.

The light through the window made Jake squint his gray eyes slightly, almost smolderingly. He looked stern, yet calm.

Thick horn-rimmed glasses and the fitted half-zip with his firm logoed on the left chest perfectly conveyed the "cool nerd" look he always insisted he wasn't going for. He'd let his beard grow in for what Ben estimated to be a week or so. His skin shone as luminously as ever, its mocha tone seeming to perfectly complement the warm wall of knotty pine at his back. He was beautiful.

"So, what's up?" Jake asked, wasting no time.

Still a bit distracted by Jake's looks, Ben hesitated before replying, "I feel I owe you an explanation."

"You already told me what happened."

"No," Ben said. "Not just about Florida. About the past year." There was a pause. "You deserve so much better than how I've treated you. With all the Grandma stuff, you've been nothing but wonderfully supportive. And I don't know if I've ever even said thank you once."

Jake lifted his elbows from the table, crossed his arms, and sat back slowly.

"So, thank you."

Jake nodded once in acknowledgement.

"I also wanted to meet because...I wanted to ask your forgiveness. I realize that might sound selfish given the situation. But I'm going to ask anyway."

Ben ducked his head when saying this, but he could see Jake had uncrossed his arms, as if signaling permission to continue. It felt like he'd rehearsed in his head a thousand times what he was about to say. Still, Ben went slowly.

"Please forgive me for never expressing how much I appreciate you. For betraying your trust by cheating. For not communicating what's bothering me. For not trusting you to understand what's bothering me. I don't think I realized how much I'd held back on really letting you in. The times I'd get annoyed when you'd just want to talk things through, understand where I'm coming from, what I'm thinking. It wasn't fair. You gave me every opportunity—you gave *us* every opportunity—to be great. And I put up barriers way too often. That's no way to go about having a relationship. You did things right, and you tried to help me do things right, too."

Ben glanced up at Jake again. His expression had softened.

"I guess I just wanted to make sure I said that. Maybe you already know it—you probably already know it. But I didn't want there to be any question in your mind as to whether *I* knew it. I felt I owed you that, at least."

Ben paused again and raised his shoulders, bracing for the impact of pain his next words would deliver him.

"I'm sure you're going to make some lucky guy very happy."

Without looking up, Ben quickly reached for his latte, half hoping to find it spiked with whiskey. In his haste to take a sip, he spilled onto his chin and coffee dribbled down his neck. "Shit," he grumbled, grabbing a napkin in exasperation. Jake smiled as Ben peevishly dabbed at his chin and the few wet spots on the table.

"Do you realize how silly it was when you suggested San Francisco?" Jake asked.

Ben slowed his cleanup. It wasn't the response he'd expected. "I know," he said, slumping his shoulders slightly.

"It's why I didn't text back right away. I mean, it's like the gayest city on the planet and you thought it would be a good place to—"

"I know, I know," Ben said, wincing. They both had to laugh a little. "It's just what came to mind. It was more of an icebreaker, I suppose."

"I thought your mom might consider moving there now, to be near Abby and the kids."

Ben hesitated. "Nope. She's definitely staying put."

"How's she doing?"

"I don't know."

"What do you mean you don't know?"

"I mean I don't know. I haven't talked to her."

"Not at all?"

Ben shook his head.

"Not even a text?"

Another head shake.

"Since when?"

"Two months? Since the night I texted you."

Jake paused to study Ben's expression. It was serious, but not sad.

Ben puffed out his chest resolutely. "I'm not sure we will again," he added.

Jake's eyes widened, like those of someone whose long-held suspicions were unexpectedly vindicated. But he didn't ask about it further. Despite Ben's willingness to volunteer details about how he and his mother had left things, Jake didn't really seem that interested or surprised. Surprised at how it ended, perhaps, but not by Betsy's words, actions or motivations. The knowing look on Jake's face said everything: It was here where Ben had been stuck. And if he ever hoped to escape from that emotional quicksand, his decision to effectively dissolve the relationship with his mother, while perhaps unfortunate, was unavoidable.

Grandma knew this. Whether she ever really expected true resolution seemed unlikely in light of how far gone the situation ended up being. But she also knew Ben wouldn't leave it alone if she pushed even a little. She'd push him off the cliff if it helped him. Only after what must have already felt like an impossible choice did Ben now seem untethered enough to really choose.

He could, like his mother had done so absolutely, choose and pursue his own version of the good life. For Ben, that life included Jake. He found himself in a position, if undeservedly, to not only atone for his mistakes, but to cultivate an environment that allowed for a truly healthy relationship. So, they began spending some time together. Not as boyfriends or partners— Jake wasn't prepared to fully reconcile just yet. But in time, Ben hoped, it would be more. He didn't expect his apology would be enough, and Jake had made that clear. Saying "I'm sorry" wasn't the end of it. If Ben was serious about recognizing the wrong he'd done, he had to be willing to honor that with a change in the behavior that required the apology in the first place. For what was possibly the first time, he felt fully up to that challenge.

<center>~~~</center>

Ben tossed the hand spade into a pail and brushed the dried soil from his hands.

"Want to grab some breakfast?" asked Jake.

"I'd love to, but I have to be to work at nine."

Jake arched an eyebrow. "On a Saturday?" he asked, incredulously. "Since when?"

"It's new."

Shortly after Betsy had returned to Florida, Ben reached out to Sid Leary to inquire about lending a hand at the clinic. Knowing they were "overwhelmed," as his father had put it, he figured Sid would take all the help he could get. Ben agreed to a few weekend morning hours each month, managing post-operative patients' medications, ordering X-rays, and advising on conservative options in lieu of surgery. In the short time Ben had been covering, Sid had already pushed for him to increase hours. "The patients love you!" he'd asserted. Ben thanked him in insisting this was the most he could manage for now, but that he'd been enjoying his time there, and would happily think about it.

Still kneeling, Jake smiled at this news before warmly offering, "I think that's wonderful."

Ben walked Jake to his car, where Jake handed him his mail.

"I'll pick you up for dinner at five," Ben said. "The show's at seven thirty."

"What are you wearing?"

"A suit, I think. But you can wear whatever you want. Really."

Jake took a deep breath. "Okay," he said, a bit reluctantly.

They hugged, and Ben turned his head to give Jake a kiss on the cheek. "Thanks for coming this morning."

Jake tried and failed to conceal the hint of tears welling in his eyes. Quietly, he pulled Ben tighter.

After they parted, Ben took a moment to sift through the stack of mail from Jake. His heart leapt when, amidst the pile of mostly junk, he uncovered another letter from Francine. Following Jim's death, a condolence card addressed directly to Ben had unexpectedly arrived from New York. His thank-you note back developed into what eventually became an almost weekly correspondence between the two—always via snail mail, which Ben found tedious at first, but grew to prefer. His new penpal's letters had actually been what prompted Ben to contact Sid in the first place. While Francine hadn't explicitly discussed any relationship she and Jim had shared, at least not yet, something about hearing from her had spurred the need in Ben to connect with the memory of his dad in any way he could find.

Ben lowered the window from inside his stuffy car and opened the letter. The beauty of Francine's penmanship alone was enough to make a person weep.

Mon cher Benjamin,

My apologies for my tardiness in responding to your most recent letter. Richard and I have only just returned from a week in Brussels. Business for him, pleasure for me. Another wonderful city. Have you been? Sadly, we were a bit late to enjoy the Floralia exhibition, but our stay happened to overlap with the last few days of the city's Pride event. I expect the color we could have seen from the spring blooms would have paled mightily in comparison to the dazzling human parade filling the streets last weekend.

I was touched to learn of your new role in your father's clinic. From the enthusiasm in describing your experience, dare I say you may have found a new niche? In any event, it's a lovely homage and I expect he would have been absolutely thrilled by the sentiment.

L'Opéra! Few things in recent memory have delighted me as much as knowing you'll soon be attending your first. And Carmen—what a first! This opera holds a special place in my heart and memory, and not just because I'm partial to the fact that its libretto is sung 'en français.' Carmen happened to be my first lead role at university. I'm afraid you may receive more than you bargained for when asking if I could offer any insights into the piece.

I won't say much about the music. Maestro Bizet brilliantly does that work for us. After the first attention-grabbing clang of the famous overture, I'm sure you'll quickly find his score, like the opera's title character, both beautiful and bewitching. In short, the 'story' is about two star-crossed lovers: Carmen, the Spanish gypsy, and the dutiful soldier, Don José. He is left a broken man when Carmen, insisting she was born and will remain free, ultimately rebuffs his advances.

For most newcomers, this background would be an ample summary of what to expect for their first time. But something tells me you'd be more interested in understanding the context in which this riveting heroine was brought to life on the stage, beyond the tunes and plot points. Hopefully you'll see fit to indulge me by reading a bit further.

On the surface, Carmen may inaccurately appear to be a typical femme fatale. Quite the contrary. She's the one being chased. Yet in the original novella that served as the opera's source, she was portrayed as a direct manifestation of the devil. There was therefore some early shock at what many considered the indecent nature of the opera. Few at the time had seen such overt realism on stage, *compared to the historically sanguine productions they'd come to expect. Still, it's not difficult to see why its first performances were targeted to the conservative audiences of Paris's Opéra-Comique— the depiction of a racial and cultural outsider who deserved nothing less than the violent denouement unfolded in act four.*

Earlier in the performance, perhaps fittingly for a would-be villain described as a fiery gypsy, her fortune cards predict her untimely demise, which from the outset almost feels like an inevitability. I don't think I'm giving anything away by saying she dies by Don José's hands at the end. It is opera, after all.

But I take issue with the conventional notion of Carmen being resigned to her own tragic destiny. Despite an indignant nineteenth-century audience's likely satisfaction at the punishment of such an unapologetic figure, I don't see it as Carmen being punished for her 'amoral' ways. Rather, my experience has been that she is the driver of her own fate. I've witnessed multiple productions where Carmen doesn't believe Don José has the courage to kill her—even to the point where she almost dares him to do it, until ultimately deciding to fall onto the blade herself. She is the one who chooses. She is the one who will not tie herself to anything or anyone who attempts to hold her back or force her into 'propriety.' To be asked to do so is not love. It's possession. She will be herself, and the rest can take it or leave it. Or she can and will leave them. All without regret. So, in a way, unlike most other autonomous women whom we see or read about since time immemorial, Carmen gets to keep her power, even in death. In her first scene she says,

"L'amour est un oiseau rebelle, que nul ne peut apprivoiser. Si tu ne m'aimes pas, je t'aime."

"Love is a rebellious bird that no one can tame. If you don't love me, I love you."

It's a brave thing to let yourself love someone when you're not loved back for who you are. I have great admiration for anyone who can face that—that frightening prospect of ending up alone. I suppose it's why I adore this woman so much. The sheer individuality she exudes against the powerful forces trying to drag her back to the status quo. It is utterly and beautifully human. To rebel is to love, even if it means saying goodbye. That's what Carmen has meant to me.

I look forward to hearing all about your first experience at the opera, Ben. Until then, sending you my sincerest wishes for continued happiness and health.

Bises,
Francine

Ben crumpled the elegant stationery slightly when pressing the letter against his chest. Somewhere above him he could hear a small chorus of birds, assembled as if there only to trill their morning hymns to the faithfully departed interred nearby. Just for a moment, he thought of that alien, illusory world to which his mother had so eagerly retreated. And with its closeness at long last feeling galaxies upon galaxies away, his weary heart, but now leaping, rested.

THE END

about the author

Jeff Wiemiller has maintained his blog, WordontheStreep.com, since 2011. When not busy writing, he can be found treating patients as a physical therapist in the Twin Cities metro area, losing cribbage to his husband, and vacuuming up after his two feline children, Puss and Boots. The Cypress Club is his first novel.

Made in the USA
Monee, IL
22 September 2021